Jawbone Walk
A DCI Finnegan Yorkshire Crime Thriller
Ely North

Red Handed Print

To contact ely@elynorthcrimefiction.com

Author's website at https://www.subscribepage.com/ely_north_home

https://www.facebook.com/elynorthcrimefictionUK

Cover design by Cherie Chapman/Chapman & Wilder

Cover image © Philip Silverman / iStock

Published by Red Handed Print

First Edition

Kindle e-book ISBN-13: 978-0-6489684-9-8

Paperback ISBN-13: 978-0-6455982-1-6

1

Saturday 29th August – Somewhere in North Yorkshire

A crisp, clear night. Sky, admiral blue. Moon, a vanilla button framed in a shimmering halo.

Screen door slams shut.

Subtle, sweet aroma of woody heather hangs in warm air.

Heavy footsteps scrunch over gravel.

Hoot of a tawny owl nearby. From far away, a reciprocating call.

Van door is thrown open.

Arms reach inside and tug violently at trussed ankles.

Musical warbling from a nightingale.

The squirming body hits the ground with a thud.

Muffled, desperate cries.

Ankles unbound.

Perching on a gnarled, dying apple tree, silhouetted by the creamy glow of the lunar satellite, a blackbird sings a sweet, melancholy melody... oblivious to evil.

Arm yanks at the sliding door of the shed, overdeveloped biceps bulging.

She leads their prisoner inside, holding the leash around his neck as though taking a dog for a walk.

Gloom until lights flicker on to assist in their torture.

Moths materialise.

Everything in position.

Sturdy board expertly strapped to a reclining gym bench angled at twenty degrees downward.

With prisoner secured, she kneels at the side of him and whispers in his ear.

'I hate to do this, but I must. You have betrayed us, and we need to find out the truth. I cannot say I was ever fond of you. After all, although you worked for us, you are still one of them—the enemy. I had a certain amount of respect for your work, and you were useful... sometimes. That is why I want to give you an easy way out. *Talk*. Tell me everything and your death will be quick and painless. Hold out on me and it will be long, drawn-out, brutal.' She rips the gag from his mouth. 'What's it to be?'

Fear has an acrid, bitter smell.

The T-shirt is placed over his head, which is girdled by a leather strap tied to the bench. Movement is impossible. Water trickles out from the bucket and falls upon the cloth, seeping through to the prisoner's mouth and nose. He coughs and splutters fluid from his lungs, gasping for oxygen, as acidic bile stings his throat. The giant keeps on drizzling the water until he receives a slight nod from his boss. He puts the bucket down and pulls the rag away.

'Ready to talk yet?' she queries gently.

The prisoner is too busy expelling water from his lungs to make any comprehensible reply. She nods again as the giant yawns and places the cloth back over the prisoner's mouth and nose and resumes his duties. The captive convulses violently, experiencing the horrific sensation of dry-drowning as his tormentors discuss options for their evening meal.

With a full confession extracted, their work is done for the night. She allows the prisoner to fill his lungs with air before replacing the gag.

'Well, well, well... most interesting. Your information is fascinating. Why didn't you tell us right at the start? You could have saved yourself a lot of pain.'

'What are we to do with him? Should I dig a hole?' the lackey asks.

She smirks. 'No. I have a dramatic ending for the traitor. It's befitting and will send a message to the others, cause great consternation and confusion amongst the bungling police, and send a shiver down the spine of the public.'

'And what about the others?'

She pauses, reflects, pouts.

'The others will receive a similar death... god willing. On Monday evening, the hordes of mindless holidaymakers will leave Whitby behind... like lemmings, back to their baked beans on toast, soap operas—fawning over snippets of gossip about their imperialist monarchy. I have checked the weather and the times of the tides, and Monday night favours us. That is when he dies. We will create chaos because *chaos* is our friend, Maxim. Remember that.'

'Yes, Kira.'

2

The tines of the garden fork slide effortlessly into the friable soil, and with a deft flick of his wrist, Frank unearths a clutch of potatoes, then chuckles.

'Welcome to the sunshine, King Edward, and brood, you little beauties.'

Picking up a large specimen, he rubs dirt from it, releasing an earthy aroma. He works steadily, methodically, for forty minutes, bagging potatoes, picking tomatoes, and nipping off the heads of cabbages and cauliflowers with a bone-handle pruning knife. He picks up two old wooden crates overflowing with an abundance of garden vegetables and loads them into the boot of his car. He returns to his allotment and pulls out a handkerchief.

'Hell, I've worked up a bit of a sweat,' he murmurs to himself as he mops his brow.

As he takes a gulp from a bottle of water, he gazes out past Whitby Abbey to the becalmed North Sea.

'It's a sight for sore eyes. It doesn't matter how many times I witness that view, I never weary of it.'

His focus fixes on the horizon where dark, clouds are gathering. It's a bright sunny day, but there's a definite chill in the air as the broiling summer reluctantly surrenders to the cool blanket of early autumn.

He wipes down the gardening tools and enters his shed. It's a rustic affair, but in true Frank Finnegan style, it's neat, tidy, functional, and furnished with all the essentials a man needs in a retreat. In the centre of the confined space is a cast-iron, pot belly wood stove. It rests upon a cement sheet, its flue punctures the roof. Behind the stove is a layer of aluminium sheeting fixed to the wooden slats, providing heat protection and also helping to radiate warmth when a fire is in full flow. At one end of the shed is a well-worn but comfortable armchair, with a couple of woollen blankets resting on the backrest. At the opposite end is a Georgian mahogany bureau, an heirloom once belonging to his father, and his father before him. Meera had earmarked the old-fashioned desk for resettlement about five years ago when she and Frank were in the midst of renovating their home. Frank was aghast at his wife's callous indifference to a majestic piece of craftsmanship. He pleaded his case in defence of the bureau, but Meera said it was a piece of old junk and told him to take it to the tip or try to sell it to a second-hand furniture shop—but it wasn't staying in their refurbished house. He found a new home for it in his man-cave, and still lovingly polished it once a month.

That was when his police diaries began. He bought five leather bound journals from an antique shop along with an iconic Sheaffer Imperial fountain pen. It was an impulse purchase. He hadn't intended to spend four hundred pounds to kick-start his journalling, but he figured he'd got a bargain. He conveniently forgot to tell Meera how much his antiquities cost—she didn't appreciate the expertise and artistry of such objects.

He gently pulls the desk flap down and opens one of the little box drawers at the back, and retrieves a cigarette and a box of matches. Pulling up a chair, he opens a larger drawer beneath the writing flap and extracts a bottle of Glenfiddich whisky and a small glass tumbler. The match crackles into flame as he lights the cigarette and breathes in deeply.

'Oh, how I miss you,' he groans. 'I know, I know. I'm not in denial. Smoking is a killer, and I must admit, since I quit, I've felt a lot healthier, not to mention the money I've saved. Nevertheless, I miss you. This is like having a secret affair. If Meera found out I was with you once a week, she'd have my guts for garters. It's our little confidential rendezvous. Hush-hush.'

The rich amber fluid sloshes into the glass. He pulls out a journal, unscrews the top off the fountain pen, and takes a sip of whisky.

'Right, let's begin,' he says with gusto as he neatly writes a heading on the cream coloured paper.

"August - The Case Of The Missing Schoolgirls, The Armed Robberies, And The Unsolved Murder Of Shirley Fox."

———◇———

His mind is lucid as recollections, dates, and times are swiftly transcribed to the history book. As well as a factual, chronological retelling of the prior month's investigations, he intersperses the record with his own thoughts and feelings, giving life to the cold, dry words on the page. Two hours fly by with an occasional brief intermission for a cigarette and a nip of whisky. He glances at his wristwatch—one o'clock. Thirty minutes and Meera will make her way from the church to his allotment. He picks his pen up and finishes his summary of the month.

Diary Entry.

"In summing up, August was a mixed bag. Finding Emma Tolhurst and Zoe Clark alive and physically unharmed was a major achievement. Their kidnapping and subsequent ransom was a testing time for everyone on the team. God only knows how it must have been for their parents and family. Emma Tolhurst has carried on with life like nothing happened, whereas from what I understand from Acting DI Prisha Kumar, Zoe Clark is struggling mentally with the events. Poor child.

Although it was a win, and the kidnapper—Mark Bridges—is safely behind bars awaiting trial, there's a lot of unfinished business. Bridges didn't take long to crack once we began putting forward the evidence we'd found against him. We discovered Emma's hair-tie in the back of his Kombi van—the same Kombi van with one orange door that was seen near Saltwick Bay on the morning the girls disappeared.

Then there was the huge haul of cigarettes and loose tobacco we unearthed in his workshop in the basement of Carston Hall School. It means one of two things: he is one-half of the of the armed robbers who have been holding-up petrol stations over the last eighteen months; or he is a fence. I suspect the former, as his insistence he met a guy in a pub and agreed to buy the stolen goods, is an insult to my intelligence. Yes, it's still an ongoing case, but won't take long for us to trip him up and get the truth out of him.

There are aspects of the kidnapping case that still keep me awake at night. Bridges insistence that Emma and Zoe's form teacher, Tiffany Butler, was the mastermind behind the kidnapping, still rings true. However, she has a watertight alibi, as at the time of the girls' disappearance, she was at Frodsham Spa getting pampered. Is Mark Bridges simply an ex-boyfriend out to sully her name and reputation in revenge for being spurned? Or is he telling the truth? I don't believe Bridges has the brains for such an elaborate kidnapping plot. Armed robber—yes! A Machiavellian mastermind who exacted twenty million pounds and squirreled it away in offshore bank accounts—I don't think so!

Now to Dudley Fox's involvement in the case. I like Dudley, having been a casual acquaintance of his for many years at the bowls club. But that's personal, and I always leave personal feelings outside the station door. It was Dudley who spotted the Kombi van with one orange door, only later to renege his account and inform us his dead wife, Shirley, had texted him the information. And of course, it was Dudley who passed a scrambled message to us the night we launched a massive search for the girls—a message that once again came from his dead wife.

delta sewer egg ran

An anagram of Westerdale Grange, the place where the girls were imprisoned.

Down to some damn fine police work, DI Kumar discovered Dudley Fox was on strong anti-depressants, supplementing them with self-prescribed lithium drops, all washed down with copious amounts of whisky. There is scientific evidence to suggest this unholy cocktail can create hallucinatory effects in people—especially hearing or seeing things. This would explain Dudley's communication with the dead. It was *he* who spotted the Kombi van, obviously in a drug induced stupor, then imagined it was Shirley who texted him the information.

The anagram he supplied about Westerdale Grange is a little trickier to explain away, but I'll try.

Dudley Fox is an intelligent man who studied botany and herpetology at Oxford University, before moving to Whitby, then working on top secret government projects at Menwith Hill. About a decade ago, he was asked by the Deputy Principal of Carston Hall School, Charles Murray, if he would take some of the older students out on the moors to educate them in the local flora and fauna. As an aside, Dudley and Charles Murray met each other while at university. Carston Hall has six outdoor education buildings across the country, four of them in Yorkshire. Although, to use the term—buildings, does them a disservice. They are mostly Georgian and Victorian era manor houses, one of which is Westerdale Grange.

How Dudley came up with the anagram for Westerdale, which led us to the girls, I'll never truly know. But I assume in his psychotic state, his brain picked at random pieces of information and memories. He knew Zoe and Emma attended Carston

Hall. Somewhere in that addled mind of his Westerdale Grange appeared on the radar. I suppose the correlation of Carston Hall, Emma, and Zoe, and Charles Murray helped join the dots for him. It was pure fluke Westerdale just happened to be where the girls were being held captive.

I've been a copper now for longer than I care to remember. I'm a rational, logical man. I have no time for gods, or the afterlife, the supernatural, aliens, ghosts or talking with the dead. Neither do I believe in coincidence, which to me, is merely information we detect, select, and give credence to. There is a term for it—confirmation bias. Meera, however, believes in all sorts of nonsense. I've lost count of the number of times over the years she's said she was thinking of someone, then her phone rang, and it was the person she was thinking about. How many times has she thought of someone and *not* had them call her? But no credence is given to that. Although I have no time for coincidence, I believe in serendipity, which is subtly different from the former. Chance, random events that end in a fortunate outcome. Dudley Fox's anagram was purely and simply serendipity at play.

So, that was August, a brutally hot month in more ways than one. There are loose ends that need tying up. First, we find out if Bridges is part of the armed robbery duo. If he is, then we find his accomplice. Secondly, Prisha is keen to re-investigate Tiffany Butler's alibi, despite Superintendent Banks telling us to drop the matter. Lastly, and most importantly, we need to find the killer of Shirley Fox. I have a good team in DI Kumar and DS Stoker. We all gel, and work well together. I'm hoping September will be a quiet month on the crime front to let us all focus our minds and resources onto the unsolved murder. I'll be back with my monthly round up at the end of September.

DCI Frank Finnegan, signing off."

He pats blotting paper over the drying ink, then splashes another drop of whisky into the glass, reclines in the chair, and drinks, savouring the burn and the aftertaste of complex aromatics. The latch on the allotment gate clinks.

'Frank! Are you ready?' Meera calls out.

He slips the scotch bottle and glass back into the drawer, screws the top on his fountain pen, gently shuts his journal, and closes up the bureau.

'Be right with you, my love!' he shouts back as he slips into his ancient corduroy jacket. He pulls the shed door shut, turns the key, then fastens the padlock, as Meera crunches up the gravel pathway. He pauses for a moment and studies the key in his hand as Meera eyes him suspiciously.

'Whatever are you doing?' she asks.

'If people were honest, there'd be no keys and no locksmiths. Imagine a world where you didn't have to lock your car, or your front door?'

Meera shakes her head. 'Your mind works in mysterious ways, old man.'

They set off down the path, arm in arm. 'Talking of mysterious ways. How was church?'

'Wonderful! The vicar gave an excellent sermon on forgiveness. He said it is the pinnacle of all the human virtues to find forgiveness in your heart.'

'Forgiveness, my blue arse!'

She slaps him on the shoulder. 'Frank! Curb your language. The vicar was merely pointing out it's cathartic to forgive and helps people move on with their lives.'

'And what about the murderers, rapists, child sex offenders, and people who rob you blind—should we forgive those buggers as well?'

'The vicar thinks so.'

'Aye well, the vicar should walk in my shoes for a few bloody weeks. He'd soon change his mind about forgiveness. What hymns did they sing?'

'Oh, my favourite—All Things Bright and Beautiful. And we sang one of your favourites, too.'

'The Lord is My Shepherd? Jerusalem? I Vow To Thee My Country?'

'No. We Plough the Fields and Scatter.'

'That's a bit quick off the mark. Another two days before autumn begins.' He drops the car keys into her hand and gives her a peck on the cheek. 'You drive, love.'

She stares at him disdainfully. 'Had a little tipple, have we?'

'Just a drop to jog the memory and make the ink flow. Did you put the roast on before you left for church?'

'Yes. A leg of lamb. Should be ready in about an hour.'

Frank rubs his hands together in delight. 'Grand! I've got some fresh veg to go with it. How does roast cauliflower, mash and sauteed cabbage sound?'

'Sounds wonderful,' Meera says with a hearty laugh. 'But back on the diet tomorrow.'

'Yes Meera. Back on the diet tomorrow and back to solving crime. Thank god for Sundays.' As he steps into the car, he throws one last glance out to sea. 'We might need to get the heating on when we get home. That weather change they predicted has arrived early.'

3

Monday 31st August – Bank Holiday

The rain comes in icy squalls, lashing the few hardy holidaymakers brave, or stupid enough, to have ventured to the seaside for the public holiday. The British are accustomed to finding entertainment during atrocious weather. They may not enjoy it, but that's not the point. It's in their genes, hardwired. They cannot control it.

A quiet hum pervades the CID room as people address their work in a calm, systematic manner. The three detectives are sitting around DS Zac Stoker's workstation discussing their caseloads.

Frank pulls his eyes from the rain spattered windows. 'It's a lot quieter now we've wrapped up the kidnapping case,' Frank states as he surveys his domain. 'And the schools return tomorrow from the summer break, which means most of the holidaymakers decamped over the weekend. But we still have plenty of niggly little cases to put to bed, and two big ones to solve, and no doubt new ones will crop up daily.'

'What's our main priority, Frank?' Prisha asks.

'Definitely the Shirley Fox murder, and the armed robberies. We're pretty certain Mark Bridges is one of the robbers or is a fence for them. Either way, he's up to his neck in it and we need to nail him. When are you due to interview him?'

'Tomorrow. I finally received some batch numbers from the tobacco suppliers and they match with those delivered to the service stations, and what we found in Bridges' workshop.'

'Good work. Anything else?'

'No. I could interview Tiffany Butler again. She said their affair ended six months ago, but she may be able to give us some info prior to that.'

'I think you'd be wasting your time. If she knew he was involved in the robberies, she could have exacted her own revenge when we interviewed her about the kidnapping, and dropped him right in it, muddying the waters further.'

'I suppose,' Prisha says thoughtfully.

'You don't like that woman, do you?'

'Can't stand her. Arrogant, conceited cow! I still believe she's the brains behind the kidnapping.'

'I tend to agree, but she has a watertight alibi, and we have no evidence against her. All we have is Bridges' confession—the jilted lover. Don't let it get personal, Prisha. It can cloud your judgement.'

'Yes, boss.'

Frank focuses his attention on the back of Zac's head.

'Don't let us interrupt you, Sergeant Stoker,' he says, annoyed at the lack of input from Zac.

'I'm eating my dinner,' Zac mumbles with a mouth full of food.

'And surfing the bloody internet.'

'I am entitled to a lunch break, boss. Anyway, I'm looking for a new car, or should I say, a second-hand one.'

Frank nods as his own stomach awakens. 'I'm peckish, myself.'

'What's on the menu today?' Prisha asks with a cheeky grin.

Frank's expression is glum. 'Alfalfa and beansprout salad with haloumi,' he replies morosely.

'Ooh, that sounds nice.'

'No, it bloody doesn't. How can a man of my size be expected to survive on that? I'd give anything for a couple of pork pies and a dollop of HP sauce.'

Prisha rises and laughs. 'Think of the brownie points you'll be racking up with Meera. How much longer before you're off the diet?'

'End of September. It's a bloody life sentence.'

'Frank, has Superintendent Banks said anything to you?' Prisha asks with a hint of concern.

'About?'

'My position as acting inspector.'

He smiles. 'No. Which means she must think you're doing a good job. Why? Do you want to go back to being sergeant?'

'Of course not.'

'Well then, head down, bum up and the position may become permanent.'

Frank reluctantly finishes his lunch, feeling empty, and heads through into the main CID room. Prisha and Zac are excitedly camped around Zac's monitor.

'Frank!' Zac yells. 'Over here.'

Frank sidles up behind the pair and stares at the screen, displaying vehicles under the headline banner—Pre-Loved Cars.

'Have you found something suitable?' Frank asks, slightly bemused.

'No. But take a look at this,' Zac replies, pointing at a vehicle.

Frank fumbles his spectacles on and peers intently at the screen.

'A Range Rover, eight grand, 2007 model. Aye, looks a smart enough car. You'll need to get it fully checked out by a mechanic, though. You don't want to buy a lemon.'

'No, the one next to it,' Prisha says with a hint of impatience.

Frank leans in closer and reads the brief description. 'Land Rover Defender, no MOT, 2000 model. £1500. No offers. Nay lad, I wouldn't touch it with a twelve-foot barge pole.'

'It's not for me!' Zac declares, exasperated at his boss' opaqueness.

'Land Rover Defender, 2000 model, not registered, a pale green or grey colour, missing passenger-side wing mirror... ring any bells, Frank?' Prisha says with a cheeky smile.

The penny drops. 'The vehicle used in the petrol station armed robberies.'

'Correct.'

'And have you noticed how all the other cars are photographed in colour, whereas this one is black and white and slightly out of focus? And it only shows the view of the driver's side, not the passenger-side,' Zac adds.

'Okay, get in touch with the seller and let's see where this leads,' Frank says, with a spring in his step.

'Already messaged them asking for their phone number. I'm waiting for a reply.'

'Good work. When they get in touch, come into my office and we'll call them. It could be nothing but definitely worth checking out.'

'Hang on! Here we go boss. They've replied with their number.'

'Right, in my office now, the pair of you.'

They each take a seat as Zac enters the number into his mobile and hits the speaker button.

'Hello?' a gruff Yorkshire voice answers.

'Hi there. You messaged me your number a moment ago. I'm interested in the Land Rover you're selling?' Zac says quietly in his soft Scottish lilt.

'Oh, aye?'

'I wondered if I could come out and take a look?'

'I'm only taking cash, mind,' the voice hardens. 'Fifteen hundred.'

'Yes. That's fine. What's your address?'

'It's Little Beck Farm in Eskdaleside cum Ugglebarnby. Do you know the area?'

Frank's eyes nearly pop out of his head as he grabs a pen and paper, then makes hand gestures for Zac to prolong the conversation.

Zac shrugs, clearly confused. 'Erm... yes. I'm in Whitby. You're near Sleights, right?'

'Aye, that's right. Just off the Blue Bank Road. You realise it has no MOT?'

'Yes. I just want a run-around for the farm. It looks perfect.'

'When yer coming?'

Frank hands Zac the note.

'Within the hour. Although, it won't actually be me. I can't get out of work, so I'll send the missus instead.'

'Knows about cars, does she?'

'She knows if they go or not.'

'Right. Tell her if I'm not in the house to blow her horn. I'll be around somewhere. And yer best be quick as I've another fella coming for a butcher's. First in, best dressed.'

'Okay, thanks.' The line goes dead.

'What is it, Frank?' Prisha asks.

'We know that bloke,' he says to Zac.

'Who is it?'

'Jack Turner.'

'Ah, of course. I thought I recognised those friendly, happy-go-lucky dulcet tones,' he says with a chuckle.

'Who's Jack Turner?' Prisha asks.

'A local rogue,' Frank explains. 'Been in and out of nick for the last twenty-odd years. He was the first villain I arrested when I started on the force. Caught him red-handed, breaking into a car. He got out of prison about eighteen months ago.'

Zac puts his phone away. 'Low-level stuff. Selling stolen goods, breaking, and entering, robbery.'

'Eighteen months ago is when the armed robberies started,' Prisha says.

Frank drums his fingers on his desk. 'That's right. Looks like Jack Turner has moved up a notch, knocking over petrol stations armed with a sawn-off. That's why you need to go, Prisha. He'd recognise Zac.'

'Hang on, Frank,' Prisha says with mild alarm. 'I'm not keen on going to some remote farm owned by a crook who has a shotgun lying around.'

'Zac can follow you and park up nearby. You'll be fine. He isn't going to suspect anything untoward.'

'He's not known for his violence,' Zac adds, trying to reassure her.

'And what am I supposed to do when I get there?'

'See if it matches the description of the vehicle used in the armed robberies. If it's missing a passenger-side wing mirror, then we're on the money.'

'And if it does, then what?'

All eyes turn to Frank.

'We get a warrant to search the place, impound the vehicle for forensics, and arrest Turner. Hopefully, we'll get some prints that match Mark Bridges. Then, it's game over.'

Zac turns to Prisha. 'Do you know where Eskdaleside cum Ugglebarnby is?'

'Do I hell! I swear to god you two make up some of these place names.'

Frank and Zac both chuckle. 'Welcome to North Yorkshire,' Frank says.

4

Lush greenery surrounds the single vehicle road on either side. Prisha glances in the rearview mirror to check Zac is still behind.

'You'll go down a steep hill, then a mile further on you'll see a tiny Methodist church to the right, on a sharp corner. I'll park up there,' his voice crackles through her phone.

'And where's the farm?'

'About a hundred yards further on.'

'Left or right?'

'Left. It's a bit of a dirt track, but once you pull into the driveway, you'll see the farmhouse and outbuildings dead ahead.'

'I'll keep my phone on so you can listen in. When I arrive at the farm, put yours on mute. I don't want your voice suddenly blurting out.'

'Okay. Let me know when you've parked up.'

She drops into low gear descending the steep incline. At the bottom, she notices the church on the right as she swings the car hard to the left.

Zac pulls up outside the church. 'Good luck,' he says.

'Thanks,' she replies glumly.

A little further on, she slows down, trying to decipher a small wooden sign sticking up from behind a stone wall.

'Okay, I'm here,' she says. 'Little Beck Farm.'

'Good. I'm putting myself on mute.'

The car rattles and shakes on the uneven ground as it passes a dilapidated tractor outside a rundown barn with part of its roof missing. The farmhouse is built from the obligatory Yorkshire stone with tiny windows. It wouldn't be out of place on the lid of a biscuit tin. She pulls up outside the front door and grabs her phone.

'I'm getting out of the car now,' she murmurs.

Scanning her surroundings, she cannot see, nor hear, any sign of life. She raps on the front door and waits. Butterflies in her stomach tell her how vulnerable she is. The place is completely invisible from the road. She knocks again.

'I'm not sure about this,' she mutters under her breath. 'Something doesn't feel right. Mr Turner!' she yells. 'I'm here to look at the Land Rover!'

Zac's voice unexpectedly calls out. 'Prisha! You...'

'Idiot,' she hisses, putting him on hold. 'What the bloody hell is he thinking?'

Knocking harder, she tries the handle of the door. It opens, and she pokes her head inside.

Muted speech emanates from what she assumes is the kitchen. Stepping over the threshold, she turns her ear towards the voices. They're coming from a radio. She walks into the dining room and scans the table. A newspaper, open at the racing guide, rests next to a cup of half-drunk tea. An overflowing ashtray accompanies it.

'Mr Turner!' she yells again.

The low ceilings and tiny windows give the room a claustrophobic feel. Taking one last glance around the room, she has an uncanny feeling she's not alone. A creaky floorboard sets her nerves on edge.

She spins around.

'Who the hell are you?' the man shouts, a pitchfork inches away from her neck. Rough grey stubble sits beneath a hooked nose, which lies below dark hooded eyes. She steps back.

'Mr Turner. You scared me. Can you put the pitchfork down please? I'm here to see the Land Rover. You spoke to my husband about an hour ago.'

He eyeballs her suspiciously but lowers the weapon. 'I thought you were a burglar, or worse, the filth. Often let yourself into other folk's homes, do yer?' he grizzles as he rests the fork against the back of the chair and sparks up a cigarette.

'No. I apologise. I heard voices from inside, but it was the radio.'

'Meh,' he grunts before coughing violently, open mouthed in Prisha's direction as she instinctively recoils. A few seconds elapse until he regains his composure. His face creases as he snuffles intensely. It's followed by the revolting sound of phlegm being ingested.

Christ! This guy knows how to charm the ladies.

'Come on, lass. I ain't got all bloody day,' he moans, as he scratches at his groin, then turns and heads out of the entrance. As she follows him outside, she takes Zac off hold.

'Very good, Mr Turner. You lead the way,' she declares loudly.

He heads across the farmyard, past the broken-down tractor and pulls back a wooden barn door.

'There she is. Keys are inside. Take her for a drive but keep off the bloody road. Plenty of fields for you to choose from. You'll find nowt wrong with her. Served me well. Leave her outside the front door when yer done. I'm back inside for a spot of late dinner.'

She watches him head off in his dirty green wellies, baggy corduroy trousers and moth-eaten cardigan.

'What a lady killer,' she says when he's safely out of earshot. She slowly circumnavigates the vehicle. The Land Rover is pale green and is missing a passenger-side wing mirror.

'Looks like this is the car,' she says to Zac, knowing she'll receive no reply. 'I suppose I better give it a quick test drive. Don't want to make the old bugger suspicious.'

The engine emits a beefy rumble as she reverses out of the shed. Her skin crawls as she scans the interior. The passenger footwell is littered with cigarette butts, sweet wrappers, coke tins, and scrunched up paper tissues. As she turns her head to navigate around the battered tractor, her eyes fall onto the back seat where a pile of porno mags rest.

'Oh my god!' she whispers. 'I'll need a hot shower and an incinerator to burn my clothes after I get out of here. It's a health hazard.'

The car bumps its way up a long, winding dirt track to the top field. She parks in front of a farm gate behind which a flock of sheep are happily grazing on lush grass. The occasional bleat and idyllic vista are a welcome relief from the distasteful Mr Turner and his disgusting four-wheeled-drive. She spins the car around and heads back down the trail before hitting the brakes violently. Staring at the detritus on the floor she's taken back to her first day on the job in Whitby, just over two weeks ago.

Frank drove her out to a petrol station that had been robbed the night before. They'd questioned the manager and a young lad who had been on night-shift. Nothing much was gleaned that uniform hadn't already told them. But she remembers one thing. As the robber left, he picked up three Mars bars. Put two in his pocket and tossed one to the attendant, then left. Her eyes are gazing at the assortment of wrappers on the floor of the vehicle, specifically, the Mars bar wrappers.

Pulling out a snap lock bag from her jacket, she gingerly nudges the two wrappers into it with the back of her knuckles, desperately trying to avoid touching the scrunched up tissues. With mission accomplished, she seals the bag and drops it back into her jacket pocket. An unexpected shiver runs through her.

'I honestly feel nauseous,' she says, heading towards the farmhouse.

Jack Turner is already coming out of the house as she pulls the handbrake on and alights.

'How'd yer go?' he asks, cigarette dangling limply from the corner of his mouth.

'Yes, all good. It's perfect for what we need.'

He smiles, revealing a row of yellow teeth, before his eyes narrow.

'You're not from around these parts, are you?'

'No. I'm originally from Birmingham. My husband is from Edinburgh.'

'So what are you doing here?'

'Oh, we both worked in Birmingham and decided we'd make a tree-change.'

'A tree-change,' he repeats suspiciously.

'Yes, it's when...'

He rudely interrupts. 'I know what a bloody tree-change is. Do you think I'm thick or summat?'

'No. I wasn't sure if you...'

'So where you living now?'

'In town, Whitby, for the moment. But we've put an offer in on a smallholding. Hence why we're after a farm run-around.'

'Whereabouts?'

'Whereabouts what?'

'Where is this smallholding located?'

Shit!

'Erm.... Just outside Rusholme.'

'How many acres?'

'Ten.'

He snorts derisively. 'Ha! You mean yer playing at it! You can't make a living off ten acres.'

'We'll see. Anyway, I best get going. I'll tell my husband the Land Rover is fine, and he'll be in touch.'

He loses interest. 'Whatever! Just remember, I have another bloke due any minute. Whoever turns up with the cash first gets it.'

'Yep. Understood, Mr Turner,' she calls after him as he heads back to the house.

Thank god that's over.

As she climbs back into the relative safety of her own car, Turner stops and slowly spins around. His eyes are like slits as he rubs at his chin. She starts the engine and reverses the car, glancing over her shoulder. A loud slap on the side of the door makes her jump. He taps aggressively on the window as her heart thumps against her chest. She presses a button and the window lowers a smidgen. His mouth presses up against the opening, emitting a waft of putrid breath. She closes her eyes and shrinks away for a second.

'How'd you know my name?'

'What?'

'I said, how'd you know my name—Mr Turner? I said nowt to yer husband about my name over the phone.'

'Erm... I got lost looking for the farm, so I stopped and asked a passer-by if they knew where Little Beck Farm was. They said it was Turner's place and gave me directions. I assumed they were referring to you.'

He glares at her as his lips curl up towards his nose, thinking, ascertaining. He pulls a gurner, then turns tail and heads towards the house.

5

Prisha washes her hands for a third time then splashes water over her face, pulls three paper towels from the dispenser and dries. She stares in the mirror. Young, attractive, she sometimes wonders whether she's cut out for the job. Her father wanted her to be an accountant.

'You will have respectability, status. And it's very well paid,' he used to lecture her in his Pakistani accent.

Her mother was more lenient. 'All I want for you, Prisha, is to be happy. Find a nice young man, settle down, and have a family. Preferably, your young man will be a good Muslim... I'm just saying.'

How she hated those teenage years, and what she considered her parents' draconian rules. No alcohol, no sex, no boys unless you invite him *and* his parents to tea and definitely no parties. Her brother's got off a lot lighter. She finally escaped to Leeds University and studied architecture for no other reason than to annoy her father.

'Architecture, architecture?' he used to say with arms splayed, bearing a confused expression as though she said she was studying aliens. 'Women don't do architecture. That is man's profession.

Women don't have the required attributes to build things. That's why all engineers are male.'

She made up for lost time at uni. Drink, drugs, sex with virtual strangers at parties. She was wild and loved every moment. That was seven years ago. Her decision to join the police was another dig at her father.

'No, no, no! I forbid it! The police are racist. It's not a woman's job to enforce law. They will eat you alive. You are weak. You are a girl.'

His words only hardened her resolve. She had no inclination whatsoever to make it a career. She did it simply to piss her father off.

She figured she'd give it a year, then resign and settle down at some well-to-do architectural firm, having taught her father a lesson. She didn't hate him. On the contrary, she loved him. But he needed to realise that women can do whatever men can do.

However, it didn't work out quite as she envisaged. As she was nearing the end of her first year, and planning to leave, she was on night-shift with a more experienced male constable in a patrol car. They were called to a possible suicide situation. A young woman on the top of a multi-storey carpark in the centre of Birmingham.

As her male colleague called for backup and paramedics, Prisha took off her uniform, stripped down to her underwear, climbed onto the parapet and sat alongside the woman. She still wasn't sure why she disrobed. It was a spur-of-the-moment decision to shed the suit of authority and show her own vulnerability.

It worked. They talked... Prisha about her own strict upbringing, the woman about her abusive one. The conversation continued for a good hour.

Her name is Kelly. She is now happily married and has three children. Children who would not exist today if not for Prisha's actions on that dark night, the night when Prisha *realised* she could make a difference in the world. Unfortunately, she picked up the nickname Lady Godiva for a while.

The main bar in the pub is sparsely populated as Prisha returns from the toilets.

'I got you a cheese and salad sandwich,' Zac says as he pushes the plate towards her.

Prisha stares at it with disdain as Zac puts the remnants of his sandwich into his mouth and washes it down with a refreshing glug of shandy.

'Thanks, but no thanks,' she replies, pushing the plate away.

'Suit yourself,' he says as he picks it up and takes an enormous bite.

Prisha fidgets. 'Sorry.'

'For what?'

'For putting you on hold. I now realise what you were going to say.'

Zac throws his head to one side and grins.

Prisha continues. 'You were warning me about calling him Mr Turner. It was such a rookie error.'

'Did he twig?'

'Yes, just as I was leaving. I gave him some cock and bull about getting lost and a passer-by mentioning his last name.'

'Good comeback. Did he buy it?'

'Not sure. I've been in some situations over the last seven years, but this was the scariest. At least with inner-city drug dealers, pimps, and stand-over men, you know what to look out for. But this old guy gave me the creeping abdabs.'

Zac chuckles. 'Old guy, you say? He's only early fifties.'

'What! He looks early seventies, if he's a day.'

He finishes the roll and takes another drink. 'That's what chain-smoking, drinking, gambling and being locked up inside can do to you. Take it as a warning,' he grins.

Prisha wriggles as if to shake the dirt from her body. 'Hey Zac, do me a favour?'

'What?'

'Don't mention it to Frank about my stuff up?'

'As if.'

'Oh, and can you cover for me when we get back to Whitby—I need to nip home and take a shower. Fifteen minutes—max. I feel dirty.'

'No problem.'

The two patrol cars speed through the farm gate with sirens screeching, lights flashing. The Skoda and Ford Focus trundle sedately behind in their wake.

'What's with the sirens?' Prisha asks, turning to Zac in the passenger seat. 'Wouldn't it have been better to creep quietly up to the front door?'

He chuckles. 'Frank likes to go in with all guns blazing in situations like this. He calls it psychological warfare. Puts the willies up them. Gets their heart rate racing. More likely to say or do something which incriminates themselves.'

Prisha shakes her head. 'Has he any other eccentricities?'

'You don't know the half of it. The last Friday of every month he wears different coloured socks.'

'You're joking?'

'I jest ye not. He says it brings him good luck for the following month. It stems from when he was a boxer.'

'I didn't know he used to be a boxer?'

'Oh, yes. He was pretty good, by all accounts. A light heavyweight. He got to the semi-finals of the Olympic Games before being disqualified.'

'What happened?'

'He was up against a guy from Algeria who kept hitting him below the belt. At the end of the second round, Frank got another punch to the cobblers and the red mist came down. Battered the shit out of the guy after the bell had rung. It was pandemonium.'

'Did he tell you this?'

'No. I occasionally attend retirement dinners, police functions. A few of the old-timers told me some right tales about Frank. The boxing anecdote was just one of them. Right, here we go!'

Six uniformed officers are already fanning out in different directions as Frank and DS Jason Cartwright jump from their car and march up to the front door, quickly followed by Zac and Prisha.

Frank barges into the house. 'Jack Turner!' he bellows. 'I have a warrant to search your property.'

Jack is sitting at the dining room table calmly smoking a cigarette.

'Frank bloody Finnegan,' he spits with contempt. 'Are you ever going to leave me in peace?'

'When you start being a good boy, then I'll leave you alone. Zac, cuff him. Jack Turner, I'm arresting you on suspicion of armed robbery. You do not have to say anything, but it may harm your defence...'

'Here we go. Another fit up,' Jack growls as Frank completes the caution.

Jack spots Prisha and sniggers derisively. 'I bloody knew it! I thought you were a copper. I can smell them a mile off.'

'And I can smell you a mile off, Jack,' Zac says as he clamps the cuffs around his wrists. 'When was the last time you had a bath? I know we're supposed to conserve water these days, but you are taking the fucking piss.'

'Ha, bloody ha. You smarmy Scottish git. Still Frank's little poodle, are we?'

'Now, now, Jack. Be nice.'

Frank grabs Jack under the arm and yanks him to his feet.

'Stand up! No, on second thoughts, sit down!' he shouts, pushing him forcefully back down.

A uniformed officer appears at the threshold. 'Can't see the vehicle, inspector,' he says to Frank.

Frank nods. 'Okay Jack, where's the Land Rover?'

'What business is it of yours?'

'I'm the police, you bloody clown. Everything's my business. Now where is it?'

'I sold it not long after bitch-face left,' he says, nodding towards Prisha. Frank slaps him hard across the back of the head.

'Oi, show some respect.'

'I'll have you for that. I'm gonna file a report of police brutality.'

'Police brutality?' Zac says in mock surprise. 'Did you witness any police brutality, Inspector Kumar,' he says, glancing at Prisha.

'No. I was too busy admiring the soft furnishings.'

'And what about you, constable?' he asks the uniform in the doorway.

'No, boss. That sort of thing doesn't happen these days.'

'You pigs make me sick,' he grizzles, to which he receives another clip to the head.

Frank turns to the constable. 'Search the fields, just in case.'

'Yes, boss.'

'And make sure you shut the bloody gates after you!' Jack shouts. 'I don't want my flock getting out.'

'So, you sold the car?' Frank quizzes.

'That's what I said.'

'How much did you get for it?'

'Fifteen hundred.'

'Who'd you sell it to?'

'A bloke.'

'Very funny. What's his name?'

'Don't know. Never asked, and he never said.'

'Where does this bloke live?'

'Never asked and he...'

'Okay, smart-arse. Where's the money then?'

He nods towards a dirty, threadbare couch in the corner.

'Under the cushion.'

'Zac, do the honours,' Frank commands.

'Do I have to, boss?' he winces. 'Who knows what mutated microbes are living on that couch? It's like a giant petri dish.'

He lifts the cushion and picks up a wad of notes rolled into a bundle.

DS Cartwright clatters down the stairs. 'There's no sawn-off upstairs, boss.'

'Look Frank, what's all this about? I think you're under some misapprehension.'

Frank pulls out a small photo of Mark Bridges from his coat pocket and places it on the table.

'Do you know this man?'

'Never set eyes on him.'

'Really?' Prisha says as she throws a pile of newspapers onto the table. The face of Mark Bridges is on the front cover of two editions from the previous week.

Jack Turner shrugs. 'So what? I only get it for the racing guide. Don't bother with the news,' he says as he scans the article. 'You're not trying to link me with the kidnapping of those young lasses, are you?'

'Stop playing silly buggers, Jack. You know why we're here. Over the last eighteen months, there's been over two dozen armed robberies on remote petrol stations late at night, targeted in the North East and now North Yorkshire. Cash and cigarettes are the haul. Your Land Rover matches the description of the vehicle caught on CCTV. No number plates, a missing wing mirror and light green colour. We believe Mark Bridges is your partner in crime.'

'You can believe what you want, Frank... you always do. Look, since I last got out of the nick, I've gone straight. The past is behind me. I'm focussing on my farm. I've turned over a new leaf.'

'You must think I'm as daft as a brush. I know you think knocking off cigarettes is a victimless crime, but you're wrong. I sometimes call in to the petrol stations you've robbed and ask how things are going. For instance, the one you did recently, the young lad working that night, is now out of a job and on medication for his nerves and depression. He's terrified to even leave the house. That's what happens when a guy in a ski mask jabs a sawn-off shotgun into your face late at night. Have you ever given him a second thought?'

Jack stares off into the distance for a moment. 'You've got the wrong man, Frank. I don't know Bridges and I know nowt about any armed robberies.'

Frank bends over until his face is inches away from Jack's. 'You really are a piece of low-life scum, aren't you? You're one of life's takers, never giving back. Everything is about what's in it for you and the rest of the world can go to hell.' He yanks Turner to his feet for a second time and pushes him in the back. 'Get him out of my sight. Stick him in the cells overnight and let him reflect on the errors of his ways. We'll interview him tomorrow.'

'Come along, Jack, it will be a home from home for you. We should really get a nameplate for the door—Jack's Retreat.' Zac says as he leads him towards the exit. 'Have you ever thought about investing in deodorant? It's not that expensive.'

Frank sidles over to Prisha. 'I take it you got photos of the Land Rover earlier?'

'No,' she mumbles as she averts her gaze.

Frank rubs a hand wearily through his silver locks. 'For crying out loud, Prisha. You're a senior police officer, not a bloody schoolgirl,' he murmurs.

'I'm sorry, Frank. It's not been the best of days for me. I let him spook me earlier, and it threw me off my game. Hopefully, the Mars bar wrappers will have Bridges' fingerprints on one of them.'

Frank slides into a seat. 'We have no vehicle, no shotgun, and both Turner and Bridges deny any involvement. Even if Bridges' fingerprints show up on the wrappers, it's purely circumstantial. He could say he was hitching a lift somewhere.'

'In an unregistered vehicle without number plates? Hardly believable, boss.'

'A defence counsel would make it sound very believable to a jury. Right, I'm heading back. Go over everything with a fine-toothed comb. If the vehicle doesn't turn up here, then visit the surrounding farms within a five mile radius. If someone bought it, they won't have wanted to travel too far in an unregistered vehicle. We need something, and quickly.'

6

The rigid inflatable boat bobs gently in the water. A few strands of Kira's jet black hair flutters in a delicate breeze. She pulls the binoculars from her eyes and smiles.

'The gods have favoured us, Maxim. Almost perfect conditions. Cold, overcast, drizzle; one could almost be on the Baltic. And the holidaymakers have gone home. I can see one old man walking his dog, but other than that, no one.'

Maxim replies in Russian, for which Kira swiftly rebukes him.

'How many times must I tell you before it gets into that thick Chechen skull of yours? Speak English at all times, Maxim. No one bats an eyelid at hearing a foreign accent, but a foreign language is a different matter. There is danger in drawing attention to oneself.'

'There are only the two of us here, Kira.' A groan from beneath a heavy-duty canvas tarpaulin makes Maxim hold his hands out in apology. 'Sorry, three.'

'That's not the point. You must make it a habit. Speak English at all times. That way, it becomes second-nature to you. And try to soften your accent.'

'Yes, Kira.'

'Good. Once the doddering old fool is out of view, we'll move in closer. Try to keep the boat shielded by the big rock.'

The rock—Black Nab, watches on... dark, silent, a sentinel over an evil deed.

The minutes tick by as Kira scans the cliff top and the beach below.

'On Stalin's grave!' she exclaims in exasperation. 'Now another stupid old fool is speaking to the first old fool. Have these crazy old men nothing better to do on a night than wander around aimlessly on cliff tops in the cold?'

'It's getting dark, and the tide is coming in quickly. Maybe we should make another plan?'

'You give in too easily, Maxim. The first pancake is always lumpy,' she replies softly, lowering the binoculars. 'Okay, the old men are moving off. Let's do it.'

Maxim reaches for the pull start on the outboard motor. Kira slaps his hand away.

'Imbecile!' she hisses. 'Use the oar. The noise could attract attention.'

Another muffled groan escapes from the tarp. Maxim gives it a kick as he picks up the oar. Kira pulls at the zip on her wet suit and adjusts the straps on her neoprene boots.

'Get in as close as you can, but avoid the rocks.'

The rubber boat edges slowly towards Black Nab as the tide aides its progress. Kira slips from the boat into waist high water, grabs the bowline and pulls the boat along, keeping Black Nab between her and the mainland.

'Okay, drop the anchor,' she whispers.

Maxim obeys and throws the bungee anchor overboard as Kira continues to drag the boat forward until she feels resistance. She takes the bowline and wraps a loop around a rock and secures it with a couple of hitches. Maxim throws a backpack on and drags the body to the edge of the boat. He drops into the water and pulls at the binding around the canvas. It's heavy, but Maxim is a tall powerful man, and although he meets a little defiance, the wrapped body falls into the water with barely a splash.

Gurgling and desperate coughing can be heard. Kira joins him to lend a hand. Within seconds, they haul the body out of the water and lay it down at the base of Black Nab.

'You fix the anchors to the rock, and I'll cut the ropes. Oh, and Maxim, only put the anchors in as deep as they need to go. We need as little sound as possible.'

Maxim nods as he pulls the steels and a lump hammer from his bag. The clank, clank, clank of metal on metal carries on a stiffening breeze as the light prematurely fades and the temperature drops.

Kira pulls a knife from her ankle sheath and hacks through the cords encircling the tarp. Wild eyes stare up at her, the desperate pleas for mercy muffled by a gag.

Maxim finishes his task, his giant biceps making little work of driving spikes into ancient shale. As he hauls the naked body upright, Kira busily attaches ropes between the anchors.

'Okay, ready,' she says.

Maxim holds the man by the throat as Kira secures three ropes around the body and ties them to the anchors with a trucker's hitch, crude but effective in creating the right amount of tension. They both stand back to admire their handiwork.

'I suppose I should say a few words,' Kira begins. 'Ahem. You have served us well over the years and in return we have recompensed you generously. But we must make an example of you for the benefit of the others. If you run from the wolf, be careful not to run into the bear.'

They both drop their heads and perform a cross sign over their chests.

'Svin, predatel,' Maxim snarls, then spits at the body.

Desperate eyes scrunch up in unbearable fear. There is now no escaping a slow, excruciating death.

'And there you go again?' Kira chastises.

'What now?'

'Speaking Russian. Will you ever learn?'

They wade back to the boat as Maxim unzips a pocket on his wetsuit and pulls out a walnut. He places it between the crease of his elbow and jerks his forearm upward. A slow splintering sound is lost on the breeze. He picks at the kernel of the nut as Kira shakes her head at him.

'Murder makes me hungry,' he says with a grin.

Ten minutes later, the boat is a dot on the horizon as the faint throb of an outboard motor starts up.

7

Tuesday 1st September

Frank squirts foam into his hands and liberally smears it over his face and neck. He picks up the safety razor and pulls it vertically up his throat, cocking his head to one side. Tapping the razor head in the warm water, it clinks against the white enamel of the sink.

'It's been a while, Frank.'

His wife's voice drifts in from the bedroom where she's getting dressed. He arches his eyebrows and gazes at his reflection. His mind trawls back in time. It was only two weeks ago since they last had sex... maybe three. He glances at his watch, already running late.

'If you're in the mood, it will have to wait until I get home tonight,' he calls back.

Meera's head appears in the mirror, sporting a disapproving stare.

'I wasn't talking about sex!'

'Oh,' he says, repositioning the blade on his cheek. 'What were you talking about, then?'

'The last time you went to church.'

His hand twitches. 'Ouch! Damn it!' he cries, reaching for a tissue. Tearing a tiny square off, he sticks it over the red globule that wells on his chin. 'Now look what you made me do,' he grumbles.

'Did you hear what I said?' Meera continues unabated by Frank's cut.

'I heard. And it's not true. What about that wedding of your friend... you know, the one who got remarried to the guy who sells edible knickers.'?

'Debbie. And her husband doesn't sell edible knickers. He sells organic underwear, made from sustainable, natural fibres.'

'Damn funny business for a man to be in if you ask me,' he mumbles as he resumes shaving. 'Wants to get a proper job.'

Meera applies a thin smattering of makeup. 'Don't try to change the subject. Anyway, do you know how long ago their wedding was?'

Frank squints at himself. 'About four, possibly five months back.'

'Ha! Eighteen months, actually.'

Frank eyeballs her through the glass. 'Are you sure?'

'Yes, certain.'

'Time flies when you're having fun.'

'I'd like you to attend church with me this Sunday.'

'Why? What's the occasion?'

She glowers at him. 'There doesn't have to be an occasion. It's a time of reflection and thanking the Lord for what we have in life.'

He winces as he taps the razor in the sink again. 'I was thinking of getting a big day in at the allotment on Sunday. My cherry tomatoes are ready, and my rhubarb needs thinning out.'

'You can pluck your tomatoes and thin your rhubarb after the service. It's only two hours.'

'Two hours I'll never get back,' he groans under his breath.

'And how are you going with the diet? I can't be watching over you all the time.'

He averts his eyes and rapidly finishes his shave. 'Good,' he says, splashing cold water onto his face.

'Come on then. Let's have a weigh in.'

'I haven't really got time, love,' he says, dragging a towel across his face.

'Don't speak rubbish. It will take ten seconds,' she says as she taps the scales with her foot, the electronic dial springing into life.

She carefully stands on the plate and waits for the numbers to settle. Clapping her hands together with glee, she turns to her husband.

'I've lost nearly two kilos in a week!'

'What's that in pounds?' he grumbles, resigned to his ignominious fate.

'About four and a half pounds.'

'Hell,' he mumbles as he takes his position, sucking his gut in as though it will confuse the scales. It doesn't. The digits stare up at him, almost laughing their contempt. 'I think this bloody thing is broken. It needs a recalibration.'

His wife glares at him. 'It's you who needs a recalibration. You've gained a kilo.'

'What's that in pounds?'

'Two and a bit.'

'That's not bad,' he says as he slopes off into the bedroom.

'You're supposed to be losing weight, not gaining it! And when was the last time you took your blood pressure?' she yells after him.

'Yesterday. All good. Anyway, got to dash, my love. I'll skip breakfast. See if I can shake a couple of pounds.'

8

The three detectives hurry down the damp, sandy steps towards the beach. The sky is a grey swab of misery, with the biting wind a willing ally. The tide has turned from ebb to flow, meaning they are fighting time, already a lost battle. As they reach the sands, they encounter the blue and white police barrier tape with the words—POLICE LINE DO NOT CROSS—emblazoned across it for people who are not sharp on the uptake.

DCI Finnegan hands out three sealed plastic bags containing crime scene protective wear; jumpsuits, gloves, goggles, masks, and booties.

He fumbles the booties over his shoes, grumbling. 'I've already got bloody sand in my socks.'

'Look on the bright side, Frank,' DS Zac Stoker says, sporting an impish grin.

'It's early Tuesday morning, the weather's turned to crap, we have a dead body, I've had no breakfast—what bright side?'

Zac breaks into song. 'Oh, I do like to be beside the seaside, oh, I do like to be beside the sea.'

Frank cannot resist a chuckle as acting DI Prisha Kumar rolls her eyes.

'You have the sickest sense of humour of anyone I've ever met,' she says with a mock scowl as she pulls at the hood on her bodysuit and zips up.

As Frank struggles into his protective gear, he surveys the scene. A uniformed constable is sauntering towards him. He looks chilled to the bone. Halfway down the beach, heading towards Black Nab, Special Constable Kylie Pembroke is placing a blanket around a man who is sitting in a camp chair, head down. A swarm of forensics are already busily at work around the geographical feature in the distance. The flashlight from a camera constantly catches the eye.

Frank addresses the constable as he approaches. 'What have we got apart from a dead body?' he asks.

'Pretty gruesome, sir. A guy strung to Black Nab. Rope around the throat, midriff, and shins, holding him tight to the rock. You can't see him from this angle. He's facing the sea. The bloke down the beach with Kylie is Trevor Kinglake, a professional photographer. Came out here at five-thirty to set up and catch the sunrise. Didn't notice anything untoward until he zoomed in on some of his shots and noticed something odd. He took a look around the back of the Nab, puked, then dialled a nines. Forensics have been here for a good thirty minutes.'

'Who's the forensic supervisor?'

'Charlene Marsden.'

'Oh, good. Charlene's a safe pair of hands. Has the pathologist arrived yet?'

'Yep, he's here,' the constable says wearily, with a shake of the head.

Frank detects the signal. 'No... please don't tell me it's Raspberry?'

'Afraid so, Frank.'

'I thought he was on long service leave?' he groans.

'He cut it short. Apparently, he couldn't adjust to enjoying himself.'

Prisha turns to Zac as she slips her booties on. 'Who's Raspberry?'

'Bennet Whipple—a.k.a. Raspberry Whipple. The local pathologist. He had a humour triple bypass on the NHS when he first arrived in the country. Nigerian born. Knows his shit, but you wouldn't want to be stuck in a lift with him for more than a few...'

'Minutes?'

'Seconds.'

'Christ, that bad?'

'Yeah. A bundle of joy. He makes Frank look like Coco the Clown on meth amphetamine.'

'Oi, I heard that, sergeant!'

They head across the beach towards Black Nab.

'Zac, get a statement from the photographer. Prisha, you come with me.'

As Frank and Prisha near the rock, the imposing figure of Bennet Whipple appears as he studies something attached to the Nab.

'Ah Bennet, what a pleasant surprise?' Frank says, trying his damnedest to sound positive and friendly.

Bennet stops his inspection and eyeballs Frank. 'During work hours, I'd appreciate it if we could address each other with the correct nomenclature regarding our allotted duties—Detective Chief Inspector Finnegan.'

'My apologies, Doctor Whipple,' he replies, shooting Prisha a knowing glance. 'May I introduce you to Acting Detective Inspector Prisha Kumar. A recent addition to our squad.'

'Pleased to meet you, Doctor Whipple,' Prisha says, holding her hand out.

Bennet stares dismissively at the outstretched appendage as though he's been handed a shitty stick.

'We're not attending a garden party, Acting Inspector Kumar.'

'What happened to your long service leave, doctor? I thought you and Mrs Whipple had a round the world trip booked?' Frank says as he gingerly navigates the slippery shale.

Bennet Whipple stares at the ground, momentarily distracted from his work. 'It was a monumental misjudgement on my part. I've concluded I don't make a good tourist.'

'You don't say,' Frank mutters.

'I find people—at best—damn annoying, at worst... grotesque. Sitting on an aircraft while individuals cough and sneeze; making banal small talk with strangers; dealing with the bureaucracy of

security checks, passport control. That's before we even arrived at our hotel. I took a black light with me to inspect the room. I detected semen stains on the carpet and, most worryingly, on the ceiling. God only knows how it ended up there. I couldn't sleep. We curtailed our trip and returned home the next day.'

'How far did you get?'

'Paris. I spent a week redecorating the spare bedroom before returning to work.'

'I see. They say a change is as good as a rest. Right, let the dog see the rabbit,' Frank says as he and Prisha sidestep the doctor and edge around the rock.

Prisha turns away, horrified, repulsed by the sight.

Frank's jaw drops as he gazes at the body. 'Sweet merciful mother of Mary! No one deserves to die like that.'

9

The naked body of a tall male is strapped to Black Nab with rope across his neck, waist, and legs. A gag is in his mouth, hands tied behind his back, feet bound. Eyes—deep black holes, the tip of his nose missing along with his earlobes and part of his bottom lip. Incisions, bite marks, and grazes cover every part of his body, too numerous to count. The scrotum flaps loosely in the sea breeze, ripped open, the penis all but gone apart from a bloodied, fleshy stub.

'I've seen some things in my time, but nothing like this,' Frank whispers.

For a copper with almost forty years on the force, he thought he was unshockable, immune to man's inhumanity to his fellow man. Today—he's sickened to his core.

Prisha reluctantly fixes her eyes on the scene, appalled at the depravity. She can barely look at the cadaver's face. Bennet Whipple joins the pair as they all gawp at the gruesome vision.

'I won't know the cause of death until I get him back to the mortuary and perform the post-mortem. But I'm hoping for his sake he was already dead or at least unconscious when he was tied to the rock.'

'I share your sentiment, doctor. If he were conscious, it would have been an insufferable and terrifying death.'

'This is no ordinary murder, boss,' Prisha says as she finally controls the urge to regurgitate her early morning porridge.

'No, it's not. Whoever did this was exacting revenge.'

'And sending a message, a warning to others,' Prisha adds as she screws her eyes up and takes a step forward. 'And it would have needed two people, minimum, to carry it out.'

'I suppose it's obvious, doctor, but what caused the injuries?' Frank asks.

'Sea life; crabs, fish, sand fleas. The crabs will have definitely snipped open the scrotum and feasted on the testicles, possibly while he was still alive. Probably responsible for the penis, too.'

Frank screws his eyes up, winces and involuntarily clamps his thighs together.

'Fish maybe took the lobes and lip. The eyes... hmm... could have been birds, seagulls, before the tide washed over him. I'll have a better idea once I put samples under the microscope.'

'I can't think of a worse death. I'd rather be burnt at the stake,' Frank says.

'Truthfully, being burnt at the stake would have been a doddle compared to this. Most people would have passed out with smoke inhalation before the heat or flames reached them. It was quite humane for the dark-ages compared to some of the horrors they perpetrated. It's a pet subject of mine; death and torture in the middle ages. A fascinating topic.'

'You do surprise me.'

'I'm astonished you haven't asked me for the estimated time of death, yet inspector?'

Frank turns and stares at the waves rolling in about fifty yards away.

'Because I know what your answer would be. If he was tied to the Nab while still alive then I can hazard a guess,' he says, studying his watch briefly. 'The tide is coming in. Another hour and the base of this rock will be under water. High tide three hours later and only the tip of Black Nab will be exposed. That will take us to 1:00 pm, which means the last high tide would have been about 12:30 am this morning with the preceding low tide, at 6:30 pm last night. There's probably a three hour window when the Nab is accessible, which would mean he was secured to the rock somewhere between 5:30 and 8:30 pm last night. The tide would have washed over him probably about 10–11 pm.'

'Impressive, inspector,' Bennet Whipple says drily. 'If speculative.'

'It's ballpark, I know. But it narrows it down.'

'You have an excellent knowledge of the tides.'

'I'm a keen angler and I've lived around these parts all my life.'

Prisha studies the rope, which is tight against the victim's neck. She traces it a few feet to the left and inspects the anchors.

'These are pitons, boss,' she says. 'Used in rock climbing to secure ropes.'

Frank moves cautiously to her side, wary of the algae on the fractured slate bed.

'Are you sure?'

'Yes, boss. I do a spot of rock climbing in my down time. I know a piton when I see one. And this rope they've used, it's old school.'

'What do you mean?'

'Unless I'm very much mistaken, I'd say it was a natural hemp rope, similar to the type they used in old sailing ships.'

Frank spins around surveying the forensics team. 'Hang on, there's Charlene. She's a forensic fibre expert as well as a crime scene supervisor. Charlene! Can you spare a mo?'

An elderly, diminutive woman makes her way forward. 'Morning, Frank,' she says in a brittle, croaky voice. 'This is a rum do if ever I saw one.'

'Yep, it's a curly one all right. Fingerprints from the body?'

She nods. 'We've captured the deceased's fingerprints with the mobile scanner, but no match. They were tricky to get because of the damage caused by sea life.'

'I see. Charlene, what type of rope is this?' he replies, nodding towards the cord attached to the metal anchor.

'It's Manilla. Sometimes called hemp rope. You don't see it much these days as it's been replaced by synthetics. It's extremely durable and strong, but the length shrinks when wet.'

'Why's that?'

'The width of the fibres expand with moisture. As it expands width ways, it shortens lengthwise.'

Frank chuckles. 'You learn something new every day. And what's the shrinkage rate?'

Charlene tilts her head to one side. 'Varies, depending on many factors, but it could be as little as three per cent up to ten per cent. This rope used to restrain the poor chap is about two metres long, which means it may have shrunk by between six and twenty centimetres.'

'What's that in old money?'

'Roughly—two and a half inches to nearly eight inches. I'd suggest it be towards the lower end of the scale.'

'Still, if you're pinioned to a rock with a rope across your throat, any shrinkage is going to increase the pressure.'

'Very true. I'll test the shrinkage rate back at the lab.'

The three of them return to the body as Zac saunters across the beach and clambers across the base of the Nab. He pulls his chin back as he spies the corpse.

'Fuck me,' he murmurs. 'I take it we can rule out suicide?'

Prisha rolls her eyes and shakes her head at him.

Frank addresses Charlene. 'Silly question, but it needs to be asked; any form of ID been found?'

'No. And absolutely no evidence. We've taken samples and swabs from the body, but immersion in sea water has wiped it clean. We may retrieve something from the rope, the gag, or the cloth binding his feet, but it will be a long shot.'

'What is that wrapped around his feet?' Zac says as he crouches to take a closer look.

'Not sure yet,' Charlene says. 'It looks like an old cotton rag or T-shirt.'

Frank eyes the incoming tide. 'Thanks for your help, Charlene. I'll let you get back to work. You've probably less than an hour to finish up before the old man of the sea pays you a visit. Unless you have the powers of King Canute,' he adds with a grin.

'You're forgetting your history, Frank; King Canute failed to turn back the tide, proving he was a mere mortal compared to the omnipotent power of Mother Nature.'

'I stand corrected.'

'Holy shit!' Prisha exclaims with alarm, her eyes glued to the body.

'What?' Zac asks.

'I think I know who it is... I think we *all* know who it is!'

10

A plump gull emits a melancholy, resonant mew, swooping low over Black Nab, a perfect harmonic accompaniment to the bleak backdrop of the merciless, unremitting North Sea.

'It's the Deputy Principal of Carston Hall... Charles Murray,' Prisha declares.

All eyes gape at the corpse.

Zac edges forward, face wrinkled in doubt. 'Are you... shit, I think you're right.'

'It's definitely him,' Prisha confirms.

The development alarms Frank. 'I need this like a hole in the head,' he mumbles before refocusing. 'Prisha, Zac, did you ever suspect Murray had anything to do with the kidnapping of the two girls?' he demands.

Prisha bites her lip. 'No, boss. He was odd, peculiar in his mannerisms. And according to Tiffany Butler, he gave some girls the creeps... wandering eye syndrome. But he was never on our radar. Mark Bridges and Butler were our only suspects.'

Zac strokes his stubble. 'I agree. A wee bit peculiar, but I never thought for a moment he was involved.'

Frank huffs. 'Could we have missed something?'

Prisha falters, questioning her judgement. 'Well... I suppose we... we can always miss something, but I don't know what.'

'Come on Frank, think about it,' Zac begins. 'If Charles Murray had anything to do with the kidnapping and ransom demand, don't you think Bridges would have snitched on him too? He was quick enough to implicate Tiffany Butler.'

Frank has a hollow feeling in the pit of his stomach, which he doesn't welcome one little bit. It comes from experience.

'Maybe, but I hate coincidences with a passion,' he growls. 'Two girls who attend Carston Hall, abducted not more than a mile away from where we're standing, last seen wandering towards Black Nab. The caretaker confesses to the abduction but accuses Tiffany Butler, the girls' form teacher, of being the mastermind behind it all. Fifteen days later, the Deputy Principal of Carston Hall is murdered in the most brutal fashion, strapped to Black Nab. Slowly eaten alive.'

'Actually, it was Charles Murray who gave me the tip-off that Bridges and Butler were having an affair,' Zac adds.

Frank rubs the ball of his thumb against the inside of his index finger, repeatedly.

'This smells worse than an old tramp's jockstrap,' he says with deep introspection before he snaps to his senses. 'Right, look lively, we have work to do. Prisha, you're heading over to Full Sutton Prison today to interview Bridges about the armed robberies, right?'

'Yes, boss.'

'Good. When you interview Bridges, he'll no doubt have heard about a death at Black Nab, but let's hope he hasn't heard who it is. Once you've finished with the robbery questions, go over the kidnapping case again, then towards the end, tell him about the fate of Murray. See how he reacts.'

'Will do, Frank. But I don't see how Murray's death could be in any way related to the kidnap case.'

'Just keep an open mind, Prisha, an open mind. Zac, you need to get a warrant to enter Murray's house and obtain fingerprints. If you get a match with what we've already got, then we need to contact next of kin and get them down to the mortuary for a physical ID. Was he married?'

'Separated, boss, according to Tiffany Butler,' Prisha says.

He spins around, agitated yet invigorated. 'Dr Whipple! Dr Whipple!' he bellows, scanning the vicinity for the good doctor.

'No need to shout, chief inspector. Calm, quiet, methodical is always a shorter route to your destination.'

Frank ignores his advice. 'How long before we can bring a relative in for an ID?'

'Inspector, I have many cases running concurrently. Tomorrow, maybe Thursday.'

'Bullshit, Whipple! I'll give you four hours to make the body at least half presentable to a family member. We need a positive identification asap!'

'Chief inspector, that is imp...'

'Damn it man!' Frank explodes. 'Make it happen! This isn't your run-of-the-mill murder. Whoever did this could strike again.

The sooner we confirm this is Charles Murray, the sooner we can start to piece together the jigsaw.'

They both pull a Mexican standoff as the seconds tick by. Bennett Whipple is the first to blink.

'Four hours... I'll do my best, chief inspector.'

'Good. Thank you.'

'I'll also call to let you know when I'm planning to do the autopsy. I assume you'll attend?'

Frank's stomach churns. There are many things which sicken him about the job, but watching a once living body being sliced, cut, and hacked open is the worst. And as for extracting the gloopy organs...

He swallows hard. 'Of course. It goes without saying,' he replies, stoically. His colleagues follow him as he clambers off the rocks to the surety of the sand. 'By the way, give my regards to Mrs Whipple when you see her.'

Whipple has already resumed his work. 'I can ascertain no benefit in passing on a third-person's salutations in retrospect, inspector. It is meaningless... but I'll mention it all the same,' Bennet Whipple replies with no emotion as he uses a small wooden paddle to poke at a flap of skin dangling from the scrotum. 'Hmm... interesting.'

The three detectives march across the beach in quick time.

'Prisha, you organise uniform to go door to door at the holiday park. Maybe someone was out walking late last night. Although I doubt it. It was wild and woolly. Zac, what did the photographer have to say?' Frank demands, now in full battle mode.

'He's legit, boss. Checked his website. He's local. Robin Hood's Bay. Arrived five-thirty. Twenty minutes to set up. Light levels, finding his spot, all that malarky. Started shooting just before six. Before he moved his tripod, he reviewed some of the photos. Noticed something odd and zoomed in on a few of them. An army of crabs seemed to be converging around the back of Black Nab. He assumed it would be a dead fish or seal and went to check it out. Chucked his arse up then called a nines.'

'You've got a certain way with words,' Prisha states. 'You could have been a poet in a different life.'

'Thanks,' Zac grins. 'He's agreed to come down to the station for fingerprinting and DNA. He's pretty shook up... you know what artists are like, they only see the good in the world, not the bad.'

'That's what they're there for, Sergeant Stoker, otherwise there'd be no point living, would there?' Frank states reflectively.

'Erm... Not sure, boss. There's always football.'

'The best football is art, Zac. It's the gladiator and the sculptor—combined in one.'

Zac holds his hands out in front of Prisha, confused. She pulls a face and shrugs. They duck under the police tape and disrobe from their protective suits.

'One other thing, Zac. Persons unknown murdered Charles Murray, which means everyone is a suspect until proved otherwise—understood?'

'Yes, boss.'

'Repeat Finnegan's ABC.'

'Assume nothing. Believe nobody. Check everything,' Zac replies like a weary schoolboy, much to Prisha's amusement.

'Which means what?'

'Dig into the photographer's background and story.'

'Correct! He could be the next Lord Olivier for all we know.'

'Who?'

'Give me strength. Robert De Niro?'

'Oh, I get it, boss.'

Frank claps his hands together. 'Right, who's for a bacon and egg butty? My shout.'

Prisha and Zac grimace as they resist the urge to vomit.

'What about your diet?' Prisha asks.

'Bugger the diet for this morning. Well?'

'Thanks for the offer, but I'll give it a miss.'

'Me too,' Zac confirms.

Frank stares at them, bewildered. 'You young 'uns! Don't you know an army walks on its stomach?'

'A bit like a crab?' Zac replies.

11

Prisha parks the Skoda on the driveway of a modern bungalow on the outskirts of Whitby. Pulling on the handbrake, she glances at Zac.

'You're a hundred per cent sure about the fingerprints?'

Zac chuckles. 'Prisha, there's no such thing as one hundred per cent. We took a dozen prints from Charles Murray's flat, and they match with what we got off the body from the beach. That means they're ninety-nine per cent accurate. I enjoy an occasional bet, and I'd take those odds any day of the week.'

She winces, then sighs. 'God, I hate this part of the job. Especially when it's a murder.'

He places his hand on her arm. 'I know. It stinks. The only comfort I can take from these situations is telling myself I'll do everything I can to find the bastards responsible.'

'But we don't always, do we?'

'Don't what?'

'Find the murderer.'

He stares wistfully out of the window. 'Come on. Let's do it. Do you want to play mother?' he says as he exits the car.

'Not really,' she replies, following him towards the front door. 'But I suppose I will.' She knocks on the door, calmly but firmly. 'How long will it take me to get to Full Sutton Prison?'

'About an hour.'

Prisha checks her watch. 'You'll have to accompany Mrs Murray to identify the body, as I'm due at the prison at one o'clock.'

'That worked out nicely for you.'

'It wasn't planned. Here we go,' she murmurs, peering through the frosted glass as a blurred figure approaches.

A middle-aged woman with long, grey hair elegantly styled opens the door. Laughter lines nestle at the corners of her mouth, crow's feet adorn her soft blue eyes.

'Hello, can I help you?'

'Are you Mrs Nicola Murray?'

She nods. 'Yes.'

'I'm Detective Inspector Kumar and this is Detective Sergeant Stoker from North Yorkshire Police,' she says as they both flash their cards at her.

She clasps her hand to her mouth. 'Oh, you've found him. Thank god for that. Is he all right? Where was he?'

How the hell could she have found out already? Prisha muses as she swaps a fleeting, puzzled look with Zac.

'I'm sorry, but how do you know we've found him?'

The woman blinks and pulls her chin back. 'Because I filled in a missing person's report last Saturday at the police station. I assume that's why you're here.'

Shit! How come we didn't know about this?

'Oh, I see. May we come in? I think we may be at cross purposes.'

The living room is decorated tastefully and as neat as a new pin. Prisha shuffles uncomfortably on the settee, with Zac at her side. They decline the usual offer of refreshments.

'I'm sorry, but we weren't personally aware he was recorded as missing, Mrs Murray,' Zac explains in his soft Scottish brogue. 'Contrary to the widely held belief, we take all missing persons cases seriously the moment they're lodged. But with an adult, there's maybe a little less urgency as most people turn up after a couple of days.'

'I'm sorry, but you've lost me. Have you found my husband or not?'

Prisha swallows hard. 'Yes. Yes, we have. And it's not good news, I'm afraid, Nicola.'

'Oh no! No, no, no!'

'I'm sorry to inform you that your husband has passed away.'

Christ! I need to work on my delivery. I made it sound like he'd fallen asleep in an armchair and never woken up. Then again, I could hardly give her the full-blown details... not yet, anyway.

Nicola rocks back and forth as one hand clinches the side of her neck as though she's been stabbed. Her face is elongated in pain as tears tickle her cheeks.

Prisha turns to Zac. 'Maybe we will have that cup of tea, after all.'

He nods and makes his way to the kitchen.

The initial shock has momentarily subsided. Prisha stares at her watch, wondering when the Family Liaison Officer will turn up.

Nicola pulls a handkerchief from the inside of her sleeve, then blows her nose noisily. 'Please forgive me,' she stammers.

It's funny the things people say in their moment of grief.

'You take your time, Nicola,' Zac replies with a warm, friendly smile as he brushes his long, black locks back over his head.

'I'm fine, really. Okay, I'm ready. What happened to him?'

Prisha clears her throat. 'A professional photographer who was taking photos of Black Nab found his body early this morning. Black Nab... that's, erm, a natural geographical...'

Nicola cuts her off. 'I'm aware of Black Nab, inspector. I've lived here most of my life. So, you're telling me he drowned?'

'It is a possibility. We'll know more once we have the pathologists report. But it wasn't misadventure or suicide. We suspect he was murdered.'

'Murdered! No way! Are you sure you have the right man?'

'We obtained fingerprints from his flat earlier and they match with the body, so yes. We're certain.'

'I'm confused. Charles wasn't fond of the water even on a hot summer's day. There's no way he'd have gone for a swim at Black Nab. The waters around there are treacherous.'

'He wasn't swimming, Nicola. He'd been tied to the rock with ropes around his body.'

Her eyes close as she silently rocks back and forth, either imagining the horrifying death or trying to push it from her mind. Rising wearily to her feet, she gazes at a photo of her husband on the mantlepiece.

'Who would want to murder Charles?' she murmurs.

'That's what we aim to find out, Nicola... with your help.'

Tears erupt again. 'Charles had no enemies. He was a deputy principal at an elite private girls school, for Christ's sake! The most aggression he ever had to deal with was from irate, over-privileged parents complaining about their daughter's English score. This can't be happening.'

'I'm led to believe you and Charles were separated?' Zac says.

'What? Yes, about eighteen months ago,' she replies as she sits back down in an obvious fog.

As callous as it sounds, now is always a good time to get the good oil. While their brain is addled, Prisha thinks.

'Can you tell us about the separation?' she asks. 'It may offer up some clue.'

'It happened suddenly. I thought we were a loving couple, childless, but loving. Then one day he came home from work and told me he still loved me, but like a sister, not as a wife, not as a lover. He said we would always remain close friends, but life was too short, and we should separate, and both try to find new love.'

'That must have come as a shock,' Prisha offers gently.

'I was devastated. But my upbringing... well, I was taught not to make a fuss and just get on with things. I hoped it was a mid-life crisis, and he'd return after a few months with his tail between his legs. But he didn't,' she adds as she gazes longingly out of the window, almost expecting her estranged husband to amble up the driveway.

'Do you know if Charles was presently, or recently, in a relationship?' Prisha asks.

She clasps her hands together, dazed. 'He said not.'

'You seem uncertain?'

'Not long before our separation, we attended a party. It was held by one of the teachers from the school. That's when I thought something might be going on.'

'Can you elaborate?'

'On two or three occasions I caught him making eyes across the room, you know, flirting. I told myself I was being ridiculous. The woman was at least fifteen years younger than him and could have had any man she wanted. I'm not the jealous or suspicious type, but I know what I saw.'

'And who was this woman he was flirting with?'

'Tiffany Butler.'

Zac stiffens and murmurs something incomprehensible.

'Did you confront him about it?'

'No, of course not.'

'Apart from the flirting, did you see or hear anything to suggest he was having an affair with Miss Butler?'

'No.'

A hush falls over proceedings, the only noise the occasional screech of a distant seagull.

'Can you think of anyone who would want to hurt your husband, Nicola?' Zac continues.

A shake of the head.

'Had you noticed anything different about him over the last few days, weeks, months? A change in mood, or peculiar behaviour?'

She rocks back and forth, thinking, playing a morbid drama out in her head. 'Not really. Apart from...'

Hesitation.

'Apart from?' Zac nudges.

'Apart from the day the two girls from Carston Hall went missing from Saltwick Bay. Zoe and Emma, I think they were called.'

'That's right,' Prisha whispers.

'He visited me that night, after he'd finished at school. He was running the place as the principal was overseas on holiday.'

'And how was he?'

'Very upset.'

'In what way?'

'Agitated. Edgy. Distressed, rubbing his hands together. I sympathised with him. Even though he didn't know the girls too well, it was still a shock to the system. He even had a shot of whisky, and he rarely drank.'

The recollection doesn't reconcile with Prisha's impression of Charles Murray the day she visited him after the girls went missing. He was more concerned with the reputation of the school than with the fate of the girls.

'That was the last time I saw him.'

'Did you see him regularly?' Prisha asks.

'Yes. Once, sometimes twice a week, he'd call around for a cup of tea and a chat. As I said, we were still on good terms. That's why I reported him missing. A week without seeing or hearing from him wouldn't have been unusual. But by the second week, I became slightly unnerved and tried his mobile. It was dead. I called around at his flat and saw no sign of life. I rang Carston Hall last Friday, and he hadn't been seen there since the day you arrested the caretaker, Mark Bridges. That's when I knew something was wrong.'

'Just to confirm—the last time you had any contact with Charles was the day the girls went missing?'

Another nod of the head.

'You said he was agitated, nervous... is there anything he said specifically which was out of character?'

'No, not really. Although,' she adds, reflective, puzzled. 'He did say something odd.'

'What?'

'He said, thank god I don't believe in the afterlife.'

12

Prisha takes a left turn and drives past the rather unassuming sign for HMP Full Sutton. Visiting prisons isn't her favourite part of the job, especially category A prisons. First of all, there's the ghastly smell. An unholy fusion of stale food, body odour, and disinfectant which clings to your clothes and lingers on the skin. There's an overbearing claustrophobic atmosphere which hems you in, squeezing the air from your lungs. But worst of all is the pervading cloud of depression and hopelessness that sucks the marrow from your bones.

The interview room is standard fare. White painted breeze block walls, fluorescent lighting, plastic chairs, bare table apart from the recorder. A prison officer stands mute in a corner, Mark Bridges, and his solicitor are sitting opposite her, expressionless, as she goes through the usual rigmarole of risk assessments and the caution.

'How have you been?' she asks with a friendly smile once the preamble is complete.

'Never better. It's like being on holiday,' Bridges replies drily.

'A shock to the system?'

'Just a little. How are Zoe and Emma doing?'

'Good of you to ask. Emma's doing really well, as though nothing happened. She's a tough one, that girl.'

'And Zoe?'

She pauses. 'Not as good. Withdrawn, depressed, stays in her room all day. She's seeing a psychologist.'

He sighs and drops his head. 'I never... I mean... I didn't think it would affect them too much.'

There is remorse in his words and also stupidity.

'You drug two young girls, tie them up, gag them, then imprison them in a cellar for three days. How did you think it would affect them?'

He doesn't reply, merely fidgets with his fingers.

'You didn't think it through properly, did you?'

He lifts his head. 'The girls weren't hurt physically. She said they had a toilet, a sink, a kettle, beds, books, and food and water. She said it would be like an adventure for them.'

He's either a damn good liar or his words are true.

'She? You mean Tiffany Butler?'

'Yes, who else would I mean?'

'Mark, you're not doing yourself any favours by keeping up this fantasy. Miss Butler has an alibi. There is not a scrap of evidence to link her with the kidnapping. No fingerprints, no DNA, not even a hair fragment. And more importantly, the girls never mentioned her name once.'

'I told you, she's clever. She outsmarted me and now she's outsmarted you lot.'

She's not here to talk about the kidnapping, but a thought has just occurred.

'You mentioned the girls were provided with food and water?'

'Yes, that's what she told me? Was that another lie?' he says with some alarm.

'No, they were given bottled water and food.'

He relaxes. 'Good,' he mumbles.

'Do you know what the food was?'

He shrugs and shakes his head. 'No. She never said. I assumed it would have been biscuits, fruit, cheese sticks.'

Again, he's either a brilliant actor, or he genuinely doesn't know the girls were provided with forty-eight pot noodles, hence the kettle. It once again stirs her dormant suspicions that Tiffany Butler had some part to play in the crime, and she set it up to be in the clear if things didn't work out as planned.

She pulls out a packet of Polo mints and offers him and his solicitor one. They both shake their heads as she pops one in her mouth.

'Mark, for what it's worth, I believe you. I think Tiffany *was* involved.'

'She wasn't just involved. It was her who dreamt the whole thing up,' he snaps angrily.

She sighs. 'Then give me something I can nail her on?'

He huffs. 'Christ, I've given you everything. I don't know what else to say.'

Her mind trawls back over all the inconsistencies in his original statement until a couple of things jump out.

'Let's go back to the drop-off point for the girls. You said when you arrived, Tiffany Butler was already there.'

'Yes.'

'And she then transported them to Westerdale Grange?'

'Yes. But I didn't know it was Westerdale. Tiffany said it was better I didn't know.'

'But obviously, you didn't actually witness that because you weren't there.'

'Obviously.'

'Who took the girls out of the back of your Kombi van?'

'I did.'

'And you put them into the boot of Tiffany's car?'

'No. I laid them on the grass at the side of her car.'

A tingling sensation shoots down Prisha's spine. 'Why not put them directly into the boot?'

'She had a tarp on the backseat. Said she'd lay it out in the boot to stop any contamination, forensics, and all that. She was keen for me to set off back to the school as soon as possible.'

'Did you see her put the girls in the boot?'

'No. As I was leaving, she was untying the tarp. I don't see how any of this helps,' he adds, becoming restless.

His solicitor leans forward. 'Inspector, I believe you are here to interview my client about another matter. Can we please address that, as we are all busy?'

'I'm not,' Bridges smirks.

'Yes, of course.' Prisha unbuckles her leather satchel. 'Mark, are you aware of a spate of armed robberies on petrol stations that have occurred over the last eighteen months, around the North East and North Yorkshire?'

'Yes. You'd have to be deaf and blind not to have seen or heard about it on the news.'

'And are you aware that as well as cash from the till being stolen, the main haul was cigarettes and pouch tobacco?'

'Yes. The press nicknamed them the Tobacco Raiders,' he replies with a grin.

'The media like a catchy name. And as you know, during our investigations into the disappearance of Emma and Zoe, we searched your workshop in the cellar of Carston Hall School.'

He shrugs.

'During the search, we found cigarettes and tobacco products with a retail value of over thirty thousand pounds, with an estimated street value of about half that.'

'You're not telling me anything new, inspector.'

'You said you bought them from some random guy you met in a pub.'

'That's right.'

'Which pub?'

He pushes his lips out and waggles them from side to side.

'I can't remember now.'

'What was this bloke called?'

'Didn't get a name.'

'How did you get your hands on them? The tobacco and cigarettes?'

'I arranged for him to drop them off at the school late one night.'

'What vehicle was he driving?'

'Some sort of transit van, a Nissan, I think. White.'

'And what did this mystery man look like?'

'Average height, build, weight. Mousy hair. Non-descript sort of guy.'

'Any distinguishing marks—scars, tattoos?'

'Not that I noticed.'

'Accent?'

'Northern. Maybe Manchester.'

'If you saw him again, would you recognise him?'

'Maybe, maybe not.'

'And how much did you pay for the cigarettes and tobacco?'

'He wanted ten grand, but I haggled him down to seven.'

'And you paid him cash?'

'No, I paid by cheque! Of course I paid him cash.'

'That's a lot of money to find for a man on a caretaker's wage.'

'I'm careful with money. I had some savings. It was a good way to double my investment.'

'And how did you hope to offload them?'

A flicker of doubt shoots across his face. 'Yeah, that bit I didn't fully think through.'

'Seems to be a failing of yours.'

He glares at her, then softens. 'I was thinking about selling them on the internet but hadn't quite figured out how. There was no rush, they weren't going anywhere, and the price of smokes is only ever going to rise. It's like investing in gold.'

Prisha has outlined the many plot holes in his ridiculous version of events. Bridges is a poor liar, and it's easy to detect when he's telling lies... and also when he's telling the truth. Now she gets serious.

'Do you know a man called Jack Turner?'

Eyes stare at her, impassive. He shakes his head.

'Can't recall such a name.'

'Maybe this will jog your memory.'

She pulls a photo from her satchel and places it on the table.

'For the benefit of the recording, I'm showing Mr Bridges a recent photograph of Jack Turner.'

A cursory glance is all the image gets. 'Nah, never seen him before.'

She shows him three photos of the Land Rover, two taken from grainy CCTV footage and one downloaded from the Pre-Loved Cars website.

'Do you recognise this vehicle? It was involved in the armed robberies.'

Another shake of the head. 'Nope.'

Now to reveal her hand, after a long pause, of course. Their eyeballs lock. She slowly extracts the snap lock bag containing the Mars bar wrappers and carefully places them on top of the photos.

Eyes blink rapidly as the cogs in his head go into overdrive.

'Mars bar wrappers. What of them?' he asks.

'They were found in the Land Rover.' His right shoulder involuntarily lifts, as though trying to relieve an ache. 'One of them has your fingerprints on it.'

She's gilding the Lilly somewhat. It was a partial print and certainly not enough to get a conviction, but he doesn't know that.

'Can you explain how a chocolate wrapper with your fingerprints on it could find its way into a vehicle you've never seen before, owned by a man you've never met?' Arms are now crossed, face hardened. 'Cat got your tongue?' she adds softly.

Silence ensues as she stares at him, and he gazes at the wrappers. He's desperately trying to think of a plausible explanation that a jury might buy. But he's struggling to find one.

'Come on, Mark, help me out here. We know you were involved. Were you part of the gang or were you just the fence?'

He takes a deep breath. 'Can you stop the recorder, please? I need a break.'

Prisha states the time and acknowledges his request, then hits the pause button.

'Can we talk off the record?' he pleads.

'Sure. Anything you say now cannot be used in a court of law. Fire away.'

'What's in it for me? I'm already going down for a long time. Why would I want to increase my sentence?'

'The kidnapping case will take a long time for the Crime Prosecution Service to put together. Whereas the armed robberies, as serious as they are, will be far quicker to get to court. We can make a note to the judge about your cooperation in both cases. No guarantees, of course, but a guilty plea and acknowledgement of your assistance can sway judges in handing down shorter sentences.'

'It's a gamble, you mean?'

'Yes, but it's all you've got, Mark. You're going down for both crimes either way. It's just a matter of time until we find more evidence against you, or for Jack Turner to slip up. It's your last roll of the dice to minimise your time in here. A few years of good behaviour and they may move you to a category C prison. A couple more years and you could end up in a "D Cat". An open prison will be a doddle compared to this place.' She doesn't believe a word about the prison transfers. He'll be serving twenty in maximum security without a doubt, but she has to leave the door open for him.

'Maybe when I eventually get out, we could go for that drink we talked about?' he says with that attractive boyish smile of his.

Prisha blushes. 'Yes, maybe we could,' she hears herself replying softly.

His face drops. 'I'll be an old man by then. Probably early fifties,' he laments, fully realising the enormity of his actions.

'Fifties are not old these days. They're the new forties.'

His eyes tear up as he sniffs. The atmosphere is heavy. He regains his composure and sits bolt upright.

'Okay. I want a few minutes alone with my solicitor,' he states pragmatically.

'Sure. I could do with a coffee, anyway.'

'Okay, Mark,' she says, pulling a clutch of papers from her satchel, 'this is going to take a long time to get through. We can certainly make a start today, but if you'd prefer me to come back another day to finish off, then we can arrange that.'

He sighs. 'No. Let's get it all done today, then it's out of the way.'

'Fine,' she replies, desperately trying to remain calm despite her euphoria running rampant at convincing him to confess to the robberies.

His solicitor is less than impressed. 'Wonderful! You'll have to excuse me for a moment. I need to make a call to my office and ask them to rearrange all my appointments. I wasn't expecting this!'

'Pardon me for breathing,' Prisha mutters as the solicitor leaves the room.

'She's a laugh a minute, that one,' Bridges says with a chuckle.

13

Zac knocks once, then slouches into Frank's office and closes the door. Frank is busy signing papers and barely looks up.

'Getting anywhere with him?' he asks.

'No. It's the usual performance from Jack Turner. No comment, no comment, no comment. Have you heard from Prisha?' Zac says as he flops onto a chair and runs a hand through his hair.

'I tried a moment ago, but it went to message-bank. She must still be at the prison. Her phone will have been left at the guardhouse.'

'That sounds promising. Pushing three hours. She may have had a breakthrough.'

'It's looking that way,' Frank replies absentmindedly as he swishes his signature across the last of the documents and reclines in his chair. 'Bloody paperwork,' he grumbles.

'How's the search for the Land Rover going?'

Frank shakes his head. 'Nothing in the vicinity of Little Beck Farm. I've called it off. Like looking for a needle in a haystack.'

He picks up his pen and twiddles it between thumb and forefinger.

'Zac, a personal question?'

'Go on.'

'Prisha—you've worked closely with her now for a few weeks. What are your thoughts?'

Zac puffs his cheeks out. 'She's a team player. No ego. Keen, a sharp mind. She's got balls. Easy to get along with and easy on the eye. Why do you ask?'

'Hmm... Yesterday, at the farm, if she had the nous to take a photo of the vehicle, we'd have Turner by the short and curlies.'

'True. But we all make mistakes, Frank. There is a lot of pressure that comes with the job. She's a city girl and being catapulted into a remote area and coming face to face with Jack Turner would be enough to put the fear of god into anyone. He's harmless enough, but you wouldn't know that looking at him. Anyway, she had the nous to get the Mars bar wrappers. I'm not sure I'd have picked up on that.'

'Aye, fair point. It's a bit of a black mark against her name, though. I hope the superintendent doesn't start asking too many questions. I'd hate to drop her in it.'

Zac thinks of Prisha's other blunder from yesterday when she called out Turner's name. He decides not to mention it.

'Talking of the insalubrious Mr Turner. What do you want me to do with him?' Zac asks.

Frank checks the clock on the wall. 'His twenty-four hours are nearly up. Let him go.'

'You could get a twelve hour extension from the superintendent.'

'No. She's funny about granting extensions unless we have hard evidence, and the suspect is wavering. You know what Jack's like. We could keep him here for a month and he'd still be repeating no comment like a bloody parrot. We'll get him, eventually. I can't envisage any more petrol stations being held up. That's one little scheme that has run its course.'

'Okay, Frank. I was developing a migraine from his body odour, anyway.'

'It's a dirty job, Zac, but someone has to do it. I've been there, done that and bought the T-shirt.'

'Ah! That reminds me, I called in at the forensics lab earlier and caught up with Charlene Marsden,' Zac says pulling his phone out.

'Oh, aye?'

'The rag around Charles Murray's feet was a T-shirt,' he replies handing Frank his phone. 'I got a photo.'

Frank is baffled. 'What in hell's name! Mortician—Hacked Up For Barbecue?' he mouths, as he studies the macabre image emblazoned across the T-shirt.

'Russian death metal band,' Zac explains.

'Death metal? What in all buggery is death metal?'

'You've heard of heavy metal?'

'Just about.'

'It's like an extreme form of that. Hundred miles an hour, heavy fast drumming, deep growling vocals like the devil.'

'Not quite The Carpenters, then?'

'Who?'

'I'm sensing a definite generation gap between you and me, Zac.'

14

Prisha's finger jabs down on the stop button of the recorder.

'How do you feel?' she asks Bridges with a pleasant smile.

He sucks in air, his muscular chest rises, then expels breath in a long, slow whoosh.

'Exhausted, mentally, and emotionally, but relieved it's all over. I was never cut out to be a criminal.'

A wave of empathy washes over her. He's not actually capable of hurting anyone. He has a simple and gentle nature, but he's made some bloody stupid decisions. Prisha packs away the documents and buckles up her satchel.

Hell, I almost forgot. Charles Murray.

'Oh, Mark,' she says as his solicitor rises and thumps her briefcase shut. 'Did you hear about the body found on Saltwick Bay early this morning?'

He stands, raises his arms above his head and performs a stretch.

'Yeah. Who was it, swimmer, surfer?'

'No, it was actually someone you knew.'

The solicitor glares at Prisha. 'Inspector! Are you now wishing to question my client about another matter?' she demands.

'No. It's simply a bit of idle gossip. It has nothing to do with Mark.'

'Good. Right, I must be on my way. My afternoon has been thoroughly disrupted enough. Good day.'

The prison guard remains silent in the corner as the solicitor departs, slamming the door behind her.

'Who was it?' Bridges asks as he performs neck exercises.

'Charles Murray.'

Confusion creases his features as he slowly sits back down and rests his arms on the table.

'Charles Murray, old Twitchy,' he mumbles. 'How?'

'Murdered in the most brutal fashion. Naked and strapped to Black Nab as the tide came in. The crabs and fish had a beano.'

His eyes crease. 'Poor bugger? Who did it?'

'That's what we aim to find out. You worked alongside him at the school for many years. Do you know of anyone who may have had a grudge against him?'

He ponders, whilst shaking his head, staring into the distance.

'No, not old Twitchy. He was as straight as they come. Or at least that's the impression he gave.'

'So nothing odd that jumps out, no peculiar behaviour, sudden outbursts, or shady characters you may have seen visiting the school?'

'No. Not that I can think of. Hang on... actually, now you mention it.'

'What?'

'Something I overheard. About six months ago, I was up in the school's loft placing rat bait. We get a lot of them in the winter months, and they can wreak havoc with the electrics if they chew through the insulation.'

'Yes?'

'As you can imagine, it's a big old loft, so I was up there some time. Anyway, I heard a mobile phone go off right underneath me, then the sound of Charles Murray's voice. I was directly above his office. I knelt down to get a closer listen. Bit rude of me I suppose, but we all like a good eavesdrop, don't we?'

'I suppose we do, especially if we're unseen.'

'I obviously couldn't hear what the caller was saying, but Murray's replies were peculiar.'

'In what way?'

'Hang on, give me a moment. I want to get this right.' He closes his eyes for a few seconds before they blink open. 'That's right. He said, "tonight?" as though he was surprised. Then he said "the safehouse" as if he was repeating what the caller had said. He followed that with, "this is not what I'm paid to do" or something like that, in an angry tone... no, not angry, more indignant. And he ended by saying "there are always options" he said it in a sort of superior, laughing manner. Then it went silent. I assumed the call had ended.'

'Are you sure he said safehouse?'

'Positive. If it hadn't been for that, I wouldn't have given it a second thought.'

'I don't suppose by any miracle you can remember the day of the call?'

'Yes, I know exactly what day it was.'

'Go on.'

'It was Friday afternoon, the twentieth of February this year.'

Prisha's surprised at his excellent recall. 'Why would the date stand out for you?'

'It was the night that woman was murdered near the 199 Steps.'

'Shirley Fox?'

'Yes, that's her. I even joked with Tiffany the next night. I told her about me overhearing Twitchy and I suggested maybe he was the murderer. It was only a joke, of course, with hindsight in very poor taste. Tiffany got annoyed and told me not to be so bloody stupid and not to repeat to anyone about what I'd heard Twitchy saying.'

'Why?'

'She said it could get me the sack, snooping on teachers. Apart from the tragedy of the poor woman being murdered, I was worried about it being bad for business.'

'Obviously, you were still involved with Tiffany at that time?'

'Inspector, I was involved with Tiffany right up until two weeks ago when you arrested me. I don't know what horseshit she's been shovelling you, but our relationship never ended. I loved her.'

'Okay, okay. Let's not go down that path again. Did you ever suspect anything going on between Charles Murray and Tiffany?'

He laughs. 'Tiffany and Twitchy! Do me a favour.'

'You said you were worried about it being bad for business. What business?'

'I manage a holiday rental, on Church Lane.'

'Sorry, I get confused between Church Lane and Church Street.'

'Church Street merges with Church Lane on the corner opposite the Prince of Wales pub. Church Lane continues up towards the 199 Steps. The holiday house is directly opposite to where Shirley Fox was murdered. I manage it for my aunt... or at least I used to.'

Prisha is gathering in the pieces of the puzzle, if not yet putting them together. 'One last thing about the kidnapping case?'

'Go on.'

'How did you obtain your fake passport?'

'Ha, from none other than Jack Turner. Cost me twenty grand. Hence why I got involved in the robberies in the first place.'

'Turner doesn't look like an expert forger to me.'

'Jack's not an expert at anything. He knew someone who could get it done.'

'Who?'

'Some Russian guy he knew.'

She swallows hard. 'Russian?'

'So he said. You never know what to believe with Slippery Jack.'

'Did you ever meet this Russian?'

'No. All he said was he was a big guy, not to be messed with.'

'I see. And is that where Tiffany got her fake passport from?'

'No. She said she'd take care of it herself. That was one thing she always insisted on—separation of everything. She said it was a safeguard so the police couldn't link us if it all went pear-shaped. She certainly got that one right!'

'Yes. Apparently to her own benefit.'

15

Frank and Zac are sitting with mouths agape as Prisha finishes her account of the interview with Mark Bridges.

'I've made a duplicate of the recording and the original is getting transcribed as we speak. That's only the robbery details, of course. All the other stuff about Charles Murray and Butler was off the record.'

Silence descends as Prisha stares first at Frank, then Zac and back at Frank.

'Well?' she says, irritated at their gawping faces.

'Congratulations,' Zac murmurs.

'Aye, bloody well done,' Frank concurs. 'A full confession from Bridges, not only implicating himself but also Jack Turner in the armed robberies.'

'We better round up Stinky Jack and give him the news,' Zac says, still gobsmacked at Prisha's resounding success.

'Hang on, before we finish, can we discuss what Bridges told me about the kidnapping case, and Charles Murray?' Prisha requests.

'Feel free,' Frank replies.

'Do you mind a bit of conjecture?'

'No. I encourage all my officers to look at things laterally as long as they don't get obsessed with their speculation.'

'There's going to be a lot of—what ifs, Frank. Tiffany Butler's name crops up again and again,' she begins.

'Only when talking to Mark Bridges,' Zac interrupts.

Prisha glares at him. 'Can you let me finish?'

'Sorry.'

'From day one, I've always thought she was up to her neck in it. She's a manipulative cow and a control freak. On the drive back to Whitby, I was thinking about Bridges managing the holiday rental on Church Lane, and also about him overhearing Charles Murray's telephone conversation. Bridges has always stuck to his story that he was only *one* part of the kidnapping team, and that he abducted the girls but handed them over to Tiffany Butler. In his original statement, he said when he arrived at the drop-off point, Tiffany was already there waiting for him, and it was her who transported the girls to a safehouse of which he didn't know the location. I asked him a few more questions. And here's an interesting thing—he never actually *saw* the girls in Tiffany's Subaru. He laid them on the grass, then hightailed it out of there. Now, strap yourselves in. Here's the biggy—what if Tiffany didn't transport the girls to Westerdale Grange?'

'Then who did?' Zac questions.

'Charles Murray.'

Frank pulls his head back, brow furrowed. 'How come he's suddenly appeared on the radar?'

'I'll explain in a moment. Forensics had Tiffany's car for three days and found not one jot of evidence; not a single strand of hair belonging to the girls, not a fingerprint, absolutely no DNA.'

'That's right,' Zac confirms. 'Even the sniffer dogs lost interest after about five seconds. Her car was clean.'

'I think it was clean because Zoe and Emma were never in it. What if after Bridges left, Charles Murray arrived, and it was *he* who took the girls to Westerdale?'

'But why Charles Murray?' Frank queries less than convinced at Prisha's fishing trip.

Prisha waggles her cheeks from side to side. 'Charles Murray's wife, Nicola, reckoned Tiffany and Charles were flirting with one another at a party. What if Tiffany Butler was having an affair with Bridges and Charles Murray at the same time?'

Frank grimaces. 'Then why hasn't Bridges ever mentioned Charles Murray in relation to the kidnapping?'

'Because Bridges didn't know Murray was involved. Don't you see? It's almost perfect. This is why I think Tiffany is a devious bitch. She gets Bridges to do the first part of the plan, and Murray the second part. She was making sure she had absolutely no physical contact with the girls. If the wheels fell off, as they did, then Bridges points the finger at Tiffany, and we focus our attention on her. But she has her alibi, and her car is clean. We have absolutely nothing on her, and Charles Murray doesn't even come into the reckoning. Frank, do you remember this morning on the beach when you asked me if we could have missed something?'

'Aye.'

'Well, I think we did. Charles Murray was Tiffany's invisible man.'

Frank leans back in his chair, fingers tapping the desk. 'As theories go, it's got legs, but still no evidence. We'll need a search warrant for Murray's car. See if forensics come up with anything.'

'Hang on Frank, I haven't finished yet,' Prisha states, her imagination in full flight.

'Hell, have you had too much coffee today? Go on.'

'What if Charles Murray was involved in the murder of Shirley Fox?'

'Woah! Back up your horses and stagecoach, a bit there, lass,' Frank says. 'I can see how he could have been involved in the kidnapping, but the Shirley Fox murder? You're pushing the boundaries now.'

'Hear me out. Murray would have known Bridges managed a holiday let on Church Lane, yards from where Shirley was killed. It would have been the perfect spot to hide, unseen. As Shirley walked past, he could have slipped out of the door, clonked her on the head and strangled her.'

'Why?' Zac asks, now appearing as incredulous as Frank.

'That I don't know... yet.'

Frank scratches at his stubble. 'Let's run with your theory for a moment. If Murray was the mystery killer waiting in Bridges' holiday house, he'd have needed a key from Bridges. You said Bridges overheard Murray's conversation about the safehouse and he remembered the exact date because it was the same day as Shirley's murder.'

Prisha nods. 'Yes.'

'He even made a poor joke about her death and Murray being involved.'

'That's right.'

'Don't you think he'd have also recalled giving Murray a key to his holiday house?'

'Yes, he would have. But what if it was Tiffany who gave the key to Murray? She could have taken it, then replaced it without Bridges ever knowing.'

'Strewth!' Frank exclaims, puffing out his cheeks. 'Have you finished yet?'

'Not quite. Tiffany could have used the knowledge of Murray's crime as a bargaining chip to get him to aid and abet her with the kidnapping of the girls.'

Frank rises, exchanging a dubious glance with Zac. 'Okay, let's assume all that is true. The question still remains; why would Charles Murray want to murder Shirley Fox?'

Prisha bites the inside of her cheek and glances out of the window at the distant rolling waves. 'That I don't know, apart from it may have something to do with Dudley Fox's work at Menwith Hill. If Murray killed Shirley, I don't think he meant to. Maybe he intended to abduct her, hence mentioning the safehouse, which was probably Westerdale Grange. If Shirley Fox recognised him during the attempted abduction, then he'd have had no other choice but to kill her.'

Frank slowly shakes his head. 'One minute Charles Murray is a respectable deputy principal at an elite private girls' school, the next minute he's some cunning Jack the Ripper knocking off innocent women and abducting young girls. It's fanciful in the extreme.'

Prisha raises her eyebrows. 'I would totally agree with you—if it was yesterday.'

'What does that mean?'

'Respectable deputy principals don't typically end up strapped to a rock as the tides coming in. Murray was entangled in something serious. His death wasn't just a murder... it was vengeance on an industrial scale.'

Frank pulls on the lobe of his ear. 'It's got more holes in it than a Swiss cheese factory,' he says with a sigh, resuming his seat. 'Having said that, Dudley Fox *was* working on a top secret project at Menwith Hill at the time,' he murmurs as his gaze takes in the panoramic vista of Whitby. 'If someone wanted to get Dudley to divulge secret government information, then abducting Shirley as leverage would have been one way to do it.'

'Shit! This is getting bigger than Ben Hur,' Zac says, as all three of them now stare outside.

Prisha nods, her mind on fire. 'Maybe this is what it's been about all along—Dudley Fox. Shirley's murder, the armed robberies, and the kidnapping could all be interwoven. And if they are, there's one common denominator between all three.'

'Tiffany Butler?' Frank says.

Prisha nods. 'Yes... Tiffany Butler.'

'As speculation goes, it's not a bad hypothesis, Prisha. But we need facts, eye-witnesses, and evidence, and you're overlooking one thing.'

'What?' Prisha replies.

'Bridges could be feeding you a crock of horseshit. Maybe he was the one who masterminded the kidnapping, and he alone was the one who enacted it. All this stuff about overhearing Murray's conversation, and still trying to implicate Tiffany, could be lies. Bridges could be playing you, Prisha.'

'He could be, but I don't think he is. He's admitted his part in two crimes and knows he's going down for a hefty spell. He has nothing to gain but a clear conscience. And as you noted when you first interviewed him, he's a terrible liar. The flip side of that is when he is telling the truth, he's completely believable.'

'Okay. We don't have much else to go on at the moment, so let's keep your speculation in our minds to guide us but not control us. Are we done?'

'Yes,' Prisha says with a grin.

'Good.'

'Oh, one last thing,'

'Hell fire!'

'Not that it really fits in anywhere, but Bridges obtained his fake passport from some Russian guy using Jack Turner as a go-between.'

'I'm glad we've cleared all that up then,' Frank says with a sardonic sigh.

16

Wednesday 2nd September

Frank grunts into the mouthpiece, receiver at his ear.

'Yes, yes, I see.'

He glances out of his office window as Zac and Prisha amble into the incident room, laughing and joking, buoyed by their recent success on several fronts. Frank gently taps on the window to attract their attention. He waggles the back of his fingers at them, indicating for them to come into his office.

'Yes, of course,' he continues on the phone. 'No, I fully understand. It's out of our jurisdiction. I'll liaise with our colleagues in Humberside.'

Prisha and Zac enter the office, all smiles, ribbing each other. They fall silent as they notice Frank in mid-flow.

'Once again, thanks for notifying me so promptly. It's appreciated. Yes, and the same to you. Bye.' He hangs up the receiver and stares at his proteges.

'No news on Jack Turner, I'm afraid, Frank,' Zac begins. 'Looks like he's gone to ground. We've got his ugly mug on all the social media sites and uniform have a photo of him. The local TV news will include him in their early evening and late night bulletin.

He's not the sharpest tool in the shed. He'll turn up sooner or later. It's just a matter of time.'

Frank nods but says nothing.

'And I have some good news and some not so good news,' Prisha says with a bounce in her step. 'I spent all last night thinking about Tiffany Butler's alibi.' She laughs. 'I know we're not supposed to take our work home with us, but it's been niggling away at me. My spider senses were twitching. Anyway, this morning I paid another visit to Frodsham Spa, the lynchpin of her alibi. We know that on the morning of the girls' kidnapping, she was getting pampered at the spa. Her swipe card recorded her entering and leaving. She was at the spa between ten and two o'clock. Now remember, according to Bridges, he says he dropped the girls off with Tiffany about 11:35 am, give or take. Therefore, Tiffany Butler is in the clear, right?'

Frank and Zac glance at each other. 'It appears that way,' Frank mumbles.

'Except—no one at the spa actually *saw* Tiffany between eleven and one because she was in the flotation tank for two hours—or so everyone thinks. I went back to the room where the flotation tanks are located. They face out onto deserted moorland. And guess what, they have big, beautiful windows offering you a stunning view. Turn a security key and they push wide open. It's a two-foot drop to a gravel path which runs around the perimeter of the spa. However, the building has numerous security cameras on every aspect, but they point outwards and not directly down. So, I conducted a little experiment with the help of the woman on reception, monitoring the cameras. I slipped out of a window, hugged the side of the building, bent double, and made my way around to the rear which is no more than ten feet from the main road separated by a small wall behind which are a row of dense trees and shrubs. There's a security camera on the corner, so I was sure it would pick me up as I climbed over the wall and disappeared into the trees. When I went back to reception via the main entrance, you should have seen the look on the receptionist's face. She thought I was an illusionist. She had seen nothing of me. The camera, which I thought would have captured me, is completely out of focus and is pointing at the horizon. Completely useless. Ta-dah!' she finishes with her arms held out, expecting a round of applause which Zac obliges her with.

'Nice work. What's the bad news?' he asks.

'Oh, the bad news, yes. It's impossible to *prove* that's how she was able to be at the rendezvous with Bridges at eleven thirty. But I'm damn sure that's how she pulled off the miracle. All she had to do was park her car on the roadside instead of the spa carpark.' She finally ends with a chuckle.

'I think it's time one of us paid Tiffany Butler another visit,' Zac says.

'The pleasure will be all mine,' Prisha replies with a mean glint in her eye.

Frank's face is downcast and ashen. Slowly, the two detectives notice his countenance.

'What's wrong Frank? You look as white as a sheet.' Prisha asks, concerned.

'Don't tell me Meera's extended the diet until the end of October?' Zac says, instantly regretting his words.

'Sit down,' Frank says. They both pull up a seat. 'Some bad news, I'm afraid.'

'What is it?' Prisha asks, as a twang of anxiety ripples through her body.

'Early this morning, Mark Bridges was found unresponsive in his cell with a rope around his neck. He died in hospital a few moments ago.'

'Suicide?' Prisha questions in a distraught whisper.

'Unlikely. The rope has been identified as hemp rope. The same type used to tie Charles Murray to Black Nab.'

17

Their eyes peer out from behind plastic goggles. Dressed in white protective body suits, from head to toe, the three of them cut an odd assortment; the giant hulking physique of Doctor Bennett Whipple; the stocky and broad build of DCI Frank Finnegan; and lastly, the slender, almost delicate figure of DI Prisha Kumar.

How the hell can a man of his size be a surgeon? His hands are like Christmas hams, Frank thinks to himself as he girds himself for the forthcoming horror show.

'No sign of bruising to the skull. A few minor abrasions to the back of the head probably caused by the waves pushing him against the rock,' Bennett Whipple begins, bending over the body of Charles Murray, fascinated with his work. 'The toxicology report will be some weeks away, but for what it's worth, this is not the body of a man who indulged in drink or drugs. That is conjecture, inspector, conjecture!' he bellows, his voice echoing off the harsh surfaces of the mortuary walls.

'Okay, no need to shout,' Frank says.

'I find it helps people pay attention.' His focus returns to the cadaver. 'I can confirm the scrotum was ripped open by a Carcinus Maenas.'

'What the hell's that?' Frank asks.

Doctor Whipple pauses and eyes Frank impatiently. 'A common sea crab, inspector. May I continue?'

Frank nods. 'Aye.'

'No doubt there was a veritable scrum as they feasted on the delicacies inside the pouch,' he continues. 'The eye sockets definitely show signs of aggressive avian peck marks. Probably a Gelochelidon Nilotica or possibly a Larus Argentatus, or Larus Fuscus, or even Larus Canus.'

'You mean a seagull?' Frank queries.

The doctor stops again and straightens to his full, imposing height, sighing wearily.

'Yes, inspector—to you, a seagull. May I continue?'

Frank nods. 'Aye.'

Bennett leans over the body once more. 'Numerous fine bite marks are consistent with the frenzied feeding habits of the Scomberomorus.'

Frank opens his mouth but doesn't have time to ask his question before Bennett forcefully thrusts his palm out in front of him.

'Mackerels inspector, damn mackerels! Right, let's open him up and see what we have inside. My favourite part. I'm expecting an abundance of sea life to rain forth,' he adds with a certain amount of macabre glee as he reaches for the scalpel and deftly splits the flesh open from the collarbone to the lower abdomen.

Frank closes his eyes. A gushing noise resonates around the room. As he opens his eyes, Bennet Whipple reaches for the rib shears. Frank closes his eyes, swallows hard and braces himself for the brutal sound of cracking bones.

———◦———

'There we are. All done. Quite fascinating,' the doctor says as a rare smile briefly pays him a visit. 'I'll have my interim report to you by tomorrow.'

'Thanks, but in layman's terms, what killed him?'

'All his vital organs were in tip-top shape apart from the damage caused by the Talitrus Saltator—sand fleas—inspector!' he yells. 'Although, that is a misleading nomenclature. They are, in fact, from the amphipod family, a crustacean. The damage they inflicted was initiated post-mortem. I've never seen so many in a cadaver before. It's amazing how much flesh they can gnaw through, the cheeky little critters,' he adds with a chuckle. 'Of course, they don't have teeth. Their mouthparts comprise the labrum, mandibles, paragnaths, and maxillae, which amount to the same thing.'

'I appreciate the biology lesson, doctor, but what was the cause of death?' Frank reiterates, desperate to leave the grisly chamber.

'Carcinology is the study of crustaceans, inspector—not biology, which is a very wide umbrella.'

'Thanks for the clarification. Cause of death?'

'Definitely drowning, you could tell by the...'

Frank cuts him off. 'You can spare me the details. Would he have been conscious as the tide washed over him?'

'I don't see why not. The eating of the testicles and penis by crabs would have been quite painful, but it's unlikely it would have caused him to black out.'

'Quite painful!' Frank says with incredulity as he suffers an imaginary shooting pain through his own genitals.

'The cold seawater would have numbed the pain.'

'We should be thankful for small mercies,' Frank replies as he and Prisha turn towards the exit. 'Christ, that was brutal,' he adds under his breath.

Doctor Whipple whistles a cheery tune as he scrubs at his hands under warm running water.

Frank pulls open the door for Prisha. 'Now there's a man who enjoys his work just a little too much for my liking. By the way, did you call on Miss Butler?'

'Yes. No one home. Her next-door neighbour said he hadn't seen her for a few days. Which is odd, as the school term has just begun. So I rang the school, and they said she was on carer's leave visiting her sick mother.'

'Okay. Leave it a few days, then call again.'

18

Thursday 3rd September

Frank removes his Tupperware salad bowl from his backpack and stares at it with contempt. There's a knock on the door.

'Come in.'

'Morning,' Zac says in a cheery tone.

'Correct,' Frank replies curtly.

Zac chuckles. 'What's for dinner today? Looks delish.'

'Paleo grains, shredded carrot and beetroot with a dollop of low-fat cottage cheese,' he replies glumly as he deposits it into the tiny bar fridge nestled in the corner of his office.

'Yummy, yummy, yummy. I envy you. I wish my missus would pack me off with such goodies each morning. Unfortunately, I'll have to pay a visit to the chippy today. Or maybe I'll go for a big juicy beefburger smothered in fried onions and dripping in ketchup; then again, I might just pig out on half a dozen freshly minted donuts washed down with sweet black coffee.'

Frank slams the fridge door shut and glares at his detective sergeant through slits.

'You're about as funny as a fart in a spacesuit.'

Zac grins and picks up the overnight reports from Frank's desk.

'What's the latest?' he asks as he focuses his attention on the papers.

'Pretty quiet. Two stolen cars, a domestic at Hawsker, and a fire at Birch Hill Farm near Beck Hole,' Frank replies as he makes himself comfortable in his chair.

'What was torched?'

'An old barn.'

'Suspicious?'

'Not sure yet. Still waiting on a call from Fire Services.'

'Hmm...' Zac ponders.

'What?'

'As the crow flies, Beck Hole would only be about five miles from Jack Turner's abode, Little Beck Farm.'

'Good call. It would be just like Jack to try a stupid cackhanded attempt at a cover-up. Why don't you have a drive out there and check it out? Take Prisha with you if she's around.'

'Already on my way, boss.'

Prisha is enjoying the rugged scenery as they take the short twenty-minute drive to Beck Hole. Her mind is weary from constantly regurgitating the various aspects of the cases and their apparent crossovers. The clues, snippets, leads, the information from Bridges. She gives herself a break and focuses on something else.

'Are you any good at translation?' she asks Zac, as she flicks the indicator to take a left turn.

'No. I didn't do languages at school. Why?'

'I meant Yorkshire translation.'

Zac laughs and sits up straight. 'Oh, I get it. Frank?'

'Yes.'

'Go on then, what's he said that's bamboozled you?'

'I have a list in my notebook, but I'll reel a few off from the top of my head. The other day we were driving through the town, and he looked out of the car window and said—it's neither mickling nor a muckling. What the hell does that mean?'

Zac grins. 'Neither one thing nor the other. Usually said when he's referring to the weather.'

'Ah, I see. Okay, next one—what a palaver.'

'Uttered when referring to a long-winded series of tedious events that at the outset appeared to be straightforward.'

'Got it. Falling arse backwards into the butter?'

'The individual he's referring to is extremely lucky.'

'A bit like—they always come out smelling of roses?'

'Exactly. Next.'

'Hear all, see all, say nowt?'

'Observe everything, but keep it to yourself.'

'Appen?'

'Perhaps, or possibly that's true.'

'Faffing?'

'Stop messing about... wasting time.'

'Manky?'

'Something that has gone off. That sausage roll was manky.'

Prisha giggles. 'In another few months, I'll be an expert in the Yorkshire dialect.'

'You can put it on your CV.'

'Okay, last one, and the most baffling. Put wood in... oil, I think he said.'

Zac guffaws. 'Put wood int 'ole,' he corrects.

'Meaning?'

'Shut the bloody door!'

'Christ! I'd never have got that one.'

As they near Birch Hill Farm, a faint aroma of smoke filters into the car.

'I can't believe last week we were basking in golden sunshine and this week it's like the middle of winter,' Prisha complains as she takes her eyes off the road for a second and fiddles with the heater.

'Let me do that. You focus on driving,' Zac says as he cranks the heater up. 'If you think this is cold, wait until the middle of February when it's blowing its arse off, and the snow is three feet deep.'

'Aww, I bet it's beautiful and romantic. I can imagine Heathcliff and Catherine running across the open moors towards each other, arms outstretched.'

'Who? Anyway, if they did, I can assure you Heathcliff's balls would have frozen, and Catherine's tits would have dropped off before they reached each other.'

She purses her lips and throws him a disparaging glance. 'You know who you are—a young Frank Finnegan.'

'Bullshit! Slow down. Next left.'

As they turn onto the farm track, the one remaining fire truck is parked next to a smouldering building. The roof and doors are completely gone, but the stone exterior remains intact. They park up and alight as the senior crew manager greets them. His face is streaked with soot, and he appears weary.

'I was about to leave. Come on, I'll give you a quick heads up.' He leads them into the heart of the building. 'A trailer, and a four-wheel-drive. Plus, over a thousand hay bales... or so the farmer says.'

'Is he insured?' Zac asks.

'Yes, apart from the four-wheel-drive.'

Prisha is already circumnavigating the burnt-out car.

'Arson?' Zac asks the crew manager.

'Definitely. Whoever did it tried to make it look like faulty wiring.'

He pulls at a sliver of wire next to a charred power outlet and holds it up to Zac.

'What?' he asks, perplexed, as he stares at two insulated wires and a bare one.

'They cut the insulation. But if it had caused the fire, then all the insulation would have melted. Very amateur. Anyway, the seat of the fire was from underneath the four-wheel-drive. Diesel was the accelerant. At least they had the sense not to use petrol. Right, I'm already four hours over my shift and I'm bushed. Is there anything else I can help you with?'

'No, thanks.'

The crew manager turns and heads back to the fire truck.

'Watch yourself, parts of those wrecks are still hot,' he calls out as the rest of his crew packs their equipment away.

'Only the farmer can tell us if this was Jack Turner's vehicle or not?' Prisha comments as she gingerly sticks her head inside the window and peers at scorched metal and coiled springs from the seats.

Zac joins her, trying to avoid the pools of water. He carefully orbits the body of the wreck, eyes taking in everything, mind computing.

'Funny how both wing mirrors are now missing,' he notes.

'Could the other wing mirror have simply melted during the heat of the blaze?'

'Possibly, but you'd still expect to see fragments of glass near the door, and I can't see any,' he replies, crouching as he pushes through the debris with the metal arm of a windscreen wiper. 'This is definitely Jack's handiwork. He's got previous for arson, and he's certainly not improved his technique over the years. Come on, let's have a chat with the farmer.'

It's nearly midday as Prisha and Zac enter Frank's office and confirm the farmer had indeed paid Jack Turner fifteen hundred pounds for a Land Rover Defender a few days ago.

'Did he confirm the colour and the missing wing mirror?' Frank asks.

'Yes, boss,' Prisha says. 'But it's weak evidence and now with the death of Mark Bridges, his confession won't have much credence in court.'

Frank rises from his chair and ambles over to the tall window that looks out over the river.

'No, it won't. But Jack doesn't know that, does he?'

'I'm sure his brief will make him aware of it,' Zac adds. 'Any updates on the murder of Mark Bridges?'

Frank huffs. 'I've been liaising with Humberside Police. The CCTV cameras leading to Bridges' cell were conveniently out of action, and obviously none of the inmates are speaking. So, it was a random attack because of Bridges' involvement in the kidnapping of two young girls, or someone wanted him dead for other reasons.'

'The armed robberies?' Zac prompts.

'Possibly. But Jack Turner doesn't have that sort of clout to get someone knocked off. The rope he was hung with is foreign to the prison, meaning it was brought in from outside,' he replies, trailing off. He snaps from his introspection. 'We've done all we can for the moment. We'll see how Jack reacts when we eventually arrest him. But for now, I want everyone to focus on the Charles Murray case. The super's due in at one and she wants a meeting with the three of us.'

Zac and Prisha are puzzled. 'That's odd,' Zac murmurs.

'It is bloody odd,' Frank agrees. 'Right, if you'll excuse me, I'm going to attempt to eat my dinner. Wish me luck.'

As plain and drab as the police station is, Detective Superintendent Anne Banks' office is about as beige as it gets. It's a tiny room with no windows, located on the second-floor at the end of the corridor wedged between the incident room and the toilets.

In winter, she employs a small fan heater located under the desk to keep her feet warm. In summer, a pedestal fan recirculates the stuffy, overbearing air. It's not the only reason she seldom visits. Whitby is small potatoes compared to some of her other jurisdictions. She's also known Frank Finnegan for over thirty years, and he runs a tight ship. Today she doesn't need a heater, as five bodies are more than capable of raising the temperature despite the nature of the inclement weather outside.

With introductions over, she turns slightly to James Carmichael, who is sitting uncomfortably close on her side of the desk. It's not through design, but through necessity. He feels as claustrophobic as she does.

James studies the three faces in front of him as he weighs his words. He has an easy languid way with the top brass of the police but never quite pulls it off with those working the coalface.

He begins. 'As the superintendent explained, I am a senior officer of JSTAT, the Joint State Threats Assessment Team, which falls under the umbrella of MI5. Our main remit is national security: foreign actors who plan to conduct assassinations, espionage, democratic interference, economic security. I'm sure you get the picture.'

Frank, Prisha, and Zac are wondering what this is about. As Anne Banks explained, she had been referred to this matter from the highest level—no other than the Chief Constable himself. This was serious shit!

For comfort or for a power-play, James Carmichael rises and clasps his hands behind his back.

'We have a slight issue that has arisen—namely, Charles Murray.'

The three detectives eyeball each other warily.

'I'm not sure how much intel you've already uncovered on Mr Murray, but let me give you a synopsis. Charles Murray studied at Oxford University between 1988 and 1993. He was an active member of the British Communist Party, a rising star. Extremely intelligent, a gift of the gab and he had the common touch, able to mix with lords and duchesses and also the gal from down the supermarket. We kept tabs on him as a person of interest, for obvious reasons. Before my time, of course.

In 1994 he got hitched and his membership with the Communist Party lapsed. For a couple of years, we kept him on our radar, but it appeared he was now a happily married man and had devoted himself to academia working as a lecturer at Cambridge University. In 2004, he moved from Cambridge to Whitby to take up the position of deputy principal at Carston Hall Girls School. As prestigious as the school is in these parts, it's hardly Cambridge. This peculiar career move raised our suspicions and, once again, we put surveillance on him. He was quiet for a few years, but eventually he showed his hand. He was in the pay of the Russians.'

'A spy?' Prisha asks.

'We prefer the term—espionage agent, but yes... a spy. We fed Charles Murray false information, which he would pass onto the Russians. Information which had just enough plausibility and substance to convince the Russians of Murray's authenticity and usefulness. Any questions so far?'

Prisha readjusts in her seat. 'Yes, why didn't you just arrest Murray?' she questions, instantly feeling foolish at the naivety of her question.

Anne Banks raises an eyebrow as James Carmichael offers Prisha a condescending smile.

'There's an old saying: keep your friends close and your enemies even closer. There may have come a point in the future where Murray could have been valuable to us, or for him to take the king's shilling and begin feeding us information.'

'You mean you were using him as a pawn in some giant game of chess?' Zac says with a hint of contempt.

'We don't deal in ethics, sergeant. Our job is to ensure the safety of the nation and its people. To protect our way of life and all its freedoms from our many enemies. It may seem cruel, callous, but the greater good is always paramount.'

'Try telling that to Nicola Murray,' Zac mutters.

'Sergeant!' Anne Banks snaps.

'Sorry, ma'am,' Zac replies with little contrition.

'Ahem, yes,' Carmichael says. 'We seem to have wondered off-piste. Last Friday, Charles Murray contacted us requesting a rendezvous with one of our intelligence operatives; the destination, the top of Sutton Bank at midnight. During the meeting, he indicated he wanted to change sides and work as a double agent in return for certain guarantees.'

'What sort of guarantees?' Frank asks suspiciously.

'Immunity from past deeds.'

'What past deeds? Do you mean spying, being a traitor?'

'He didn't elaborate. Our agent said he'd need to talk to his chain of command, and he'd be back in touch. The next time we heard of Charles Murray was when you filed your report on Tuesday after the discovery of his body at Black Nab.'

An uneasy hush falls over the airless office as each person gathers their thoughts. Frank is the first to break the silence.

'What state was he in when he had this meeting at Sutton Bank?'

'Agitated. Trying to keep a lid on things.'

'He is edgy by disposition,' Prisha says as she recalls her first encounter with him. 'He had the nickname Twitchy at Carston Hall.'

'What made him suddenly want to change sides?' Zac enquires.

'Again, we're not sure,' Carmichael replies, his eagle eyes scanning the faces in front of him.

'Do you know of Tiffany Butler?' Prisha asks.

Carmichael pulls his head back and straightens. 'We know Murray was in a casual relationship with Miss Butler.'

His intonation denotes he knows more than he's letting on, Frank thinks.

'Would she have known of Murray's double-life?' Prisha persists.

'Highly unlikely. The whole point of a secret agent is to be just that—secret.'

Frank rubs at his face. 'The scenario is, Murray got spooked for whatever reason, and decided his safest bet was to come back to the fold. He has a meeting with one of your operatives and three days later, he's murdered. Which all points to the Russians finding out about his betrayal and taking him out.'

Carmichael nods his agreement. 'It's one possibility.'

'But why go to such lengths to kill him? A lot of effort and planning went into his murder... and risk. Why not just put a bullet through his head while he slept?'

'I think that's obvious, don't you, inspector?'

'Yes. It was a warning. But a warning to who?'

'We're not sure. As far as we know, Murray was working alone. A sleeper. Anyway, I'll get to the point of why I'm here telling you all this. I want you to drop your investigation into the murder of Charles Murray.'

All police officers exchange confused glances.

'What?' Frank asks, incredulous.

'You heard, chief inspector. This goes well beyond the remit of the police.'

'No, it bloody doesn't!' Frank growls. 'Our job is to prevent *and* detect crime. And my team intends to find out who murdered Charles Murray and bring them to justice.'

Carmichael looks to the superintendent for support, but finds none.

'Frank's right, Mr Carmichael. There's no way we can stop a murder investigation. The police have a social contract with the public. We can't simply turn a blind-eye to a murder because the victim was involved in espionage. We would lose face and support. Despite his nefarious double-life, Charles Murray was a respected member of our community.'

'I was afraid you'd say that superintendent. I have no authority in police matters, but if I so wish, I could go further up the ladder, to the very top if required. It wouldn't be in the best interests of anyone's career path, in fact, the very opposite.'

Anne banks stands up. 'Is that a threat?'

Carmichael retrieves his briefcase from the corner of the room, slips into his jacket, and makes his way to the door.

'I'll give you a few days to reconsider your stance. Good day. I can see myself out.'

19

Friday 4th September

Zac places two pints of bitter, and a gin and tonic on the table. The pub is relatively quiet, and the trio have picked a spot in a quiet alcove.

'Here's to the end of a tiring and confusing week,' Frank says as they all clink glasses and take a slug. 'Right, two quick pints and a debrief, then I want you two to go home and switch off for the weekend. If you're anything like me, your brain will be addled.'

Zac sniggers. 'Got to say, Frank, this Murray murder has more tentacles than a bag of octopi.'

'You mean a consortium of octopuses? The plural of octopus is octopuses. Anyway, it keeps the grey matter alive,' Frank replies as he takes another satisfying gulp of the amber nectar. 'Okay, let's go. Thoughts, questions, theories... let's lay it all out on the table. Prisha?'

'Not sure where to begin. It's like four jigsaw puzzles mixed up in one. Okay, first off, why would Carmichael want us to drop the case?'

'That one's easy,' Frank says. 'As heinous as Murray's death is to us, and the public, to Carmichael it's a tiny cog in a big wheel. They probably have surveillance on the mysterious Russians, and god knows what their ultimate end game is. He doesn't want the plods barging in with the size twelves undermining their operation. Next thought.'

'Carmichael appeared reticent when asked about Tiffany Butler, like he was holding back.'

'I agree. He knows more than he's letting on.'

'I've got a question for you, Frank,' Zac says as he spills a packet of peanuts onto the table. 'You've been on the force for thirty-eight years. In all that time, how many visits have you had from the spooks?'

Frank rubs his earlobe between thumb and index finger. 'If my memory serves correctly—none for the first thirty-seven years and two visits in the last six months. Once when interviewing Dudley Fox shortly after the murder of his wife. And now, a visit after the murder of Murray.'

'Coincidence?' Prisha asks.

'I don't believe in them. They are random occurrences which could be logically explained if we knew the whole truth,' he replies, swiftly rounding up a clutch of beer mats. He places one down on the table. 'Shirley Fox murdered six months ago—no suspects. A seemingly random attack. Charles Murray, murdered Monday gone—a harmless deputy principal by day, a spy by night,' he adds, placing another mat down. 'The suspected murder of Mark Bridges on Wednesday morning, only hours after his confession to Prisha about the armed robberies, and some interesting anecdotes about Charles Murray and Tiffany Butler.' The third mat is placed on the table. 'Dudley and Murray knew each other. Murray worked at the school, along with Bridges and Tiffany Butler. Bridges was involved in the robberies with Jack Turner, and the kidnapping possibly with Tiffany. If we rule out coincidence, then what's going on?'

A moments silence ensues as each detective stares down at the stained beer mats. Zac takes a sip of his pint as Prisha's hand darts out and tightly grips his arm, causing him to spill beer down his front.

'What the...'

'You're right Frank! It's not coincidence,' she cries, eyes bulging.

'Spit it out, lass. Don't leave us dangling.'

'They're being eliminated!'

'Who are?'

'Anyone who knew about the armed robberies, the kidnapping, and Shirley Fox's murder.'

'Shit. You could be right,' Zac murmurs.

'Which means there could be others in danger,' Frank says, deep in thought.

Prisha knocks back her gin and tonic. 'Yes. Most notably, Jack Turner, and...'

'Tiffany Butler,' Zac says finishing off her sentence.

Frank downs his pint and slams the glass on the table. 'You know, a moment ago when I said I wanted you two to go home and switch off for the weekend... cancel that. I want you both in the station, eight o'clock tomorrow morning. We have work to do.'

20

Saturday 5th September

The blue flashing light hits Prisha's bedroom window, briefly illuminating the interior. She stirs in bed and for a moment imagines she's in a nightclub before her senses drift back into reality. She glances at the red dots on her radio alarm—5:05 am.

Sitting up, she wipes the sleep from her eyes, then gazes at the curtains. Although it's chilly outside, her window is slightly ajar. The timeless rhythm of the constant breaking waves helps her to fall asleep.

The blue light streaks across her wall again, followed by blackness. Tottering towards the window, she peers out into the becalmed night. The lights are coming from high up on the east cliff, near to the pier. She yawns.

'Probably a Friday night assault. Boneheads with too much beer in their belly and a bloodstream full of amphetamines. They think they can take on the world. Although, it's a bit late, or early, for that sort of thing.'

She pulls a dressing gown over her pyjamas, pushes her feet into a pair of slippers and heads downstairs. As she makes a cup of hot chocolate, a fresh thought niggles at her.

'Odd that I didn't hear a siren. And if it was a punch up, there's usually blazing, angry voices, accompanied by wailing and screaming women. It's a still night, but even from that distance voices would have carried.'

Dropping a marshmallow into the centre of the rich, velvety brown liquid, she grabs a book from the coffee table and climbs the stairs. She plumps up her pillows, snuggles down and opens Wuthering Heights at the first chapter. She's read the book at least twelve times, but she always returns to it when troubled. It's her comfort blanket. Something reassuring and everlasting about the story, the antiquated language, the characters. Getting lost in a timeless novel from a different age is refreshingly purifying—even if it is a tragic romance.

Her eyes read the words, but her brain cannot digest them. She puts the book down and returns to the window. There are more flashing blue lights, and also a green one.

'Hmm, the emergency doctor is on the scene. Doesn't look promising,' she murmurs, throwing a glance at the clock which has ticked over to 5:25 am. 'Damn it. This job will be the death of me.'

She quickly pulls on a pair of tight tracksuit pants, a thick hoody and slips into her running shoes, dropping her warrant card and bank card into a pocket. Pulling her front door shut, she skips down the steps, then does a few quick leg stretches before jogging through the gate. At the top of the street, she hangs a right onto North Terrace as the frigid air stabs at her lungs. Passing under Whalebone Arch, she picks up her pace down the track which leads onto the serpent-like Khyber Pass. Running along at the side of the river, a handful of fishing trawlers glide by, lights twinkling as they head towards the harbour entrance. Now at a steady click, and in a good rhythm, she soon traverses the swing bridge and heads up into the old town. As she reaches the 199 Steps, and the place of Shirley Fox's demise, she bears left onto Henrietta Street, and is quickly greeted by the smoky, fishy musk from Fortunes Kippers emporium as blue flashing lights are corralled into the narrow lane. Passing the last of the old fishing cottages on her right, she slows to walking pace as she spots the police barrier tape and a couple of uniforms standing guard, protecting the entrance to the east pier.

A constable notes her arrival and sidles forward. 'Sorry miss, but this is a crime scene and is currently out of bounds to the public.'

She pulls her hood down and flashes her warrant card.

'Oh, Inspector Kumar, my apologies.'

'That's okay constable,' she replies with a warm smile.

'Early morning jog or business, ma'am?'

'Bit of both.'

He lifts the tape up for her to duck under.

'Chief Inspector Finnegan and DS Stoker arrived a moment ago. If you hurry, you'll be able to catch them,' he advises.

'Thanks. What have we got? A death?'

'I believe so, ma'am.'

'Male, female, or non-binary?'

He appears puzzled. 'Ahem, I don't have any details as yet, ma'am,' he says, missing Prisha's dry humour.

'Who reported it?'

'A Vietnamese couple who were out for a spot of early morning fishing at the end of the pier.'

'Cheers,' she says as she sprints off. She catches up with Frank and Zac as they near the lighthouse situated before the footbridge, which leads across to the east pier extension.

'Frank, Zac, wait up!' she yells.

'Prisha, what are you doing here?' Frank says.

'I saw the lights from my bedroom, accompanied by a nagging feeling. Anyway, I could ask you the same question.'

'DS Cartwright called me and Zac about thirty minutes ago.'

'And why didn't he call me?' she asks, a tad annoyed.

'Who knows how Cartwright's mind works? It's a labyrinth of confusion. You're here now, that's all that matters,' he says as they continue walking at a brisk pace. 'Have you been on this pier before?'

'No. I haven't had as much time as I envisaged since I arrived in Whitby. Been a little busy.'

Frank chuckles. 'Don't worry, lass. It's not usually like this. It will calm down pretty soon—touch wood,' he says, patting Zac's head.

They walk single file across the footbridge and onto the extension.

'Me and my dad used to do a lot of fishing at the end of this pier when I was a lad. He had a name for this part of the pier,' Frank says with a wistful air. 'He called it Jawbone Walk.'

'Why?' Prisha asks.

Frank stops and points to his left, across the harbour. 'Top of the hill on the west cliff—what do you see?'

Prisha follows the trajectory of his arm and spots the monument and tourist attraction.

'Ah, I get it... Whalebone Arch.'

'Aye. He said if you couldn't see the arch because of rain, fog, or snow, then to turn around and head back to land. Said it was a warning. Even had a little ditty he'd recite—*If Whalebone Arch thy cannot see, then turn around, I'm warning thee.*'

A shiver runs down Prisha's spine. 'So what do we know? The constable at the cordon was a little vague?' she enquires.

'Not much, yet. A body hanging in the water, suspended by rope attached to the railings. A nines was called at about quarter-to-five. Cartwright and two uniforms were first on the scene, followed by the paramedics and fire brigade... apologies, fire service.'

Zac, who has been unusually quiet, speaks up. 'I'm betting it's either the body of Jack Turner or Tiffany Butler,' he says gravely.

Frank sighs 'I'm not a gambling man, but I wouldn't wager money on anyone else. This thing is escalating fast. But let's keep a clear mind until we find out the circumstances. Rope and dead body could equate to a suicide.'

It's not long before they reach the end of the pier and the small throng of people; four burly fire officers, Cartwright and his two uniforms and police photographer, the on-call doctor and two paramedics, and the diminutive Asian couple sitting on camp chairs looking cold and terrified—plus, a body laid prostrate with a blanket over it.

'Any ID?' Frank barks at Cartwright.

He shakes his head. 'No, boss. But you'll know who it is,' he replies as Frank kneels and peels back the blanket, a torch from Cartwright illuminating the scene.

'Jack bloody Turner,' he whispers. 'You daft old bastard. What the hell did you get yourself mixed up in this time?'

———

Thirty minutes later, forensics are on the scene as the east pier is constantly lit up with the flash from a police photographer.

Frank is pumping Cartwright for information. 'Describe the scene to me when you arrived?'

'The Asian couple were at the top of Henrietta Street, agitated, speaking at ten to the dozen. Couldn't make out a bloody word of it at first. Their English is not much chop.'

'That makes three of you,' Frank says as he casts a glance over his shoulder at the couple, who are bewildered at the developments as Zac and Prisha interview them. 'Go on?'

'They led me and the uniforms to the end of the pier, down the steps to sea level, and pointed at the railings. I noticed the rope attached and when I peered over the edge, and shone my torch on the sea, I spotted a pair of legs with the rope wrapped around them.'

'Was he in the water?'

'Aye. Head first up to his arse.'

'Hell fire.'

'I called the police photographer, who arrived twenty minutes later. He captured the scene. By that time, the fire lads had arrived, and they pulled him up and laid him on the ground. I made sure everyone was wearing protectives, boss.'

'Okay. Good work, Cartwright, for capturing and preserving the crime scene before the body was removed. We'll make a copper out of you yet.'

Cartwright appears stunned at the backhanded compliment, which renders him mute.

Frank walks over to Zac and Prisha. 'What have you got?'

Zac turns to him. 'Pretty much the same story as Cartwright's version. Mr and Mrs Nguyen arrived on the pier about 4:30 am. Mr Nguyen set about assembling his fishing rods while Mrs Nguyen got the flask out and poured them both a cuppa. Mr Nguyen cast in at the end of the pier and caught a mackerel almost immediately.'

'Jammy bugger.'

'As he reeled it in, his line became entangled on something. He peered over the side and called his wife, who shone a torch down. That's when they saw the body. He dropped his rod in the water and they hightailed it back towards Henrietta Street and called the police.'

'Did they see anyone else?'

'Not on the pier.'

'Did they pass anyone on their way here?'

'Mrs Nguyen has the better grasp of English, and from what I could make out she said they passed a black van as they were walking up Henrietta Street.'

'What sort of black van?'

'Sketchy on the details, but it sounds like a transit van. She said it was big. They had to stand aside to let it pass.'

'So that would have been about 4:15 – 4:25 am. Hmm... did they get a butcher's of anyone in the van? A number plate? Distinguishing marks?'

'No to all the above. Although, she said the windows were black.'

'Tinted?'

'Yeah, I guess so. We'll need to get an interpreter in to get a full, verified account.'

'Okay, let's leave forensics to do their job,' Frank says as he glances at his watch. 'Prisha, have you got the Nguyen's particulars?'

'Yes Frank.'

They walk briskly back along the long pier until they are back on solid ground.

Frank abruptly stops and grabs Zac's arm. 'Hell, I've just had a thought. We've missed something!'

'What?' Zac and Prisha say with surprise.

'The Nguyens... did you check to see if they had an angling licence?'

Zac grins. 'No. I thought we had bigger fish to fry.'

Both men break out in laughter as Prisha shakes her head in disgust. 'You two! A man's lost his life and you're making crap dad jokes.'

Frank places an arm tenderly around her shoulder. 'Tears of a clown, Prisha. Merely the tears of a clown. Anyway, you don't need a fishing licence for sea fishing. It's free. Enshrined in the Magna Carta. Right, I'm bloody famished. Who's ready for a spot of breakfast? My shout.'

'Now you're talking, Frank,' Zac says, rubbing his hands together in anticipation. 'Full English for me with all the mashings.'

'Prisha?' Frank prompts.

A faint smile brushes her lips. 'Okay, why not? What about your diet, though?'

'Bollocks to the diet. Prisha, I'm going to introduce you to the best greasy spoon café in all of Yorkshire—Miserly Joe's.'

'Sounds charming.'

Frank's face hardens. 'Then after breakfast we need to track down Miss Tiffany Butler... if it's not already too late.'

21

Superintendent Anne Banks is not in the best of moods as she sits behind the desk in her cramped office, glowering at Frank.

'One murder in a week could be seen as unfortunate, two, as careless, and three, as bloody incompetence! Driving over here, I was listening to the news bulletins on the radio. The media have already dubbed the killers the Vladivostok Vampires of Whitby.'

'Bit of a mouthful,' Frank mumbles.

'Do we even know if the murders are linked, and who in hell leaked to the media about the Russians?'

'I'm not sure, ma'am. It certainly wouldn't have come from any member of my team. But these things seem to...'

She cuts him off. 'I've already had two very abrupt phone calls to deal with this morning. One from the Chief Constable and the other from the local member of parliament. Let me just say, neither were in particularly good humour. Driving over to Whitby is not the way I wish to spend my weekends!'

'That's Jack Turner for you. He never gave a thought about anyone else. Picking a Saturday morning to get murdered was most inconsiderate of him.'

She slams her palm onto the desk. 'And you can drop the sarcasm!'

'Ma'am,' Frank murmurs, contritely.

A heavy silence hangs in the air as the superintendent composes herself. She adjusts the collar on her immaculate jacket, smooths her hair down at the back, then clears her throat.

'What's the latest state of play? Are we dealing with three separate killers or is it the same ones?' she asks, quietly but coldly.

'We believe it's the same killers.'

'Why?'

'The rope used to strap Charles Murray to Black Nab was old-fashioned hemp. It was the same type of rope that was found around the neck of Mark Bridges, and the same type used to drop Jack Turner into the sea.'

'I can see how Murray may have been bumped off by the mysterious Russians for his clandestine activities and wanting to switch sides, but where do Turner and Bridges fit into the picture?'

'We're not sure at the moment, Anne. But there could be a link between the Fox murder, the armed robberies and the kidnapping.'

'This is a muddled picture you're painting, Frank.'

'We don't have all the answers yet, but we have a few theories we are exploring. We believe Tiffany Butler could be in imminent danger.'

'Have you contacted her?'

'We've tried her phone a dozen times. It's dead. We've also emailed her work address and called at her house three times. The school said she abruptly finished work midday Wednesday and took carers leave to tend to her sick mother.'

'Have you contacted her mother?'

'We have no contact details for her. We believe Tiffany has deliberately gone dark.'

'Unless she's already dead.'

'That is a possibility.'

'And if it is the Russians carrying out these atrocities—why?'

'I don't know,' Frank says as he rubs at the back of his neck. 'But I've pulled in the entire team and have every officer working all the angles.'

Anne pushes back in her chair and clasps her hands together.

'I want some results and quickly, Frank. You know how it works. The Chief Constable kicks the Chief Superintendent's arse. He kicks my arse, and I kick your arse, and you kick your officers' arses. But this is your investigation, and the buck stops with you. Do you understand what I'm saying?'

'Yes. Crystal clear.'

She sighs. 'Every dog has its day, Frank.'

'And what's that supposed to mean?' he snaps back.

'You could have taken early retirement a few years ago. If you don't catch your killers soon, then I'll bring in someone who can.'

'Thanks for your support, ma'am,' he replies pointedly.

She eyeballs him. 'You do have my support, my unwavering support...'

'That's good to hear.'

'... until you don't. Right, that's all. Keep me updated on any developments,' she commands, gathering a sheaf of papers together.

'Ma'am.'

———◦———

Frank's hands are firmly on his hips, like the proverbial teapot, as he glares out of the office window. His jowls are flushed red, eyes bulging as if he's about to explode. He spins around.

'They're taking the fucking piss!' he bellows. 'Do they think I'm some half-witted, country bumpkin who slouches around in clogs with a piece of hay sticking out of my mouth?' He erupts, not at his two detectives, but they still bear the brunt of his incandescent ire.

'Frank, I think you need to calm down,' Zac suggests in his comforting Scottish intonation. 'Think of your blood pressure,' he adds, throwing Prisha a worried glance.

Frank takes a seat. 'CCTV?'

Prisha glances at her phone. 'Yes, from a jeweller's shop near the corner of Church Street and Church Lane. It captured a black transit van heading north at 3:35 am, and again, heading south at 4:20 am. Unfortunately, the footage is poor, and we can't decipher the number plate, nor see the occupants.'

'What about the Nguyens? Did the interpreter arrive?'

Zac shuffles nervously. 'Aye. Nothing more to add than what they already told us.'

Frank expels air, his anger dissipating. 'And no contact with Butler yet?'

Prisha shakes her head. 'No.'

'Okay, we can't sit around here with our thumbs up our arses. Prisha, circulate Tiffany Butler's details to customs and all airports and seaports. If Mark Bridges was telling the truth, then Tiffany has a false passport and could attempt to leave the country, then try Butler's home address once more. If she's not there, then we have no other choice than to release her pretty little face to the media and tell her to visit the nearest police station as soon as possible. I'm loathe to do that because the press will put two and two together. I can see the headlines now—Damsel in Distress Stalked by the Vladivostok Vampires—pricks!'

'Yes, boss.'

'And Zac, just to be on the safe side, speak with Nicola Murray. See if she has a relative she can stay with for a few days. Although, to be honest, I don't think she's in any danger. Meanwhile, it's time for me to pay a visit to Dudley Fox and try to locate the epicentre of this puzzle.'

22

Dudley Fox places the two coffee cups onto the side table and takes up a seat opposite Frank, who is gazing admiringly at the view of the abbey through the living room window.

'I still reckon you have one of the best views in the entire county,' he says as he takes a sip of coffee.

'It is breathtaking. Although, I take it for granted these days.' He shuffles forward in his chair. 'Frank, I have a confession to make.'

Hell fire! Have I been wrong about him all along? Is he going to tell me he killed his wife?

'Oh, aye?' Frank says, sounding casual.

'I've reduced my medication and stopped taking the lithium drops.'

'I see. And how do you feel?'

'Tired, weary. And since then, I've not received any more text messages from Shirley.' He rubs his hands together in anguish. 'I'm embarrassed. I feel foolish... what I'm trying to say is—there were no messages from Shirley. How could they be? She's dead. I did some research and the mixture of the anti-depressants, lithium drops, and alcohol can cause hallucinations in certain individuals.

And that's what the messages were—hallucinations. I checked my phone and Shirley's. There are no text messages. I imagined the whole thing.'

Frank nods. 'There's nothing to be ashamed or embarrassed about, Dudley. The mind is a strange beast.'

'It brought me comfort, to think I could still communicate with her. Pure madness, and me, a man of science,' he murmurs, regretfully.

Frank leans forward and pats him on the knee. 'She's still in your memories, your thoughts, so in a way, she is still communicating with you.'

Dudley smiles and relaxes back in his seat. An awkward silence follows as Frank carefully thinks through his words.

'Is your visit about the reconstruction of Shirley's murder that aired recently?' Dudley says.

'Yes... partly.'

'Any new leads?' he asks wearily, already knowing the non-committal answer he'll receive.

'Not really. A few things we need to check out, but no smoking gun to speak of. It goes out on Crimewatch this coming Thursday, so who knows, maybe something will crop up.'

'Hmm... fingers crossed.' More silence. 'You said, partly. I assume you have something else to talk about? Is it about the murder of Charles Murray?'

Frank places his cup back down on the saucer and pulls at his tie.

'Yes, it is. I understand you two were friends?'

Dudley grimaces slightly. 'Friends... not really. Acquaintances, yes. I knew him from my university days. I was on the debating team at Oxford, and he was on the debating team at Cambridge. We'd cross swords occasionally, as we both shared a common interest in the sciences. We'd sometimes chew the fat whenever we bumped into one another. He was a very intelligent man. I must admit it shocked me when I found out about his death, but it pales in comparison to losing one's wife. I know that sounds rather callous, Frank, but...'

'No, not at all. I fully understand. A casual connection from your past is not the same as losing a loved one. After you left Oxford and moved to Whitby, how long before you realised Charles Murray had taken the position at Carston Hall?'

He rubs at his forehead. 'Oh, we're going back in time now. I couldn't be a hundred per cent accurate, but I think it was about eight to ten years ago. It was quite serendipitous, actually. I was on the harbour front enjoying some freshly shucked oysters and who should come and stand right next to me but Charles. He told me about his new job. We chatted for several minutes. He suggested I could help on field trips with the students of Carston Hall. Introduce them to the flora and fauna of the moorlands. I was more than happy to lend a hand. It was only once or twice per term and maybe lasted two or three years until I became too busy with my work at Menwith Hill.'

'On average, how many times a year would you see him?'

'Hard to say. Sometimes I wouldn't see him at all. Other times maybe a couple of times a year, always purely by accident. I'd bump into him having a quiet drink in a pub, or even once out walking with Shirley on the moors. I remember joking with him on one occasion and accused him of stalking me,' he finishes with a reflective, sad laugh.

'I see. When was the last time you saw him?'

He takes another gulp of coffee and leans back into the chair.

'Frank, you don't suspect I had anything to do with his death, do you?' he asks with puzzlement.

'No, not at all. But you know how it is with murder enquiries... we speak to everyone.'

'Oh, I know how it is with murder enquiries,' he repeats with a sliver of bitterness. He regains his composure and leans forward. 'Let me think now... I would have seen Charles Murray some time before Christmas just gone. About nine months ago... yes, that's correct, because they had Christmas decorations hung up.'

'Whereabouts?'

'The Malting Pot Brewery. My local. I'm afraid I was a little worse for wear. I'd had a tough week and nipped out for a couple of pints to help me unwind. Shirley was at home preparing dinner. I was sitting, minding my own business, when Charles walked in. He insisted on buying me a whisky... a double. I felt it only appropriate to reciprocate and yes... one thing led to another.'

'Can you remember what you talked about?'

'We only ever talked about one thing.'

'Which was?'

'Science.'

'I'm no expert, but there are many types of science. Can you be more explicit?'

'The whole gamut, but mainly bio-science, chemistry.'

Frank stands up and walks to the window and surveys the pristine garden outside. He has his back to Dudley.

'Dudley, I know your work at Menwith Hill is top secret, so I won't put you in a difficult position by asking details, but I would like to get an overview of what you do.'

'I'm sorry, Frank, but you know I can't talk about my work.'

He turns and stares at him. 'I wouldn't ask if it wasn't vitally important.'

'Okay, you ask your questions, and I may or may not answer them.'

'I've formed a hypothesis of what you're working on and why it's top secret. I believe it's a nerve agent, something to rival what the enemy has already developed. At a guess, I'd say you hadn't quite perfected the formula but weren't far away from completing the task when Shirley was murdered. Since then, I suspect the project has stalled without you there to run the show. Am I in the ballpark?'

He stands up and walks over to the drinks cabinet and picks up the whisky, showing the bottle to Frank.

'You're in the ballpark. A wee dram, Frank?'

'I'd love to, but not while I'm on duty. But you feel free.'

He pours a generous slosh into a tumbler and takes up his seat again.

'You and I were both young men when the cold war ended, Frank,' he says as he nips at the whisky.

'You were a damn sight younger than me,' Frank says, laughing.

'The cold war served a purpose. When two sides have enough nuclear weapons to guarantee the obliteration of the planet, then who is going to hit the button first? The answer—no one. Like two bullies with the same size club facing off against each other. A stalemate.

The Russians have Novichok, a deadly nerve agent which is extremely difficult to detect and... *neutralise*. As the Western powers play by the rules, or so they say, then we have not developed binary chemical weapons as it would breach the Chemical Weapons Convention. This means one bully now has a bigger club than the other. That bully is Russia. The balance of power shifts.'

Frank considers Dudley's words carefully. 'So, if the Western powers are prevented from developing a nerve agent to rival Novichok, then I don't understand what you are...'

'Think about it, Frank. What do pharmaceutical companies do when a new virus is detected?'

'They develop a vaccine. Ah! I get it. We can't develop a nerve agent, but we can develop some sort of neutralising agent to render Novichok impotent. Meaning the equilibrium of power is restored.'

Dudley smiles. 'I don't think I breached the official secrets act. You merely went on a fishing trip and got lucky. Of course, I can neither confirm nor deny your hypothesis.'

Frank takes a seat, hands firmly clasped. 'Dudley, the night at the brewery, just before Christmas, did you unwittingly say anything to Charles Murray about what you were working on at Menwith Hill?'

He's puzzled at the question. 'No... well, I don't think... I mean, we talked in generic terms about many things but I'd never... Wait, why would you ask a question like that? You suspect Charles of espionage? For the Russians?'

23

Prisha knocks for the third time, then calls through the letterbox.

'Tiffany, if you're home, can you come to the door, please? It's very important!'

The car is nowhere to be seen and all the curtains are pulled shut, even though it's nearly midday.

'Can I help you, inspector?'

She spins around, recognising the brittle voice of the next-door neighbour.

'Oh, Mr Lee, good morning. Have you seen Miss Butler today?'

His dog Cooky saunters from the doorway onto the grass to relieve himself.

'Not today. But I saw her briefly yesterday. She's gone away for a short break.'

Prisha lifts a leg over a selection of blooming flowers in the garden bed and walks over to him.

'So she returned from visiting her mother yesterday?'

'Her mother? No, she told me her mother passed away some years ago.'

The lying little toe-rag! 'I see. What time did she leave yesterday?'

'About noon. I'd just returned from my walk with Cooky, and she was packing her car. She seemed in an awful rush.'

'Did she say where she was going?'

'She said she hadn't decided yet. Needed a short break. I found it a bit odd as she's just come off a six-week break for the school summer holidays. She said it was long service leave.'

'How was she... in herself?'

'Not the usual calm, dignified Miss Butler I've come to know.'

'In what way was she different?'

'Rushed, jumpy. Kept staring down the street as if she were expecting somebody. Is she in trouble?'

'Not yet. You said she was packing her car. Was it the white Subaru Impreza?'

He nods. 'Yes.'

'Did she have much luggage?'

'Yes, that was another odd thing. She had two large suitcases and a small bag. I thought it was rather a lot of luggage for a short break. Although, my late dear wife, god bless her, always used to over-pack for our holidays. I think it's a woman thing... oh, I do beg your pardon, I wasn't inferring...'

'That's all right. And she definitely didn't indicate where she was going?'

'No. She gave Cooky a pat on the head, then jumped into her car and sped off at a hell of a rate, which I found rather reckless. There're several young families who live on the street and the children are often outside on their bikes. She could have...'

'Yes. Thank you, Mr Lee. You've been very helpful. Here's my card. If she returns, can you call me?'

'Why yes, I'm glad to be of service.'

She clambers back over the garden beds and pulls open the car door.

'Oh, and if you notice anything untoward, then please also call me.'

'Untoward?'

'You know, anyone hanging around the house or unusual visitors, that sort of thing.'

Mr Lee's face hardens with worry. 'Oh dear, yes, yes, of course.'

As Prisha jumps into the car, she takes a call from Frank.

'Can you talk?' he asks.

'Yes. What is it?'

'I'm in the office with Zac. I've just got back from my little chat with Dudley Fox.'

'And?'

'We weren't far off the money. Dudley was working on a project developing a neutralising agent for Novichok, the deadly nerve agent developed by the Russians. It's likely Charles Murray got him pissed last Christmas and Dudley inadvertently let the cat out of the bag about the project.'

'And Charles passed the intel onto the Russians.'

'I assume so.'

'And they attempted to abduct Shirley and use her as a bargaining chip to get the good oil out of Dudley?'

'Possibly. Obviously, their abduction went tits up for whatever reason. Any luck with Butler?'

'She's on the run. Last seen yesterday by her neighbour. I'll be back at the station in ten and fill you in.'

'Okay. Good work Prisha. Oh, and the information about what specifically Dudley was working on—only us three know. If you ever need to speak about it, use generic terms.'

'Understood.'

24

Tiffany Butler is on the verge of panic, an emotion she has not encountered before. Always calm, cool, and in control, this new feeling is in danger of swamping her.

She passes the signpost for Keswick and pulls her car over into a layby, closes her eyes and leans back in the seat, slowly trying to calm her breathing. It works. After a few minutes, her soaring heart rate returns to normal as a blanket of calm swathes her.

Glancing out of the window at Scafell Pike, she half smiles at the natural beauty of the countryside. The summit is wrapped in swirling mist, which languidly spins around on itself. Tentacles detach and glide down the mountainside like the arms of a sinister spectre, reaching, clawing, grasping. Her half-smile evaporates.

She pulls a packet of smokes from the glove compartment, lowers the window, and sparks up. It's the first cigarette she's had since university nearly a decade ago. At first, it tastes like shit before the nicotine weaves its magic.

Everything had gone so well. Her meticulous master-plan had encountered only one glitch—Mark Bridges capitulating under questioning. But her contingency plan had run like clockwork. Bridges was always going to be the fall guy if the wheels came off.

She liked him, but never loved him, although *he* thought she did. Another part of the game. He was naïve, weak, simplistic, and gullible. To think he actually believed they'd set up home together on an idyllic Greek island and live happily ever after on the twenty million pounds ransom money.

Charles Murray was a different proposition. Another gullible fool, but he'd made things very complicated for her. Once she found out about his alter-ego, the mole, the sleeper, she knew she could use him to her own advantage. Men are so easy to manipulate. Their brains are in their cocks. Control the cock—you control the brain.

Her mind drifts back in time.

The night Shirley Fox was supposed to be abducted was when the last piece of the kidnapping puzzle had slipped into place.

Charles had returned to his flat, close to midnight, distraught, crying, an utterly pathetic mess of a human being. Tiffany, shocked by his confession, had taken a few minutes to absorb the situation.

She was now implicated.

It was she who had a duplicate key made to Bridges' holiday house. The perfect hiding spot for a would-be abductor.

Charles' state of mind was in tatters, which could make him vulnerable to intensive questioning if it ever arose. If he confessed about Shirley Fox, she'd go down for a good ten years for her involvement, maybe more. The British establishment loved to hate a femme fatale, the public, even more so. It would also mean the end of her kidnapping and ransom plan—her ticket to freedom.

That night, after pouring herself a chilled glass of Dom Perignon, then snorting a line of coke, she regained control of the situation.

She cuddled Charles, told him how much she loved him and how they could escape the nightmare and eventually abscond to an idyllic Greek island and live happily ever after. She was a little miffed with herself for reusing the old Greek island bullshit, but she figured it was better to keep to just the one fairy-tale.

Of course, the poor sap wanted to know how, the details. He cried and wailed for twenty minutes until Tiffany dried his tears and told him everything was going to be all right. She'd look after him. In return, he had to help her ensure their future together. That's when she told him about kidnapping one of their pupils who had an extremely rich uncle. Until then, it had been her and Bridges, alone. Now there were three of them in the mix, although Bridges never knew of Charles Murray's involvement.

This was even better for Tiffany, as it now meant that when Bridges dropped the girls off, she wouldn't be the one who transported them to their temporary holding-cell at Westerdale Grange. Instead, it would be Charles Murray. There'd be no evidence, no forensics found in her car, and she'd have her infallible alibi.

It was the perfect crime. Two besotted males manipulated by the lure of the mother-figure and adventurous sex. Oedipus, eat your heart out!

Even the international cat-and-mouse game of moving the ransom money around had gone without a hitch. Transferring the money between numerous offshore bank accounts had a left a bureaucratic paper-trail of epic proportions. Now, five million was invested in gold—always a safe option. Another five million in various stocks and shares—some high risk, some low. And the remaining ten million was sleeping in an Argentinian bank account awaiting the day Dolores Fernandez walked in to make a withdrawal. With two exquisitely forged passports, bank accounts opened in false names, and a counterfeit driver's licence, Tiffany could be whoever she wanted to be. She had wondered if the name Dolores Fernandez was a little pretentious, but she decided she could live with it.

Ah, yes... the perfect plan.

Until that stupid bloody fool, Charles Murray, lost his nerve!

Racked with guilt over the murder of Shirley Fox, and the kidnapping of two young, innocent girls, events had taken a heavy toll on Charles. Add to that the fact he was in the pay of the Russians for handing over state secrets and it was no wonder his self-esteem was low. He hated himself and what he'd become. But he still had Tiffany... or so he thought.

Then he made his biggest mistake. He was excited when he told her, convinced it was a genius masterstroke to extricate himself from the stinking, self-inflicted mess he'd created—*a covert meeting with an MI5 operative.*

He'd put forward his proposal in hypothetical terms.

What if someone who was working for the Russians decided they wanted to change sides, become a double agent? In return for this magnanimous gesture, could they expect immunity from prosecution for past crimes?

Tiffany had told him it was a terrible idea. He'd end up on trial for murder and kidnapping, as well as espionage. He was crazy!

Charles insisted she didn't understand how the secret service worked. They didn't care about domestic trifles like kidnapping and murder, which were the remit of the police. They worked on a higher level, and sometimes they had to dance with the devil to ensure the greater good.

It didn't matter what she said to dissuade him, his mind was made up. He promised he'd keep her name out of everything and say it was he and Bridges who had enacted the kidnapping.

She knew it would only be a matter of time before there was a knock on the door.

When she heard about the death of Charles late on Tuesday evening, she was shocked and saddened. She assumed he'd taken his own life at Saltwick Bay. Maybe walked out into the sea or thrown himself off a clifftop. But a glass of champagne later, a sense of relief washed over her as she realised it made her life so much simpler. There was no one to implicate her in the Fox murder.

Bullet number one—dodged.

Then, the very next day, she learnt about the death of Mark Bridges. It unnerved her for the two deaths to be so close together.

Was something going on?

She was told he'd hung himself, but rumours in the staff room soon circulated, with some saying it may have been murder. His death could have been for many reasons. Kidnappers were universally loathed; in prison they were detested. Strange how those who fall foul of society's simple rules turn into evangelical, righteous crusaders once they're staring at a prison-cell wall.

Or perhaps Bridges was murdered for something more mundane, like knocking back unwelcome sexual advances? He was a very attractive man, after all.

She fought with herself for a few hours as a flicker of remorse tickled her conscience. Then she relaxed.

With Bridges out of the way, it would end his accusations that she was part of the kidnapping. There could be no trial—it was done and dusted. The girls were alive and free; the police had their confession. Case solved, case closed, money gone.

Bullet number two—dodged.

The gods of crime were certainly smiling down on her. She was free of all encumbrances. It was now a matter of keeping a low profile and biding her time until the dust settled before she enacted the last part of her master-plan.

Disappear!

She was feeling buoyant at school on Wednesday morning during recess, although she played the part of the shocked and grieving colleague rather too well.

It was around lunchtime the gossip started in the staff room and her world imploded. When she overheard of *how* Charles had met his end and the shocking state of his body, she raced to the toilet and vomited violently. Locking the door, she trawled over events, sticking pieces together.

The death of Bridges now didn't appear so innocuous. Her imagination ran rampant. After twenty minutes of feverish exploration of the facts, she arrived at only one logical conclusion—Charles Murray's paymasters—the Russians, were coming!

She imagined Bridges was killed because of her... the conduit between Murray and Bridges. They would not stop until they'd eliminated anyone who *could* have known about the Shirley Fox murder.

And that included Tiffany.

She told the principal of the school a cock and bull story about her mother being ill, collected her belongings, and left.

———❧———

Flicking the cigarette butt out of the car window into the wet grass, she reaches under the passenger seat to retrieve a small tin of cocaine, unaware of the vehicle that creeps up behind her and comes to a halt, almost silently... stealthily.

Her arm aches as she scrabbles under the seat for the stash. She doesn't perceive the heavy footsteps on gravel as they approach from behind.

Aching fingers. Tired mind. Addiction demanding to be fed.

25

As Prisha jogs up the stairwell at the station, she nearly bumps headlong into Detective Superintendent Banks on the second-floor corridor. By her side are James Carmichael and Frank, with Zac at the rear.

'Ah, just in time, inspector. In my office now,' Anne Banks commands.

'But ma'am, I need to run a check on Tiffany Butler's car.'

Superintendent Banks stares at her impassively. 'She's still alive?'

'I think so. She left yesterday, according to her neighbour. The story about visiting her sick mother was bulldust.'

'Hmm... if she's been gone that long, then ten minutes will not make any difference, will it?'

'No, ma'am,' Prisha replies, knowing she's on a hiding to nothing to continue the discussion.

With everyone seated in Anne's office, James Carmichael, appearing slightly contrite, removes his jacket and kicks off the meeting.

'The thing is, ladies and gentlemen, we've run into a slight unforeseen problem,' Carmichael says with an embarrassed wince.

Frank, Prisha, and Zac stare at him from across the desk as Anne skim reads the updated police database on the latest series of crimes. She's still in a foul mood, as she always reserves Saturday afternoons for a game of golf with the ladies. It's her time to unwind.

'What sort of problem?' Frank asks.

'Ahem, one of our intelligence officers has gone AWOL.'

'Don't tell me—the same one who had the rendezvous with Charles Murray?'

'Yes,' he almost whistles his reply through his teeth. 'He last reported in five days ago.'

'Is that length of time unusual without making contact?'

'It depends entirely on the operation... but in this instance, yes, it is unusual. The last contact we had with our operative was on Monday, three days after the meeting with Charles Murray.'

'So the secret organisation tasked with keeping the country safe from foreign actors has mislaid one of its foot soldiers,' Zac says with a whisper of a smile.

Anne rebukes him. 'DS Stoker! Can you show a little more respect and a lot less cockiness? We are all on the same side here. It's not a case of gloating over one another's misfortune.'

'Ma'am,' he replies as Prisha purses her lips and throws him a slight shake of the head.

'And what do you think has happened to your operative?' Frank asks, trying to get the conversation back on track.

'We're not sure, but it appears things are getting a little out of control. And to make matters worse, we've lost touch with the Russians. They've vanished.'

'And what do you want us to do about it? It was only two days ago you were asking us to drop the investigation into Charles Murray,' Frank continues, showing no emotion but perhaps enjoying a slice of schadenfreude.

Carmichael sits on the edge of the desk and rolls his sleeves up.

'Tiffany Butler could be in imminent danger. We believe she may have known more about Charles Murray's activities than we first thought.'

And here's James Carmichael with the late news, Frank thinks to himself. It would normally be Frank's job to clarify, but he turns to Prisha to take the lead.

'Prisha, would you care to explain to Mr Carmichael one of the theories we're following?'

'Yes, boss. First of all, as Frank says, it's just a theory at this juncture, but a theory which is gaining more credence by the hour. We suspect Charles Murray planned to abduct Shirley Fox, at the behest of the Russians, to obtain information from Dudley Fox regarding the secret work he's been heading up at Menwith Hill.

Mark Bridges managed a holiday house directly opposite to where Shirley's body was found. We know Tiffany was in a relationship with Bridges, but we also suspect she was having an affair with Charles Murray at the same time. It's possible

Tiffany got the key to Bridges holiday rental and passed it on to Charles Murray. The abduction was bungled, and Shirley Fox was murdered. For what reason we don't yet know. Tiffany Butler then recruited Murray to play a part in her own kidnapping plan. With Bridges and Murray doing all the dirty work, and with Tiffany's seemingly watertight alibi, she'd be in the clear if anything went wrong.'

Anne Banks lets out a huff. 'But why would the Russians kill Bridges and Jack Turner?'

'Because of Bridges' affair with Tiffany. And Jack Turner was the go-between who obtained a false passport for Bridges—from a Russian guy. Charles Murray was missing for some days before his body was discovered. He could have been tortured and told the Russians about anyone and everyone who knew about the plot to abduct Shirley Fox, and why.'

'I've seen the pathology report on Murray and there's no mention of torture.'

'Electrodes to the genitals wouldn't leave any marks, or perhaps they used waterboarding, which is one of the worst tortures there is, ma'am. Again, very hard to detect.'

'Hmm... so this is all about the Russians covering their tracks.'

'Possibly. Like I said, it's a theory.'

James Carmichael taps his lips with his index finger. 'It's a good theory. I like it. And what about Tiffany Butler?'

'Tiffany is now on the run and probably has access to twenty million pounds and a forged passport and bank cards. We have contacted all airports and seaports with her description and a photo, as we believe she may try to flee the country. Her disappearance has also been lodged with the Missing Persons Squad. I was just about to run a check on the number plate recognition system to see if we can locate her car.'

Anne Banks leans back in her chair, folds her arms and peers at her DCI.

'Theories are fine, Frank, but you have no evidence to back any of this up.'

'We have four dead bodies and a missing JSTAT officer, ma'am.'

'Don't be flippant, Frank.'

'I wasn't being flippant. If we don't have some theories to follow up on, then we're scrabbling around in the dark.'

She leans forward, pensive. 'So what now?'

'I suggest my team focus on finding Tiffany Butler and that JSTAT concentrate on finding the Russians.'

'I couldn't agree more. Mr Carmichael?'

'I was going to suggest a similar thing. With your permission, superintendent, I'd like to bring in my small team and work from here. We can share intelligence and keep up to date with progress.'

Anne considers the proposition. 'Hmm... It could interfere with the chain of command.'

'I see it as two separate teams collaborating. I would have no authority over your officers, and you—none over mine. Of course, some of *our* information may be classified.'

'Okay, yes, it makes sense,' she agrees.

Frank gazes at Carmichael. 'And I also suggest JSTAT set up surveillance on Dudley Fox purely as a precaution in case an attempt is made on his life.'

'I think that would be prudent,' Carmichael says with a nod. 'Our Russian couple have outlived their usefulness and have become a definite health hazard.'

'Excuse me,' Zac interrupts. 'Don't you think it would be a good idea to give us the low-down on this pair of Russians and some photo ID? We need to know who and what we're dealing with in case our paths should cross.'

Carmichael rubs his chin thoughtfully. 'Give me twenty minutes. I'll need to get clearance.'

———◦———

Carmichael attaches two large photos to the whiteboard.

'Kira Volkov, also known as the Pearl of the Black Sea. She was born in Odessa,' he says, pointing at the photo of an alluring woman with pale skin, high cheekbones, green eyes, and jet black hair.

Zac stretches his legs out. 'My, my, she's easy on the eye,' he says with a grin, to which he receives a fierce glare from Superintendent Banks.

'Don't let her demure appearance deceive you. She is highly intelligent and ruthless. Thirty-three years old, one hundred and eighty centimetres tall, and weighs sixty-five kilos.'

Frank groans. 'What's that in old money?'

'She's around five-foot eleven and weighs about ten and a half stone,' Zac says.

'Smart-arse.'

'She's the brains behind the duo, but she's also trained in numerous martial arts, so never underestimate her. She's also an excellent forger.' He points at the next photo of a brutish looking muscular man. 'Maxim Lenkov. He's the brawn.'

'Hell, you wouldn't want to meet him down a dark alley on a Thursday night,' Frank murmurs.

'He's six feet five and weighs fifteen stone.'

'Thank you,' Frank says appreciatively.

'Maxim served for five years in the Spetsnaz, the Russian equivalent of the SAS. Again, highly trained, ruthless and a top marksman.'

All eyes stare at the large, shaven head, and mean expression.

'You said they'd gone to ground?' Prisha asks.

'That's right. They've been under surveillance for some time. They know they're being watched, and we know they know.'

'Do you have a location for where they were staying?'

'Yes. A remote farmhouse off Knott Road near North Gill. We've combed the place, but the house has been completely cleared. Not a fingerprint or so much as a chair out of place. The pair are professional to the nth degree.'

'Do you mind if we look around?' Frank says.

'Be my guest, but you'll be wasting your time. I'll get you the coordinates.'

'Do they drive a black Ford Transit van?' Zac asks.

'Sometimes. Although they regularly change vehicles; vans, cars, motorbikes.'

'Okay, we need to formulate a plan,' Superintendent Banks says.

'I don't want to sound pessimistic, ma'am, but...' Zac begins.

'Go on?'

'Let's look at the timeline of events. Charles Murray meets with JSTAT's intelligence officer last Friday night. The last contact with the IO is on Monday. Sometime on Monday evening, Charles Murray was strapped to Black Nab. On Tuesday, Prisha gets a full confession from Mark Bridges in relation to the armed robberies. Wednesday morning he's found hanged in his cell. Then early this morning, Jack Turner is upside down in the sea, hanging from a rope tied to the east pier. And now the Russians disappear without a trace. I think they may have finished their clean-up act. Which would mean the JSTAT officer and Tiffany Butler are already dead.'

'So what do you suggest we do, sergeant? Shut up shop and go home? Put it in the too hard basket?' Superintendent Banks snaps.

'I wasn't saying that, ma'am. I'm merely...'

'I don't think Tiffany Butler is dead,' Prisha interrupts. 'If she were, then her body should have turned up by now. No doubt very publicly. I believe she realises what's going on. That's why she's done a bunk.'

Anne Banks rises to her feet. 'If she is alive, we need to find her quickly. I take it your team is searching for your missing officer?' she asks Carmichael.

Carmichael slides off the edge of the desk and rolls his sleeves down.

'Yes. We have a specialist team on it now, searching for him and the Russians. With your permission, superintendent, I'd like to assign one of our officers to your team?'

'Why?'

'They're highly trained in covert operations and are licenced to carry a firearm.'

'Are you suggesting my officers could be in danger?'

'No. The last thing the Russians would want is to harm a police officer. That would cause a diplomatic stink, which would have serious consequences for them back home.'

'But it's fair game to go bumping off undercover agents and members of the public?' Zac comments.

Carmichael slips into his jacket. 'For field operatives, it comes with the territory. It's a dangerous job, and they know that. As for members of the public, well... those who are dead weren't entirely innocent, law-abiding citizens, were they?'

'Shirley Fox was,' Frank says, reflectively.

Carmichael sighs. 'True. I'm sorry about that. Unfortunately she was but a pawn in a game that has gone badly awry.'

Both Prisha and Zac throw him a sideways glance.

26

The figure moves along the passenger-side of the car as Tiffany's fingers fall onto the small tin of cocaine under the seat. Another shadow snakes its way along the driver's side.

A forceful rap on the passenger window startles Tiffany as she quickly drops the coke receptacle, sits bolt upright, and stares out of the window.

'Could you lower your window please, miss?' the police officer commands.

She obliges and gives the officer a winsome smile. 'Have I done something wrong?' she pleads.

He points his finger into the car towards the police constable standing at the driver's door. She's holding a cigarette butt between finger and thumb, sporting a disapproving pout.

'I could issue you with an on-the-spot fixed penalty fine for littering,' he says. 'Up to eighty-pounds.'

She notices the three chevrons on his lapel. 'Please forgive me, sergeant. That was so silly of me and out of character. My mind is elsewhere. I've been driving for five hours and pulled over to have a break as I was feeling weary.'

'Still, it's no excuse,' the sergeant says, sternly.

Tiffany's contrite expression disappears as it's replaced with a sad gaze.

'It's my mother, you see; she lives in Bristol, and she suffered a heart attack early this morning. I'm the only person she has left now. My father passed away last year. I'm making my way from Scotland. You're right, it is no excuse, I understand, and I never ever drop litter. It was a complete aberration.'

She now pulls her little-girl-lost pout and flutters her eyelashes. The sergeant offers her a benevolent smile.

'I see. We can all take our eye off the ball sometimes. Okay ma'am, drive safely and I hope your mother makes a full recovery.'

The young female constable walks in front of the car and shoots Tiffany an icy glare as she holds the tab-end in her fingers.

'Eh up, sarge, what do you want me to do with this?'

Tiffany watches in the rearview mirror as the sergeant pulls at his car door.

'Flick it into the long grass. One bloody ciggy stub ain't going to kill the planet, is it? It's all made from plant material, anyway.'

'Charming.'

The patrol car performs a U-turn and sedately pulls away, disappearing from view as it rounds a bend in the road.

It's the second time Tiffany combats fear.

She retrieves the cocaine, already razored into a fine powder, and places a pinch on the back of her hand then sniffs. Not instantaneous, but near enough, the illegal stimulant sets to work at regenerating energy, banishing lethargy, and jump-starts the synapses in her brain.

'You damn fool!' she exclaims. 'You've come this far. Don't blow it now by a momentary lapse of concentration. Okay... think. What's my position, what are my chances, how do I salvage this?'

———◦———

Tiffany pulls into the parking lot of a car hire company and takes in the scene. Twenty, thirty cars, all second-hand. It's a business on a shoestring. Probably an older guy running it, maybe with his wife. It's not Hertz or Rent-A-Car, that's for sure. Probably used by older locals who have given up their family car. More economical to hire a vehicle on the rare occasions they need one.

She pulls two suitcases from the boot and makes her way to the portable cabin, substituting as a business headquarters. An old-fashioned bell rings as she walks in. An elderly gentleman behind the counter reluctantly raises his head, slightly annoyed that his sixth customer of the week has walked in to disturb his peace.

'Hello, I wish to hire a car for two days,' Tiffany says with effervescence and energy. 'But I'd also like to ask a small favour.'

The man puts his paper down and slides his spectacles onto the bridge of his nose.

'Oh, aye?' he asks suspiciously. He's not in the habit of handing out favours.

'I live in Whitehaven and set off not more than thirty minutes ago to visit my ailing father in Edinburgh. He's in a hospice. It's inevitable... but still,' she adds as crocodile tears drill down her cheeks. 'It doesn't make it any easier.'

The old man's face softens. 'So how can I help?'

'Well,' she sniffles as she dabs a tissue at her eyes, 'I noticed a peculiar sound coming from my car. A rumble and a clank. I thought I'd be okay because I've been a member of the AA for over ten years... then I remembered... I'd let my renewal lapse. I don't want to take a chance on the car breaking down, so thought it best to hire a car. But I don't want to leave mine parked up on the roadside.'

She loosens the tap on the tears.

'There, there, calm yourself, lass. Don't go getting yourself all worked up over nothing.'

Another pat at her cheeks, then the eyes, followed by the beguiling damsel in distress smile.

'You're so kind. All I want is to hire a roadworthy car from you that will take me from here to Edinburgh... and I wondered if I could leave my car in your compound until I return? The palliative care nurse told me it will be two days, maximum, if I'm lucky.'

The man pats the back of Tiffany's hand, which has been deliberately left on the countertop.

'I tell you what, lass, I'll give you my best car. A BMW Mini Cooper—2010 model. She's a beauty. Plenty of storage for one. A great handler and you'll look like the bees' knees. It's a pleasure to drive. And of course you can leave your car here. It will be safe in the compound until you return.'

He turns and stares at a plethora of keys hanging from hooks.

'You're too kind,' she sniffs.

'Here we go,' he says, grabbing a set of keys. 'Now I just need your driver's licence, and a bank or credit card and you'll be on your way.'

Tiffany fumbles in her handbag, as though flustered, before handing the man her forged driving licence, and credit card bearing her pseudonym. After a quick glance, the man gives her another warming smile.

'Now, Miss... erm,' he readjusts his spectacles 'Miss Dolores Fernandez, give me five and I'll show you to your car. We are open from nine until four, but I'll give you a business card so if you should arrive out of hours you can call me and I'll make sure I open up for you so you can collect your own car. How does that sound?'

'It sounds perfect. My, your wife must be the happiest woman on earth to have such a wonderful, caring, and considerate husband!'

As she pulls away in the Mini, she goes through her mental checklist.

'Problem number one solved—the car. It's off the road and hidden amid thirty other vehicles.'

In her deliberately haphazard journey from Whitby to the west coast of Scotland and back down to Keswick, she'd kept off the main roads and away from the police automatic number plate recognition cameras. But to get to Manchester Airport, she has no alternative but to use the main roads. No one will be looking for her in a Mini Cooper, which means she's safe for at least two days, until the hire car man reports the car missing, by which time she'll be on the other side of the world.

27

The police sergeant exits the bakery carrying two small brown bags. He crosses the road and taps on the window.

'Here you go, vegetarian sausage roll,' he says with a smirk as he hands a bag to the constable in the passenger seat.

'Thanks sarge,' she replies as the window rolls down.

'It's a contradiction in terms. Bloody vegetarian sausage roll,' he chunters as he walks around the vehicle. He climbs into his seat and relaxes back as he glances at the stunning countryside of the Lake District. He squints up at the sky.

'Looks like the drizzle has set in for the day,' he comments as he takes a bite from his authentic sausage roll.

'Hey sarge, can you remember the number plate of that Subaru Impreza we pulled up behind earlier?'

'Erm... XP... 5... something. Why?'

'North Yorkshire police are looking for a white Subaru Impreza, XP51 SMR. It's just come through.'

'Shit!'

'Missing person. Report and detain if seen.'

'Bloody hell!' he cries as he reaches for the radio.

***

Prisha fastens her seatbelt and takes a quick glance around the interior of the Range Rover as the intelligence officer starts the engine.

'Your lot must have a bigger budget than ours,' she says.

'Why's that?' he replies.

'I drive around in a knackered old Ford Focus or Skoda.'

He laughs. 'It's not always Range Rovers, I can assure you,' he says, tapping at the GPS on the dash. 'Okay, Whitby to Keswick. Two hours and twenty-five minutes, according to the sat-nav. Should be a pleasant drive across the Pennines.'

'I'm looking forward to it,' Prisha says as she sneaks another quick peek at her ridiculously handsome driver.

He gives her an impish grin but says nothing.

'So what's it like working for MI5?' she asks as they trundle slowly through the afternoon traffic as they head out of Whitby.

'It's actually the Secret Service. MI5 is an anachronism left over from the old days.'

'I beg your pardon.'

'I suppose it's a similar job to the police. A lot of admin, and searching through documents and statements. It's not like the TV shows, all high-powered adrenalin and testosterone.'

'Do you enjoy it?'

'Love it. You?'

Prisha gazes out at the ocean. 'Yeah, I suppose I do. It's a bit like an addiction. The job becomes part of who you are, even though we're constantly told to switch off once we finish our shift. I find that impossible to do.'

'I know what you mean.'

'So, agent SE17, are you going to tell me your first name?'

'No. And it's intelligence officer, or IO SE17, not agent.'

'Come on! Just make up a false first name. I can't sit in a car with you for two hours and refer to you as IO SE17. It makes you sound like a bloody robot.'

He flashes her a set of pearly whites. 'Okay, call me Steve.'

'Steve! I was thinking of something more exotic, dangerous. Something that conjures up images of you sliding down ropes and diving from a burning car.'

'Okay. You come up with a name.'

'What about Zeus?'

'Piss off!'

'Fair enough. What about Lochy? You look like a Lochlan.'

He laughs.

'What's funny?'

'Lochlan is quite appropriate in the circumstances. It means—land of the lakes. And as we're paying a visit to the Lake District, yeah, why not.'

'Lochy it is then.'

They make idle chit chat for the next hour as they traverse the wild and rugged countryside. There's a chemistry between them that is palpable, and Prisha is not going to die wondering.

'So, Lochy, are you in a relationship?'

For the first time since he got into the car, his face drops.

'No. I was. It ended eighteen months back.'

Prisha's heart jumps, but she does well to hide her emotions.

'Was it a mutual break-up or did it turn nasty?'

'It turned nasty when I walked in on her getting shafted by my so-called best mate.'

'Ooh, that's not good. What did you do?'

'I packed my bag and left. Bought a new phone. Rented a caravan and have never seen nor heard from her since... or him.'

'Shit! You showed some restraint. If I'd been in your shoes, I'd have battered them both.'

'It's part of the training. Don't let emotion dictate your actions. What about you? Relationships, I mean.'

'Ended six months ago. Not as dramatic as yours, though. It just fizzled out. I woke up one day and realised I was shacked up with a right boring bastard. I like to do things in my spare time; rock climbing, kayaking, triathlons, hiking. All he wanted to do was watch the footy or go down the pub.'

'Each to their own, I suppose. Sounds like you need an action man.'

Prisha giggles. 'Maybe I've found one.'

Prisha ends the call on her mobile as they enter the town of Keswick.

'Take the third left at the roundabout and the patrol car should be parked up at the layby about a hundred metres further up.'

'Will do.'

As they navigate the roundabout, Prisha spots the patrol car ahead as it drives towards them, slows, then pulls to the side of the road.

As she gets out of the car, she flashes her badge and exchanges pleasantries with the uniformed officers.

'We were cruising along and as we rounded that corner back there,' the sergeant explains, pointing up the road, 'we see a cigarette butt come flying out of the window. Petty stuff, but it's been a quiet day. Anyway, I tap on the window and gave her a lecture about littering. She appeared genuinely sorry and said she was heading to Bristol to visit her mother, who's had a heart attack. I felt sorry for her and told her to get on her way.'

'Nothing to do with her fluttering her eyelashes at you, sarge?' the constable adds.

'That sounds like Tiffany Butler. And this was definitely the woman?' Prisha says, holding the photograph out in front of the officers again.

'Yep. One hundred per cent certain. Couldn't forget a pretty face like that in a hurry.'

'Sexist pig,' mumbles the constable.

'And she wasn't wearing a disguise of any sort; a wig or anything trying to hide her face?'

Both uniforms shake their head. 'No.'

'And she definitely said she was heading to Bristol?'

'That's what she said.'

'Was there anything odd about the way she acted? Did she appear frightened, nervous, agitated in any way?'

'Not really. She was a bit shocked when I first tapped on the window. But most people are. What's she done?'

'Nothing, as far as we can prove... yet. But we fear her life may be in danger. Got caught up with the wrong people.'

'Oh, I see.'

'Okay, well thanks a lot sergeant, constable, you've been very helpful.'

She walks to the Range Rover and climbs in, sporting a dubious expression.

'What's the go?' Lochy asks.

'Definitely Tiffany Butler. Said she was heading to Bristol, which I don't believe for one minute.'

'How long since they talked to her?'

'Over two hours ago. She could be anywhere by now.'

'What's wrong? You seem puzzled.'

'It's not like her. It's out of character. She's a sharp operator, cool, measured, thinks things out. Why would she still be travelling in her own car? She'd know by now that we'd be onto her.'

'Who knows? People act in strange ways when they're put under stress. And if she thought the Russians were going to do to her what they did to Charles Murray, that would stress anyone out.'

'Hmm... I suppose. But one thing I'm certain of—that little brush with the police would have been a wake-up call for her. If you were on the run and had been stopped by the police for a minor infringement, what would your next step be?'

Lochy drops his head to one side and ponders the question.

'I'd get rid of the car as soon as possible.'

'Exactly. But you'd still need transport.'

'Which would mean either stealing, buying, or hiring a car—or public transport.'

'Public transport is not Tiffany's style, and stealing a car would be too risky, and although she possesses many disreputable attributes, I don't think auto-theft is one of them.'

'Time to check out the garages and car hire joints of Keswick, then.'

'You took the words right out of my mouth.'

———————◦———————

The Range Rover parks up outside Keswick Car Hire, which wouldn't win any business awards for originality but leaves no doubt in the public's mind what the company is about.

'Last chance,' Prisha says as she steps from the car. 'I'll speak to the manager; you have a nosey around outside.'

Lochy nods as they walk into the car lot and part ways. Prisha opens the door to the ringing of a bell and saunters in. An elderly gentleman is sitting behind the counter with his nose stuck in a newspaper.

'With you in a minute,' he says without looking up. Two customers on the same day is testing his patience.

Prisha surveys the rather tired makeshift office. She imagines it could be a profitable little concern if the owner had the slightest interest in it. She spies the bell on the counter and slams her palm down, hard onto it, as she flicks her badge in the man's face.

'Detective Inspector Kumar, North Yorkshire Police. I haven't got all day. I have a couple of simple questions for you if you could spare me a minute.'

The man stands, sprouting an irritated grimace. Prisha pushes the photograph towards him.

'Have you seen this woman today?'

The man squints, then scratches at his cheek.

'Aye, Miss Dolores Fernandez. She came in just before lunchtime. Hired a BMW Mini Cooper. She was in a bit of a state, poor lass. What's she supposed to have done?'

'We believe she may be in danger. Did she say where she was going?'

'Edinburgh, to see her father. He's not long left, apparently. In a hospice, she said. I assumed it was cancer. She was quite emotional. Lovely lass.'

Prisha rolls her eyes. 'Could you give me details of the car she hired? Year, plates, colour and also a copy of the transaction.'

'Give me a moment.'

He disappears through a side door as Lochy enters the cabin.

'Her car's outside in the lot,' he murmurs.

'Crafty. She rented a hire car a few hours ago. She's one step ahead of us again.'

The man returns and places the documents on the counter as Prisha pulls out her mobile and takes photos of them.

'She could be anywhere by now,' she mutters.

'I can tell you exactly where she is if you like?' the man says.

'Really... how?'

'I fit all my expensive vehicles with an OBD GPS tracking device.'

She throws Lochy a look.

'Onboard diagnostics,' he says. Prisha shrugs. 'Access to the car's computer.'

'Ah...'

'I've had too many bloody stolen over the years and your lot don't give a monkey's,' the man says. 'Now, when they go missing, I hire a security firm to retrieve them.'

Prisha smiles at Lochy. 'At last, a break!'

The man invites them behind the counter and boots up an app on his computer. He types in the number plate and the screen zooms in on a map of the country.

'If she's heading to Edinburgh, she's going the wrong bloody way. There she is. On the M61, coming up to Bolton. Oh, hang on a mo... she's turning off. Looks like she's pulling into the services.'

As they watch the car move slowly along the map, Prisha radios in the details to control requesting any patrol cars in the area to proceed to Rivington Services, southbound on the M61.

'Looks like we have our prey,' Lochy says with a wide grin.

'Maybe. This one is as slippery as an eel. I'll celebrate once someone has the cuffs on her,' Prisha replies, keeping her emotions in check.

28

Frank and Zac stealthily continue their search of the abandoned farmhouse, which was the Russians' bolt hole until recently. The weathered floorboards of the bedroom creak their annoyance at Frank's bulk. In the open-plan kitchen, Zac pulls on a pair of latex gloves and yanks open cupboard doors.

'Nothing,' Frank states as he returns after his inspection. 'You?'

'Not a sausage. Did Carmichael say who owns the place?'

'Some London couple. Airbnb.'

'He was right; the place is pristine. It's funny they'd been monitoring the Russians for quite some time and the very day they raid the place, they're gone,' he says, pulling the lid from a teapot and gazing inside.

'What are you suggesting?'

'Nothing. Just thinking aloud.'

'I know what you mean, though. It's like they're one step ahead. Which suggests...'

'Someone's feeding them intel?'

'Possibly. Or they're damn lucky.'

Frank saunters over to a bookcase and rummages through a pile of neatly stacked books. He picks one up and flicks through the pages.

'Dracula,' he chuckles.

'What?'

'Dracula. Have you read it?'

Zac joins him and stares at the cover. 'No.'

Frank's eyes widen. 'You've lived in Whitby for eight years and you're telling me you've never read Dracula?'

'Sorry. I didn't realise it was a prerequisite.'

'Are you related?'

'To whom?'

Frank taps at the author's name on the cover. 'Bram Stoker. You share the same last name.'

'Yeah, we're related. He's my great grandma.'

'Very amusing.'

Frank replaces the book and saunters over to a wood burner near the back wall. He drops to his haunches as clicks and cracks pop from his legs. He pulls open the door to the fire and peers inside.

Zac's mobile disturbs the silence. 'Hi, Prisha. What's the latest?'

Frank picks up a poker and carefully prods the ashes, then reaches in and picks up a charred object and spins it around in his fingers.

'Bloody odd,' he mumbles to himself.

He replaces the shell and is about to close the door when he spots a sliver of scorched paper. Carefully, he extracts it, holding it between finger and thumb, puzzled. He pulls out his notebook and places it between the pages as he rises to his feet with a weary groan.

'Okay, good work, Prisha. Yep, I'll tell Frank. No, he's here with me now, poking the fire. No, it's not a euphemism. Bye, yep, bye.'

'Well?' Frank asks.

'Tiffany Butler hired a car in Keswick. Little did she know it's fitted with GPS tracking. She's just pulled into the services near Bolton. A couple of patrol cars are on their way now. Looks like we've got her. Anything in the fire?'

'A half burnt shell of what appears to be a walnut, and this.'

Frank opens his notebook.

metered 03999060

Zac studies the neatly typed letters and numbers, then shrugs.

'You're the cryptic queen. What do you think it means?'

'Not sure. Too short for a telephone number,' Frank says thoughtfully.

'Maybe it's the meter reading for the electricity.'

Frank shakes his head with disdain. 'This place is a holiday rental.'

'So?'

'Oh, I suppose you could be right,' he says with sarcasm. 'It's always the first thing me and the missus do when we arrive at our holiday destination. Meera puts the kettle on while I read the electricity meter. It's the highlight of our stay.'

'Okay, smart-arse, you think of something.'

He closes the notepad. 'I'll have a tinker with that later. Right, come on, look lively. Let's look around outside.'

———◦———

Zac pulls at the garage door and slides it open as Frank saunters in and hits the lights. The pair wait a moment until the buzzing and flickering fluorescents reluctantly illuminate the garage.

'Not much in here,' Zac mutters, scanning the interior. The shed is empty apart from a few items which pique Frank's interest. He makes his way to the far corner and stares at the objects.

'A gym bench, a board, ropes, and a bucket,' he says thoughtfully.

'Not unusual for a shed,' Zac says.

'All the equipment required for waterboarding.' Frank peers inside the bucket and retrieves a damp, pale pink rag. He unfolds it and stares at the gruesome picture, then reads the words.

'Abominable Putridity—Intestinal Putrefaction. Is this another one of those death metal bands?'

Zac takes the T-shirt from him and studies it. 'Aye, another Russian group—Abominable Putridity. Intestinal Putrefaction is one of their songs.'

'Catchy title. I wonder if it reached number one on the hit parade?'

'Frank, the last person to use the term—hit parade, passed away over thirty years ago.'

185

'Is that right. Anyway, how come you know so much about this type of music? Although, I use the term music in the broadest possible sense.'

'My older brother was well mad for death metal when he was younger.'

'Any hope of him being released from the psychiatric hospital soon?'

Zac grins. 'Luckily, he grew out of it some time ago.'

Frank wanders over to the middle of the garage and drops to his haunches and pats the concrete with his palm.

'Wet patch. That's the thing with concrete, it absorbs moisture.'

'Prisha was right... again. This is where they waterboarded Murray,' Zac says.

'It looks like it,' Frank replies with a heavy sigh as he rises to his feet. 'We all have our unique attributes, Zac. You may not have Prisha's incisive imagination, but you make up for it in other ways.'

'Such as?' Zac asks hopefully, fishing for a compliment.

'Can't think of anything off the top of my head. Give me a few days and I'll get back to you.'

'Very droll.'

'I've seen it before in coppers. They're rare, but you get one occasionally.'

'What do you mean?'

'Prisha. Her senses detect things, clues, inferences, oddities, then somewhere in her subconscious she jumps around, joining the dots. Whereas I'm more of a meat and two veg sort of copper. I work in a linear way, plodding along. I end up at the same destination. It just takes me longer to get there.'

'It must be nice to have her inborn intuition.'

'Aye, it must. Don't resent it, Zac. In fact, enjoy it and marvel how her mind works, and thank god she's on our side.' Frank takes a deep breath and shakes his head. 'Christ, what a hateful last few days Charles Murray must have undergone. Waterboarded, then tied naked to Black Nab as the tide approached.'

'Poor bugger. I should be used to it by now, but it never fails to amaze me the cruelty humans can stoop to.'

'I think it's a defective or missing gene. It has to be. How else could you perpetrate that on another living being? Come on, let's head back to the station. This place is tainted.'

29

She pulls the sun visor down and gazes at her reflection in the vanity mirror as she applies a fresh coat of lipstick.

'That's better Tiffany. In control. Take a break, have a coffee and a sandwich. Rest and revive. Then to the airport. Purchase a ticket to Puerto Vallarta, Mexico. A few days' respite, then a flight to Buenos Aires. Mission accomplished.' She allows herself a quiet chuckle. 'Mother always said I was too clever by half.'

As she exits the car, she takes a deep breath. A distant siren breaks its way through the continuous rumble of traffic on the motorway. She freezes, tilts her head slightly, closes her eyes and concentrates. There's more than one siren and they are rising in volume. She looks at the car, then back to the road.

'No more mistakes today, Tiffany.'

She collects the cigarettes, lighter, and small tin of cocaine and drops them into her backpack, then quickly pulls the two suitcases out of the boot. She manually flicks the auto lock button above the armrest, drops the keys onto the seat and shuts the door.

Walking into the services, she takes a quick look at her options. Starbucks, Burger King, and Greggs. She spots an elderly couple sitting at a table in Starbucks, pouring sugar into their cups.

Pulling the suitcase behind her, she marches briskly over to them.

'Excuse me, sorry to interrupt,' she says, beaming at the couple.

The man and woman look up. They have kindly, genial faces.

'Could I ask you a big favour? Would you mind keeping an eye on my luggage? I'm desperate to spend a penny.'

'Of course, love,' says the man in a thick Geordie accent.

'They'll be safe with us,' confirms the woman.

In the toilet, she takes another snort of cocaine and clears her head.

'Don't think of them as problems, Tiffany,' she murmurs. 'Think of them as challenges. It's all a game and your objective is to win.'

She formulates a couple of contingency plans and heads back to the couple at the café. As she approaches their table, she waits for the moment they spot her, then pulls an expression of agony and grabs at her elbow.

'Thank you so much,' she says, face creased in anguish.

'Our pleasure, love,' the man says. 'Are you all right there? You seem in pain.'

'Oh, it's nothing,' she replies, slipping into a chair as if she's a close relative. 'It's my elbow. They've operated on it four times and still haven't fixed it.'

'What's the matter with it?'

'A piece of floating bone. I did it in Somalia while I was working for the Red Cross bottle feeding starving infants. So where are you two from? I take it you're husband and wife or are you secret lovers eloping?' she adds with a cheeky giggle.

The couple laugh as they warm to her, then give her a brief rundown of who they are, where they're from, and where they're going. She pretends to listen with interest as she watches two police cars enter the car park and slowly cruise along. One squad car pulls up behind the Mini Cooper and two officers alight.

'Anyway, she's been nagging us to visit all year, so we decided we better bite the bullet,' the woman says.

'You don't sound keen?' Tiffany replies.

'Look, I know she's my sister, and I love her to bits, but she's so fastidious it's painful to be around her.'

Tiffany laughs as one officer talks into his radio. 'I know what you mean. My sister is exactly the same. I tell her to relax and not sweat the small stuff, but she doesn't listen.'

'That's what we say, isn't it, Malcolm?'

'Aye love. There's none as deaf as those who won't listen.'

'Where does your sister live?'

'Other side of Bolton.'

'Oh, I'm heading to Bolton myself to catch a train. My car broke down just before Preston. Luckily, I hitched a lift this far. I'll need to book a taxi now, to get me to the station.'

'What's your eventual destination?' says the man.

'Brighton, to visit my sick aunt. I say aunt, but she's more like a mother to me. She took me in when my parents were killed in a car crash when I was a little girl. She sacrificed everything for me.'

'What about your sister?'

'What? Oh, yes... she sacrificed everything for me and my sister. Anyway, I feel it's my duty to take care of her now. Kindness should be repaid, don't you think?'

'Too right, love,' the woman says.

'Anyway, thanks for the chat. It's been lovely to meet you both. I better ring for that taxi.'

She stands up and fumbles with her suitcases as the husband and wife exchange nods and winks.

'Say love, seeing as we're both heading the same way, we could give you a lift to the station. No point forking out for a cab. We've plenty of room in the car, haven't we, Carol?'

'Plenty of room.'

'Oh, I couldn't possibly.'

'Don't talk daft, woman.'

'Well, if you really don't mind? I can pay you,' Tiffany says as she extracts her purse.

The man screws his face up. 'Nonsense! Put yer money away!'

Tiffany squints a glance at the police officers as they advance towards the glass doors. She pulls at the handle of her suitcase and lets out a yelp of pain.

'Malcolm!' his wife chastises.

'Oh, sorry. Let me help you with your cases. Don't want you damaging that elbow.'

'You're so kind. I just need to nip into the shop to buy a bottle of water and some pain killers. Where are you parked?'

The woman points to a dark blue car a couple of spots away from the Mini.

'The blue Volvo,' she says.

'I'll be there in a jiffy.'

Tiffany smiles and walks off as the man struggles with her cases. She pulls a wide-brimmed hat from her backpack and slides it onto her head, followed by a pair of sunglasses.

The police enter the building, stop, have a quick chat, then split up. She walks into a Spar shop and picks up a magazine. As a police officer enters, she saunters down the opposite aisle, calm, almost elegant in the way she carries herself. She leaves the shop as the officer reaches the end of the aisle.

She briskly trots out of the building and towards the Volvo as the elderly man gallantly lifts the heavy suitcases into the boot.

'Let me help you with that,' Tiffany says.

'No. I've got it,' he huffs and puffs.

As the car makes its way past dozens of trucks in the parking bays, she spots another police car waiting in the wings. She deliberately drops her sunglasses onto the floor and bends over to pick them up.

'Damn it,' she curses.

'What's the matter?' the woman says, turning around.

'Nothing. I've dropped my glasses, that's all.'

She keeps her head down until they're safely on the slip road and accelerating away.

30

Prisha gently thumps her forehead with the heel of her hand.

'How in fuck's name could she have got away?' she curses, ending the call. 'They found the car within ten minutes of us putting the appeal out. How, in ten minutes, could she have got out of the car with two oversized suitcases and disappeared into thin air?'

Lochy grins at her. 'You said she was as slippery as an eel. Are you sure this woman has no previous? She doesn't sound like a newcomer to crime.'

'She's as clean as a whistle.'

'So what do you want to do?'

'I'm not sure. I need to think. Keep driving.'

'She could head anywhere. Manchester, Heathrow, Stanstead. Or the southern ports to catch a ferry, or maybe Holyhead to catch the boat across to Ireland.'

'Or she could have crossed over to the northbound road and hitched a lift back up north. Leeds, Hull, Newcastle, Glasgow. She's like Will-o'-the-wisp.'

Silence ensues as Prisha puts herself in the mind of a criminal on the run.

'Okay, I know what I would do. What would you do?' she asks Lochy.

He puts his shades on and flashes her a gleaming smile that makes her heart do a backward flip.

'So, I'm on the run. I assume my initial pursuers are the Russians, but I'm now aware the police are also after me. If the Russians get me—I'm dead, and it will not be quick and easy. If the police catch me, then I'm looking at a lengthy period of my life in prison. Neither option is desirable. That means I have to put as much distance between myself and my shadows as possible, and quickly. Which leaves me with one option—a flight. And as I'm near Manchester Airport, that's where I'd head.'

Prisha chuckles. 'Great minds think alike. And where would you take a flight to?'

'I'd stay away from Europe. There's a lot of information sharing between countries.'

'And also Interpol.'

'The States can be a bugger to get into even if you're a law-abiding citizen.'

'Middle East and Africa can be risky,' Prisha adds.

'Australia, New Zealand, and possibly Asia are too far away. Which leaves South America and Canada.'

'Has this car got a siren and flashing lights?'

Lochy purses his lips. 'What part of Secret Service don't you understand?'

'Pardon me for asking. Right, I'm going to call the head of security at Manchester Airport. Dolores Fernandez , indeed. She has delusions of grandeur.'

31

Tiffany slams the locker door shut and drops the key into her pocket. Pulling a suitcase, she makes her way across the departure terminal to the check-in desk.

She glances at the clock—five minutes before check-in closes and two hours, five minutes before her flight departs. There's only one person in front of her, a suspicious looking individual who looks more like an international drug mule than a passenger. Tattoos adorn his neck, from which several gold chains hang loosely down to his chest. His hair is slicked back, and he's wearing a hoody and tight tracksuit Lycra pants. It's not a good look. He turns and eyes her up, mentally undressing her.

He smiles, flashing one gold canine, then winks, puckers his lips and sucks in air through his teeth. She coughs and turns away.

The girl at the check-in desk is standard fare for an airport—cold, humourless, acting like a paying passenger is a hindrance rather than someone who is helping keep her in a job.

'You're pushing it,' she says snidely.

'Sorry?' Tiffany says.

'Another couple of minutes and you'd have missed your flight.'

'It doesn't matter whether I check-in four hours or four seconds before, as long as I beat the clock,' Tiffany replies testily as she hands the girl her false passport sporting the pseudonym—Tiffany Murray.

'Just saying.'

'Well, don't. I'm not in the mood for your passive aggressive comments.'

'Keep yer knickers on Miss Murray.'

'It's Ms Murray to you.'

She strides from the check-in desk and debates her options. She could go straight through to passenger screening, peruse the duty-free shops, grab a bite to eat, then wait in the departure lounge. It sounds like a good option, before she curses herself.

'Don't let your guard down now,' she murmurs. She realises that once through passenger screening, she's trapped.

———⋅◇⋅———

Buying a magazine and a coffee, she finds a quiet spot and takes a position opposite the main international departures entrance, but it's so vast it's impossible to monitor everyone who comes and goes.

Her eyes wander to the clock again—twenty minutes to go. Slipping the magazine into her backpack, she heads to the bathroom. In the cubicle, she pulls the small tin of drugs from the bag, has one last snort, and drops it into her pocket. Removing the lid from the cistern, she drops the locker key into the water.

With hands washed, she redoes her makeup, puts her hat and sunglasses on and exits the bathroom. Slowly spinning around, she memorises immovable objects—doors, pillars, painted numbers, toilets. Confident she has etched the information into her mind, she looks for a bin to ditch the cocaine tin. She does a double take and freezes, hit by a burst of adrenalin.

'That bitch!' she whispers. 'She's like a dog with a bone.'

Just inside the doors of the main entrance, she spots Detective Inspector Kumar, with a tall, well-dressed, handsome man by her side. They're in deep discussion with two uniformed airport security officers. Tiffany slips behind a pillar and observes. A moment passes until the group splits into two, then rushes off towards departures.

'Shit!'

Her mind computes her options, chances, and probability of capture.

'Now's not the time for faint heart,' she mumbles and strides purposefully in the direction of the passenger screening.

Her head slowly swivels like a hawk looking for a meal. She spots her prey, an older woman. Looks like a typical housewife with her husband jetting off for early autumn holidays to Spain or Greece. Cheaper and quieter after the late summer rush.

She falls in behind them. Pulls her phone out. Stumbles forward and bangs into the woman in front, at the same time dropping the cocaine tin into the woman's coat pocket.

'I do beg your pardon! I'm so sorry,' Tiffany declares, appalled at her faux pas. 'I was too busy looking at my phone.'

'That's all right, dear. No harm done,' says the woman, a little flustered.

Tiffany flashes the woman's husband a flutter of her long lashes. He smiles benevolently... his lucky day. Not often he gets a come on at his age. Tiffany apologises again, then falls back a little.

They approach two body scanners and conveyor belts. The woman places her handbag onto the belt and walks through the metal detector. A rapid buzzer is accompanied by flashing lights. She steps back, puzzled. Tiffany pulls a slightly annoyed face at the delay and moves across to the adjacent scanner as a security officer advances towards the woman. Total bewilderment rips across the woman's face as she pulls the tin from her pocket, staring at it. The guard takes it from her and lifts the lid.

Tiffany exits the scanner without fuss, unlike the woman and her husband, who are now being led away protesting their innocence in a highly voluble manner.

'Sorry,' Tiffany mumbles. 'But sometimes... needs must.'

She nervously queues up in the line for boarding, trying to suck herself in, become invisible.

Her blood pressure rises with each achingly slow, painful shuffle forward.

Hands over her boarding card, receives a stub back.

Pads along the jet bridge, head down.

Stewards greet her. She smiles politely.

One of them directs her to the seat.

Bag stowed overhead. Safe.

Headphones in.

Music on.

Sleep mask at the ready, resting on her forehead.

Main passenger door pulled shut.

Releases a long, slow expulsion of air.

Sleep mask down.

Done it.

In the clear.

Free!

Beaten the system. Evaded death. Dodged prison.

A shudder from the plane as it prepares to taxi towards the runway.

Takes a deep breath.

Music, calming, repetitive ambience piped through a wire into her brain.

Relaxation.

A sharp pain rips through her left ear.

'Tiffany Butler, I am arresting you on suspicion of obtaining and using a false passport. You do not have to say anything, but it may harm your defence if you do not mention...'

Lifts the mask and glares with hatred into the eyes of Detective Inspector Prisha Kumar.

32

Lochy nods towards the door and eyeballs Prisha. She follows him as they leave Tiffany sitting forlornly in an airport security holding room with a solitary officer.

'What is it?' she asks, once outside.

'I'm just giving you a heads up about the route back.'

'Via the M62 and onto the A64 is the quickest way. We'll be back in Whitby by six.'

'I don't like that. It's too obvious. I suggest we take the A and B roads and follow a more convoluted course.'

'You don't think the Russians are onto us, do you?'

'Nothing indicates that. I'm simply being cautious.'

'We could call on Manchester Police to provide a prisoner transit van and an escort.'

He shakes his head. 'No. The fewer people that know, the better.'

'They are *our* people.'

'Hmm... never heard of moles? Anyway, the Range Rover is safer than a prisoner transit van. Reinforced metal plating, bulletproof Armormax windows, extra-large fuel tank.'

'Optional extras when they bought it?'

'Something like that. Anyway, it's just my advice. You don't have to take it. You're in charge.'

Prisha smiles. 'I'll bow to your superior knowledge in this particular matter. The twisty route it is. But don't go too fast. I'll be cuffed to Cruella de Vil in the back seat, and I get car sick unless I'm sitting upfront.'

'I'll bear that in mind.'

'I best let Frank know the route.'

'Don't worry. My lot will track us via GPS. Anyway, even I don't know the route yet.'

'Fair enough. Oh, another thing. Absolutely no discussion of any police matters in front of Tiffany. Do not answer any of her questions. Don't engage with her in any way. And we'll need the police radios on silent. Open the door just a crack, and she'll bust it wide open and use it in her favour.'

'You make her sound like Sherlock Holmes.'

'More like Mycroft. Come on, let's get going. It's been a bloody long day, and it's not over yet.'

The Range Rover pulls away as Tiffany tilts her head and sniffs, taking in the aroma of Prisha's perfume.

'I've never been so embarrassed in all my life,' she says haughtily. 'Marched through the airport, handcuffed, like a common criminal.'

'You *are* a common criminal,' Prisha responds, already bored with her incessant complaining. 'Lochy, can you turn the heater up, please? It's freezing in the back.'

He doesn't reply but obliges as he navigates out of the airport.

'So where are you taking me?'

'You're going home, Tiffany. Back to Whitby.'

'I don't think that's a very good idea.'

'Why?'

'I believe someone is after me.'

'You're very popular at the moment, although not with the three-hundred passengers who have now had their flight delayed thanks to you. Anyway, you should be thanking us.'

'And why's that?'

'We're protecting you. You'll be safe in prison.'

'Like Mark Bridges?' she replies pointedly. 'I'd have felt far safer on the plane.'

'It's a very serious offence... false passport. Should get you five to ten. That will give us plenty of time to investigate the other matters.'

'Matters? You used the plural.'

Prisha turns to her. 'Correct. Matters.'

'Where's my luggage?'

'It's being unloaded. Don't worry, it will be dispatched to Whitby early tomorrow morning. Once it's been searched, it may be returned to you, if you get bail, although, as you are a flight risk, I doubt you'll get it. Now, if you don't mind, I'd like a little peace and quiet.'

Tiffany gives up on the loaded questions after ten minutes of being stonewalled by both officers. The journey drags on in silence.

As they pass through Skipton, Lochy takes another unusual turn and takes the B-road to Grassington.

Prisha is feeling weary as she glances at Tiffany, who appears to be enjoying a catnap. A violent buzz rings out.

'Damn,' Prisha says as she pulls her mobile from her pocket.

'What's wrong?' Lochy asks.

'Mobile's dead.'

'Pass it here.'

She hands him the phone, and he places it flat inside a small console in front of the gear stick.

'You'll need to plug it in,' she advises.

He chuckles. 'It's wireless.'

'Get out of here! How does that work?'

'It transfers power via resonant inductive coupling.'

'I thought as much. Technology baffles me. Do you mind if I rest my eyes for a few minutes?'

'No. Go for it. We're still two hours away.'

'You really are taking the less travelled road, aren't you?'

'I'm just being...'

'Cautious. Yes, I know.'

She leans back and closes her eyes, but her chin rests awkwardly on the police radio inside her jacket. She unclips it and places it on the seat next to her, away from Tiffany.

———◦———

Nothing more than a faint, distant rumble at first, the deep guttural throb of an engine creeps louder as the Range Rover ploughs on into the darkening night.

Prisha wakes, blinks, yawns, feeling slightly nauseous. Rubs at her neck.

'Where are we?'

'Just passed Fangdale Beck coming up to Grange. Another fifty minutes or so and we should be in Whitby. Hey...'

'What?'

He swivels his eyes and nods his head in the rearview mirror. Prisha turns around and stares out of the back window.

'A motorbike—so what?'

'Been with us for a while.'

'You don't think?'

'Probably not, but you never know. Just making you aware, that's all.'

'I need to pee.'

'Can you hold on?'

'I suppose.'

As the road straightens out, the blast of the motorbike engine echoes out like a gunshot. Prisha watches nervously as the black Harley-Davidson glides alongside, its solitary rider dressed head to foot in leather gear. The rider slowly turns their head until Prisha can see her own reflection in the helmet visor. The throttle is opened, and the bike roars past and accelerates away.

'False alarm,' Lochy states.

Prisha moves the handcuff up her arm slightly and rubs at her wrist. The action wakens Tiffany, who straightens and yawns.

'I'm thirsty. Anyone got any water?'

Prisha hands her a bottle. As they round a sharp bend in the road, Lochy slams the brakes on.

'Shit!' he says in a hushed whisper.

A hundred yards ahead, a motorcycle and rider are sprawled across the road.

The car slows.

'I better call emergency services,' Prisha says as she fumbles in her jacket for her mobile.

'No, not yet. I want to check it out,' Lochy says.

His hand disappears under his jacket before pulling a Glock 19 out. He pops a magazine into the pistol, racks the slide to load the first bullet, then places it back in its holster.

'Stay here,' he commands with authority, as he slams the car door shut.

Prisha's nausea takes a turn for the worse.

'He's very handsome,' Tiffany comments without a care in the world. 'I wonder what he's like in the sack?'

'I'll let you know the next time I visit you in prison,' Prisha responds in a cocky manner, deliberately intended to irk. 'Where's my bloody phone?'

She spots it in the console and leans forward, but the handcuffs impede her progress.

'Can you shuffle forward a little so I can reach my phone, please?'

'Why don't you just take the bloody cuffs off? My wrist is as sore as hell. It's not like I'm going to do a runner. We're in the middle of nowhere.'

As Prisha struggles in vain to reach her phone, she glances ahead. Lochy is advancing with caution, pistol drawn, half-crouching, crabbing forward. Reaching the stricken motorcyclist, he peers down over the body.

He kneels.

His left hand reaches out and dabs at something.

Fingers rub together.

He sniffs.

Standing, he takes a few steps back towards the car, turns, and motions to Prisha, making the "call" signal with his thumb to ear. Prisha gives him the okay sign and searches for the police radio to request assistance.

Something catches the corner of her eye.

Tries to swallow but can't.

Attempts to move but is frozen rigid.

As Lochy heads back to the motorcyclist, a gunman wearing a ski mask appears from behind a low stone wall.

'Lochy! Lochy!' Prisha screams, but the reinforced Range Rover has excellent sound proofing and mutes her warning.

Something carries to Lochy on the gentle breeze.

He stops and gradually turns, bemused.

Spots the gunman.

Prisha knows it's too late.

Lochy knows it's too late... as he reaches for his gun.

A shot rings out like the crack of a bullwhip.

A crimson geyser of skin, brains, blood, hair, and bone erupts from the back of Lochy's head. It splatters and sticks to the opposite drystone wall in a gloopy splat. By some miracle, he appears to be still alive, eyes wide open, staring at his assassin.

He wobbles.

Knees buckle.

Falls forward to the cold, hard bitumen.

The motorcyclist rises akin to Lazarus with a triple bypass.

The gunman leaps the wall like a gazelle and saunters over to the rider. They hi-five each other. He's a giant of a man, and Prisha has no doubt who he is.

The screams of Tiffany Butler go unanswered as Prisha feels woozy. Her life slips into slow-motion. She realises there's no chance against them—out of her depth by a hundred leagues.

The motorcyclist maniac advances towards the car as the giant picks up Lochy's body, drags it across the road, and effortlessly tosses it over the wall, like roadkill.

A warm trickle snakes down Prisha's leg.

Stinging pain jolts her from her catatonic state as Tiffany's palm slaps her hard across the cheek.

'Do something, you fucking bitch! Otherwise, this car is going to be our coffin, and I don't want to spend the rest of eternity with you!'

Prisha awakes... takes in the scene.

The car is parked on a grass verge next to a stone wall. Beyond, it appears to drop sharply away as she can only see the tops of trees. To her right-hand side, open fields stretch to the horizon.

She pulls the handle on the car door. 'The wall!' she shouts at Tiffany. 'We must get over the wall!'

The motorcyclist approaches, unzips their jacket, pulls out a pistol.

Prisha falls to the road, but her right arm is still inside the vehicle attached to Tiffany.

'Undo the fucking cuffs!' Tiffany screeches.

Prisha fumbles in her pocket for the key with trembling fingers. Her mind has turned to mush. The crack of a shot is followed by a whistling whoosh and a dull thwack as the bullet lodges in the reinforced glass of the open door, inches away from Prisha's head.

Her twitching fingers cannot navigate the key into the lock. She drops it and watches as it bounces under the car, then stares at Tiffany as deafness descends. Tiffany's mouth moves, but the words are clothed in treacle, as if she's underwater.

Another crack and a ding as the high velocity projectile ricochets off the metal of the door.

Her senses snap back into action.

'Prisha! Prisha!' Tiffany shrieks.

Prisha nods like a scared little girl. 'What?' she mumbles.

'Listen to me! Is this how you want it to end? A pathetic woman trembling with fear, squirming, as a bullet spills your brains out all over the road. Push your panic aside. Get angry! Now pull yourself together and pass me the damned key!'

Reaching behind the back tyre, she grips the key and fumbles it to Tiffany. The rider inexorably stalks forward. The cuff is released from Tiffany's wrist, the key still in place. The welcoming sound of an engine drifts through the air. Prisha lifts her head and peers down the road. A car comes to a halt near to the upturned motorbike.

The hulk drops onto one knee, pulls his gun out and aims the barrel at the windscreen. The gnashing of gears is instantly accompanied by a high-pitched whine as the car reverses away in a snaking, haphazard fashion. The rider stops and gazes over her shoulder at the unfolding scene.

'Now!' Prisha yells.

Both women dart towards the wall. The rider turns, fires. As they dive over the wall, a clap like overhead thunder deafens them as a spark shoots out.

Tiffany yelps.

They hit damp grass, twigs, leaf litter, and roll down the steep hill carried by their momentum.

Angry shouting in a strange tongue follows them down the steep incline, rolling, bouncing, scrabbling. Their transit ends as they crash into a grove of young saplings. Prisha stares back at the wall high above them. The ominous head of the rider peers down at her like an alien, a black orb with a wide slot reflecting light. On all fours, they scramble further into the dense copse. The last remaining daylight is snuffed out, replaced by an eerie, silent gloom.

The shouting fades as the boom of the motorbike fires. They listen, panting hard, eyes on stalks as the engine fades.

Their eyes meet. No words needed. They're in this together.

Rising to their feet, they bend at the hips and race forward, heading down the steep hill, pushing past thickets, striding through nettles, slipping on the wet carpet of undergrowth. Stings, cuts, and scratches are barely registered as the adrenaline pumps through their veins. Like wild animals being hunted, on they go, never looking back, fighting for breath, ignorant of their aching limbs and fierce thirst. The only thing that matters—survival!

———◆———

They dip their hands into the chilly water of the bristling beck and splash their faces and rub at the dirt around their necks. Prisha cups her hands and takes a large gulp.

'Do you think it's safe to drink?' Tiffany asks.

'I think that's the least of our problems.'

'Not if it causes dysentery.'

Prisha stops and stares at her, then chuckles.

'What's so funny?'

'Your face. You've got mascara running down your cheeks and your lipstick is smudged. You look like a five-year-old who's got into her mother's makeup for the first time.'

Tiffany snorts. 'Not my best look.,' she replies as she sticks her lips into the stream and sucks up the water with a gurgling sound.

They both sit on the bank as they attend to cuts and scratches. Prisha rinses her handkerchief out in the water as Tiffany takes her grimy jacket off and drops it to the ground.

'You're injured,' Prisha says as she notices blood trickling down Tiffany's arm. 'Here, let me see.'

She dabs at the wound on the elbow.

'It was the ricochet from the bullet. I think it dislodged a bit of stone from the wall,' Tiffany says as she holds her arm out.

'Yes. It's just a flesh wound, but you need to keep it clean.'

'What are we going to do?'

'I'm not sure. It's dark now. I think it best to find somewhere to rest until daylight or until we hear the cavalry arrive.'

'Cavalry?'

'Yes. The car had GPS tracking installed, a bit like your hire car. They'd have noticed the car stopped in the middle of nowhere. That should have rung the alarm bells.'

'You don't think they'd have been stupid enough to leave the car there, do you?'

'No. That's probably why they didn't follow us. If someone spotted an abandoned Range Rover in the middle of the road, the place would have been swarming with police in fifteen minutes.' A realisation dawns on her. 'Damn it! What a bloody fool I've been!' she laments as she bangs her palm against her forehead.

'What?'

'The car was bullet proof. All I had to do was remove the cuffs, lock the doors, and jump into the driver's seat and we could have got away.'

'Don't beat yourself up. It was a life or death situation. No one would think straight under that duress. I'd have rather taken my chance out in the open than sit there as those monsters approached. They would have shot the tyres, anyway.'

'Hmm... maybe. It was still a dumb mistake,' she replies as she ties the handkerchief around Tiffany's arm, then rises.

'Thanks. Where are we?' Tiffany asks.

'How the hell would I know? I've only been here three weeks. I thought I'd give up city life and start afresh in North Yorkshire, surrounded by beautiful countryside, next to the sea. A nice, cushy number. Maybe arrest a few low-level druggies; nick the occasional old biddy for shoplifting. A sea-change, tree-change.'

'You got that wrong.'

'You're telling me. A kidnapping and ransom, three, possibly four murders, and two Russian psychopaths wanting to blow my brains out. It's not what the brochure said. And it's all your fault.'

Tiffany glares at her. 'What I've done is wrong, I'll admit that, but I've hurt no one.'

Prisha snorts her derision. 'What about Zoe and Emma? Holding two thirteen-year-old girls captive for three days? And don't come the innocent, we know you were involved.'

Tiffany stands up. 'They were well looked after. Plenty of food and water. A sink, toilet, warm beds, and plenty of books to keep them occupied.'

'And what about the mental anguish for them and their loved ones?'

'What doesn't kill you strengthens you. Anyway, it was short-term pain for long-term gain.'

'Yes, your gain. Have you no remorse?'

Tiffany pulls the hairband from her head and remakes her ponytail.

'Of course. I am human, despite what you may think.'

'The two men you were in a long-term relationship with are now both dead, thanks to you. I'd be racked with guilt if I were in your shoes.'

'Ah... so you've figured out about me and Charles. Well done. Anyway, I never loved them,' she replies coldly. 'And they're dead because two crazed Russians are running around with impunity, bumping off whoever they want—not because of me. I wouldn't hurt a fly.'

'My god! You really are a psycho. No empathy, no sympathy, no feelings, no acceptance of wrongdoing.'

Tiffany reattaches the hairband and swishes her head from side to side.

'Look, if we're going to survive this predicament, can we please try to be civil to each other? You may hate me, but I'm not the one trying to kill you. I think your animosity should be reserved for our would-be assassins.'

Prisha relents as she realises it makes sense—for the moment.

'Yes, you're right.'

'Good. Now to the matter at hand—where are we?'

'I've told you; I don't bloody know.'

'Did you notice a signpost or a village we passed through?'

'Hang on, yes... when I woke up, I asked Lochy where we were, and he said we'd just passed Fangdale Beck and were heading towards Grange.'

'Christ! What the hell was he playing at? We're closer to Middlesbrough than Whitby.'

'He wanted to take the long route. Keep off the main roads. He thought it'd be safer.'

'Fuck! He got that wrong. We really are in the middle of nowhere.'

Prisha replays the images in her head of Lochy's death as a wave of revulsion and sorrow sweeps through her. Tiffany notices her expression.

'You really had the hots for him, didn't you?' She doesn't reply. 'How long were you together?'

'We weren't. I met him today.'

'Oh, I see. He wasn't a copper. I could tell that much. Special agent?'

Prisha nods. 'A sub-organisation of MI5.'

Tiffany gently rubs Prisha's shoulder. 'I'm sorry. You'd have been good together. I could tell there was a spark between you both.'

She pulls away. 'Come on. Let's find somewhere to rest until dawn.'

33

Frank glances nervously at the clock on his wall for the umpteenth time, trying hard to control his rising anger and frustration. Zac is sitting patiently in a chair opposite as James Carmichael paces the tiny office, speaking into his mobile.

'Yes. I see, very well. Keep me updated. Bye.'

'Well?' Frank growls, his low, deep baritone laced with emotion.

'We tracked them all the way from Manchester Airport. They made a brief stop of no more than four minutes north of Fangdale Beck, then stopped again at Easby eight miles further north. But...'

He pauses and rubs at the back of his neck.

'But what?'

'That's when the transponder stopped transmitting. An extensive search of the area hasn't located their vehicle, or the transponder.'

'What the bloody hell are you telling me?' Frank booms, already suspecting the answer.

'Probably that the transponder has been removed from the car and destroyed.'

'Sweet merciful shite with bells on!' he thunders. 'Fangdale Beck and Easby are way off course. What was your man doing up there?'

'From our tracking, it appears SE17 was taking the back roads to thwart any possible attack. A standard procedure.'

'Why wasn't I told the route by Prisha?'

'Probably because SE17 was making up the route as he went along. If he wasn't sure which way he was going, then how could anyone else?'

'A car the size of a Range Rover doesn't just disappear into thin air. If this is the Russians' work, then how the hell did they track the car?'

Carmichael winces. 'On that point, I'm not sure.'

'It would have to be an inside job, boss,' Zac says.

'What's the background on SE17... Jesus H Christ! Can we not give him a bloody name instead of a number?' he bellows.

Carmichael ignores his request. 'He's one of our best operatives. Smart, agile, thinks on his feet.'

'Trustworthy?'

Carmichael is shocked at the inference. 'I can assure you, chief inspector, every one of our operatives is rigorously background checked before, during and after their service!'

'It's odd they stopped at Fangdale Beck for a few minutes before disappearing at Easby,' Zac ponders.

'A toilet break, perhaps?' Carmichael offers. 'We have a team of ten scouring the area on foot as we speak, and a military chopper is in the air equipped with thermal imaging. It's only a matter of time until something turns up.'

'Try her phone again,' Frank says.

Zac taps Prisha's image on his mobile. A harsh beep blasts out.

'Still nothing, boss. Meaning it's switched off, out of range or the battery's dead.'

'Or destroyed,' Frank mutters as he puts his hands on his hips and gazes at the twinkling lights of the trawlers moored in the harbour below.

'Right, there's nothing more of value we can do tonight. Zac, go home and get some sleep. You look shattered.'

'Are you sure, boss?'

'Yes. Cartwright will begin his shift in a minute. If anything develops overnight, he'll contact us.'

Zac slips into his jacket and slopes out of the office.

'Right, I may nip back to the hotel and get a couple of hours myself,' Carmichael says. 'I'll let you know if I hear anything. Night, Frank.'

'Aye... night, James.'

Frank drops into his seat, despondent, worried, exhausted.

'What a royal cock-up,' he murmurs. 'Come on Prisha, lass, get in touch. Let me know you're all right.'

34

They fumble their way inside the barn, straining to see despite the aid of a micro keyring torch attached to Prisha's car and house keys.

'It's not The Ritz, but it will do for tonight,' Prisha says.

'I prefer Claridge's, myself,' Tiffany replies.

The sweet smell of fresh hay and the natural insulation it offers is a welcome relief from the inclement conditions outside.

'Do you think there're any rats?' Tiffany asks, with a frown.

'Undoubtably. We should be right if we get on top of the hay bales.'

'I think rats can climb.'

'Fine. You sleep outside.'

'I was just saying.'

Prisha carefully surveys the interior as her eyes adjust to the gloam.

'A ladder. Perfect,' she states as she treads towards the corner of the barn with Tiffany tight by her side.

She stumbles over something on the ground.

'What the hell's that?' she curses as she shines the diminutive light downward. She bends, grabs the wooden handle, then hands it to Tiffany.

'A rake?' she says disdainfully.

'It's a weapon... of sorts. Better than nothing.'

Manoeuvring the ladder against a large stack of bales, they climb to the top and flop out, carefully placing the hay rake well out of harm's way.

'I'm surprised. It's quite comfortable and warm,' Tiffany says.

'I'll be out like a light. I don't think I've ever felt as drained in all my life. Not even after completing a triathlon.'

'It's the shock. Fear is debilitating.'

'Hmm... How come you didn't experience any fear when it all kicked off back there?'

Tiffany rolls onto her side and pulls her knees up towards her chest.

'I did. I just didn't let it control me. You have to be in charge of your emotions, otherwise you are at the whims and fancies of events.'

'Huh... that's what Lochy said this morning.'

'What?'

'Not to let emotion dictate your actions. Easier said than done.'

'It just takes practice,' Tiffany says with a yawn.

'And how did you get so good at it?'

'I learnt it in childhood. The first few times my mother locked me in the cupboard, I was terrified. Claustrophobia is not a pleasant feeling. It's like you can't breathe. I would panic, scream, and bang my head against the wall until I passed out.'

Prisha pushes herself up on one arm and looks down at her.

'Jesus! Are you telling the truth, or is this one of your many fanciful lies?'

'It's the truth,' she replies without emotion. 'Then I realised that if I really focused on something, I could control the fear. At first, I used to imagine a gigantic clock with the second hand ticking from one number to the next. I'd see the image and count the numbers in my head. I still use that one sometimes when I struggle to sleep.'

'Why did your mum lock you in a cupboard?'

'Because she was an anal retentive nutjob. Hated mess. She was very house proud. I cottoned on pretty soon. Instead of playing with dolls, or paints or plasticine, I'd read instead. You can't make much mess with a book.'

'Where was your dad?'

'Good question.'

'You didn't have a father?'

'Obviously, someone fathered me. Whenever I asked mother about him, she'd tell me he was a worthless loser who abandoned her when he found out she was pregnant. I stopped asking in the end.'

'Not a happy childhood, then?'

'On the contrary. As long as I kept on the good side of my mother, things were fine. A little lonely. I wasn't allowed friends over, not that I ever had many. But I always had my books to escape into.'

Prisha lays back down as she experiences a stab of sympathy for Tiffany Butler.

'I'm a bookworm myself,' Prisha says, stifling a yawn.

'What's your favourite book?'

'Wuthering Heights.'

Tiffany bolts upright. 'You're joking! Me too!' she exclaims as she lets out a giggle.

'Now that is bizarre. I'd have thought you'd have been into gothic horror; Bram Stoker, Edgar Allan Poe, Mary Shelley.'

Tiffany pulls a pout. 'That's rather cruel,' she says curtly.

Prisha gazes up at her. She no longer sees a psychopath but a vulnerable young woman of a similar age to herself.

'Sorry. I didn't mean that. It was a joke.'

'Apology accepted.'

She lays back down as Prisha switches the torch off.

'Night, Tiffany.'

'Night, Prisha.'

Within a few minutes, both women fall into a heavy sleep crowded with demons. They fail to hear the hypnotic sonic down-draught caused by the military chopper or notice the blazing high-powered lamp that flits across the countryside from high above.

35

Sunday 6th September

It's five-thirty in the morning and Frank is back behind his desk; he struggled to sleep and, having disturbed Meera for the fourth time as he tossed and turned, he decided he'd be better off being in his office.

The overnight reports indicated no fresh developments in the disappearance of Prisha, Tiffany Butler, and the JSTAT intelligence officer.

He slurps on white sugary tea, his diet now fallen by the wayside. Peering through his Venetian blinds, he watches as Zac saunters in, looking dishevelled. His hair is a shambles, his stubble way past its sell-by-date and his clothes are creased.

'Hell fire,' Frank grumbles. 'He's always the same during a big case—he neglects himself.'

The expected knock on the door arrives.

'Come in.'

'Any news?' Zac asks.

'Not a dicky bird. Quiet as the grave.'

Zac sips from a cardboard cup of lukewarm, acrid coffee and grimaces.

'I couldn't sleep. I'm worried about her.'

'Aye, me too, lad. The longer it goes, the more my hope fades. If it is this Russian duo behind it, they need taking down. They've gone completely rogue.'

'Even if we do eventually catch them, they'll be exchanged for two of our agents in Russia. They'll get off Scott free.'

'Maybe. But at least they'll be off our shores.'

'To be instantly replaced by another two.'

'We can only do what we can do, Zac. We can't change the world.'

'No... I guess not. So what's our next move, if any?'

Frank stretches his arms above his head. 'I hate the waiting.'

'Me too.'

'So how about this; we jump in the car, grab a drive-thru takeaway, then head to Easby and take in the lie of the land?'

Zac grins. 'Sounds better than sitting around here on our brains waiting for JSTAT to come up with something. Give me five. I want to check the messages on my PC.'

As he leaves the room, Frank notices a new message in his own inbox from HQ. He reads it with interest.

'Zac! Get in here!' he yells.

Zac is back in an instant. 'What?'

'A statement has just been made at Northallerton by an elderly couple. They were driving home late yesterday after visiting a relative in Middlesbrough. Thought they'd take the scenic route. They passed through Easby and about eight miles further on, they rounded a bend and spotted a motorcycle laid out on the road.

They slowed down before some maniac jumped out and pointed a gun at them. They hightailed it out of there.'

'Why didn't they report it last night?'

'They're in their late seventies. They were scared to death. After a restless night's sleep, their consciences got the better of them.'

'Eight miles further south from Easby would be nearing Fangdale Beck, where the car originally stopped for a few minutes!'

'Correct!' Frank yells as he grabs his overcoat from the hatstand.

'Bloody dickheads! The Spooks have been searching in the wrong place!'

———————

A carpet of grey, fleecy clouds ominously rolls in from the North Sea as a spittle of rain activates the automatic wipers. They sporadically swish across the windscreen with an annoyed squeak. High on a hill beside a bulwark of rocks, a solitary, gnarled hawthorn tree stubbornly thrives.

Frank finishes his bacon and egg roll and passes the wrapper to Zac, who scrunches it up and drops it into a brown paper bag.

'How much do you know about Prisha's family?' Frank asks as he checks the fuel gauge.

'A little. She's first generation. Her grandparents arrived here in the mid-seventies when her father was young. Strict upbringing, but loving by all accounts. Two brothers.'

'Are they all still alive?'

'Yes, I think so. She's talked about her parents and brothers in the present tense, and she mentioned it was her grandma's eighty-fifth birthday soon and she was going back to Birmingham for the weekend. I don't think her father's happy that she's in the police, though.'

'Why?'

'Old-fashioned values, I guess. He sees law and order as a man's domain.'

'If we've no news by midday, I best give her parents a call, just to make them aware,' he says gravely.

They take the main road and bypass Easby, which is cordoned off east and west. Zac studies his phone.

'We're about a mile from Fangdale Beck, Frank.'

The car slows to a crawl as both men scan the roadside looking for anything suspicious. They see nothing to arouse their senses.

'Fangdale Beck is down there on the right, boss.'

'And Carmichael definitely said the car stopped for a few minutes *north* of Fangdale Beck. There's only one thing for it—time for a stroll.'

They park up and each man takes one side of the road as they zigzag between the centreline and the verge, creeping along, heads down, eyes flickering from left to right. Occasionally, one of them stops, bends, and inspects something of interest.

Anxiety and stress pushes tiredness from their minds and weary bones. A steady mizzle descends, coating them in a damp overcoat as a gentle breeze with teeth of ice bites at their faces.

The hundred yards takes them twenty minutes to walk. On four occasions, they have to stand at the side of the road as a vehicle thunders past.

'How much further, boss?'

Frank wipes the wet from his face with the palm of his hand and purses his lips, shaking his head.

'I think we're done. We're chasing a red herring. It was a long shot, but better than doing nothing,' he replies.

He gazes back down the road at the car parked in the distance, then turns and stares up the road. Nothing. No clues. Just a quiet country road carving its way through the rocks and moorland of North Yorkshire.

His eyes fix on the contours ahead. A thought springs from nowhere.

'Hey, Zac?'

'What?' he replies absentmindedly as he kneels to examine a mark on the bitumen.

'Do you ever watch any of those old westerns they show on the movie channel?'

'No. A bit cheesy for my tastes. Why?'

'You're right. They haven't aged well. But it's a bit of harmless entertainment. I was watching one last weekend, starring John Wayne.'

'Who?'

'Give me strength,' Frank mutters. 'He was leading a posse, chasing some outlaws. The posse was riding through this narrow ravine, you know, high rocks and cliffs either side.'

'Have you taken your medication today, Frank?'

'Bear with me. Anyway, as they rounded a bend in the ravine, they were ambushed by the outlaws.'

'Fascinating stuff. Does this rambling anecdote have a point?'

Frank nods his head to one side and points up the road.

'A sharp corner. Perfect place for an ambush.'

They stride on for another twenty feet and stop at the bend in the road and meticulously scrutinise the area.

'Frank?' Zac calls out as he crouches and dabs at the dark stain on the road.

'What is it?'

'Not sure.' He rubs his fingers together. 'It's not oil. Could be blood, but it could be from anything, a fox, or a rabbit.'

Frank drops to his haunches at the side of him and regards the small blemish

'Hmm... Not much to go on.'

He swivels around and surveys the scene. His eye picks out something incongruous to the setting. Walking over to the drystone wall, a sudden chill runs down his spine.

'Sweet merciful crap,' he mutters, eyes fixed on the blocks of aged black stone.

'What?' Zac says as he hurriedly joins his boss. 'Shit... blood splatter.'

36

The breeze sucks up hay dust from the barn floor and sends it into a swirling eddy, chasing itself around and around like a Dachshund pursuing its tail. Weak sunlight cracks through rafters and dances on the muddy shoes of the two women as they sleep. On pastures green, sheep happily graze on lush grass as an occasional fat lamb bleats for its mother. The falsetto chirrup of a joyful skylark trills across the countryside until the jumble of notes falls softly by the head of Prisha.

Behind her eyelids, movement. She can hear the rolling salty waves of the sea, unaware the stiff breeze is a roguish imposter. Her tongue is stuck to the inside of her mouth, a testament to thirst. She swallows and licks her lips.

Blinks. Confusion. Realisation. Fear. Nausea.

Her sanctuary in slumber is brutally curtailed as reality hits her in the temple with a clawhammer.

'Oh, shit,' she mutters as she pushes the image of Lochy's death from her mind. There'll be plenty of time to slay that monster if she escapes the present nightmare.

Aching limbs, blistered feet, bruises, abrasions, stinging thirst, gnawing hunger, and a throbbing headache all jostle for prime position on the pain hierarchy.

She sits up and gazes through the doorway. It's early morning. Half turning, she rubs her eyes and peers at Tiffany, who is still in a place where she is safe.

A twinge of regret pokes at her heart.

What she's done is wrong. I can have no sympathy for her. She masterminded the kidnapping of two children, and may be indirectly implicated in the murder of Shirley Fox. She swindled twenty million pounds. No... I don't care about the money, but murder and kidnapping are different. She has to pay the penalty for her actions.

But then again, if it hadn't been for her words in the car, which snapped me from my fear-induced inertia, we'd both be dead. Doesn't that even the ledger? That's not for me to decide. It's up to a jury. They'll throw the book at her. Thirty years minimum.

It's not like she's a habitual criminal. The kidnapping and ransom were a one-off. Her twisted way of ensuring she had the winning lottery ticket. Fuck... I'm all messed up.

An angry buzzing noise from outside ends the battle with her conscience. It sounds like a swarm of wasps or hornets approaching. She kneels up and gazes around at the rafters and corners of the roof, searching for a nest.

'Shit, that's all I need, an attack of the killer bees,' she mumbles.

The humming sound intensifies as it nears the doorway. Grabbing a hay bale, she pushes it towards the top of the ladder and flips it onto its side. Bobbing down behind it for cover, she peeks out around the edge.

As the object hovers in through the entrance, her stomach flips. A tiny bank of green micro lights at the front are permanently shining whilst green and red lights flash on and off in an alternating sequence beneath the propellers and to the side of the camera lens.

The drone rises until it's fifteen feet off the ground, then slowly spins, capturing the inside of the barn.

'Huh... what's that?' Tiffany groans.

Prisha rolls onto her and clasps her hand over her mouth. Wild eyes stare back as she puts a finger to her lips.

'Shush,' she whispers. 'Drone.'

They both crawl to the hay bale near the ladder.

'It could be the police,' Prisha murmurs. 'They use them occasionally to cover wide areas. Quicker than feet on the ground and more access than a vehicle.'

'Or it could belong to the Russians,' Tiffany whispers.

Prisha shrugs and nods. 'Possibly.'

The drone buzzes hesitantly around the perimeter of the building, inspecting, studying for any sign of life. As it nears their hiding spot, both women lay prostrate, cheeks pushed firmly into the rough hay. It hangs in the air as it circles around less than a foot away, its beady eye pointing away from them.

It descends like an extra-terrestrial monster on the prowl. Prisha turns her head, touching Tiffany's. Their eyes lock. Tiffany, for once, is terrified. Prisha winks at her and offers her a faint smile, which is reciprocated. The buzzing sound retreats as it glides out of the door. The noise recedes until it's replaced by nature's natural symphony. Their heart-rates subside.

Tiffany rolls onto her back, panting. 'I can handle most things, but that gave me the bloody creeps.'

'Welcome to another beautiful day.'

Prisha pushes the hay bale out of the way, grabs the rake and steps onto the ladder.

'Here, take this. Pass it to me when I get down.'

As she descends the ladder, she suddenly freezes at the halfway point.

'What is it?' Tiffany asks.

'I thought I heard something. Wait... no, it's gone.' She moves her foot down a rung and stops again. 'There, can you hear it?'

Tiffany cocks her head to one side. 'Shit! It's coming back!'

Prisha desperately scrambles back up the ladder as the drone swoops into the barn at lightning speed, does a three-sixty, then advances towards them before Prisha has even reached the top of the ladder.

The drone bobs up and down as though laughing, mocking them.

'Fuck off, you bastard!' Tiffany screams at the inanimate object which is only three feet away.

It tilts and spins around, but not fast enough as Tiffany brings the end of the rake crashing down onto the hull. Parts break off as the drone flounders and wobbles like a stricken animal. It tilts at an alarming angle and crashes to the ground. Tiffany heaves at the hay bale until it topples, landing with a dull thud on top of the wreck.

The women edge cautiously out of the barn and take stock of their position. On the horizon to the east is the sea, at least thirty miles away. They spin around and see nothing but greenery, rocks, and desolate moorland apart from sheep and the occasional tree.

'Christ, how far did we walk last night?' Tiffany murmurs.

'We were going for a good four hours, so who knows? Maybe eight, twelve miles. I don't have a bloody clue where we are. You any ideas?'

Tiffany gazes intently at the landscape and shakes her head.

'No. I can't even see any roads.'

'We know that's east,' Prisha says, pointing towards the North Sea on the horizon. 'And we also know we were somewhere between Fangdale Beck and Grange. Let's say last night we walked ten miles in any direction. Then where would that put our possible locations?'

Tiffany's mind cranks into action. 'If we walked south, then we could be near Rievaulx.'

'Rievaulx?'

'Rievaulx Abbey. It's an ancient Cistercian monastery. If we headed north, we'd not be far from Kirkby, a tiny village. If we went either east or west, then I can't think of any places we'd be near to. Why can't we see any roads?'

'Because they're all surrounded by drystone walls. We'll notice them once a vehicle comes along.'

'What are we going to do?'

'We can wait here until we spot a car on a road, then head in that direction. Or we can keep to the hills and hopefully come across a farmhouse at some point.'

'What's the safest option?'

Prisha drives the tiredness from her mind and focuses. 'Let's evaluate all scenarios. If that drone was the Russians, then they'll be heading our way right now.'

'What's the range of a drone?'

'A cheap one... maybe two or three miles. A top of the range one, possibly seven to ten miles, and that was definitely top of the range.'

'How do you know?'

'Because it still operated inside the barn, which means it had an exceptionally strong signal back to its controller. You only get that with the expensive models.'

'It could have belonged to the police?'

'If it did, there'll be a chopper here within ten minutes, but we can't take that chance.'

'And we can't wait here in the hope we see a car in the distance.'

'No. And heading towards a road is probably not the safest decision, anyway. That's what the Russians would expect us to do. If we've any chance of survival, we need to out-think them.'

'Why aren't the police and MI5 out looking for us?'

'They will be. But they obviously have no idea where we are.'

Tiffany laughs. 'They're not alone.'

Prisha smiles at her. 'I'm glad you haven't lost your sense of humour. You're going to need it today. Come on. Let's head south. If the Russians do come after us, they'll use a trail or quad bike, so keep your eyes and ears open.'

37

The road between Grange and Fangdale Beck is cordoned off with police tape as a swarm of bodies dressed in white bunny suits painstakingly dissects every inch of the area. Cameras constantly click and flash.

Frank, Zac, and James Carmichael are standing beyond the barrier tape dressed in their civvies. Zac spots a classic, silver E-Type Jaguar pull up alongside the fleet of vehicles strewn along the grass verge.

'Here he comes, the walking, talking thesaurus,' he says drily.

Frank and Carmichael turn around to witness the colossal frame of Doctor Whipple struggle out of his car. He grabs a large black doctor's bag and strides over to them.

'Detective Chief Inspector Finnegan, this is becoming rather tiresome. Since my return from my aborted holidays, I've been summoned to three suspicious deaths.'

'I do apologise.'

'If someone is running rampant around your designated locale, perpetrating outrages, then I suggest you do something about it.'

'That's a damn good idea, Doctor Whipple. Why hadn't I thought of that?' Frank replies.

Whipple eyeballs him suspiciously. 'Are you being facetious, chief inspector?'

'Not at all, doc.'

'Please refrain from using the abbreviated short-form. You are well aware I find it irksome. Now, what have we?' he says as he writhes and wriggles into his hazmat suit with a certain degree of difficulty.

'He's one of ours,' Carmichael says, his face ashen.

'Ours, ours? I am a forensic pathologist, sir, not a mind reader,' Whipple roars.

'Forgive me Doctor Whipple,' Frank begins. 'This is James Carmichael. He's the Senior Case Officer for Covert Technical Operations Specialists with JSTAT. That's a part of...'

'I know what JSTAT is, chief inspector. I am not an ignoramus. So the deceased was one of your operatives?' Whipple says staring at Carmichael as his giant hand becomes stuck halfway down the arm of his suit.

'Correct,' Carmichael confirms.

'Who found the body?'

'We did,' Zac says.

'We, we?' Whipple bellows.

'Me and the chief inspector.'

'And what is your preliminary discernment regarding the body?'

'He's dead.'

Whipple's hand eventually materialises at the end of the suit, much to everyone's relief, as he shuffles and squirms inside the protective wear, grimacing as he does so.

'Yes! I had formed the conclusion he's deceased, otherwise I would not have been summoned, Detective Sergeant Stoker! Could you explicate upon the nature of his demise?'

'A gunshot wound to the head.'

'And why would you presuppose that is what killed him?'

'A bullet hole in the forehead and an exit wound at the rear sort of gave us a clue.'

Whipple glares at him. 'Do I detect a soupcon of impertinence, sergeant?'

Frank steps between the two. 'Look, Doctor Whipple, we found the body at approximately 6:30 am this morning. He has a gunshot wound to the head, probably from a pistol. His body was moved by person, or persons unknown from the road to the field beyond the wall. That's all we are sure of at the moment. Now, we'll leave it in your expert hands.'

Whipple pulls the hood over his head with some effort and finally dons shoe coverings, gloves, mask, and goggles.

'And where exactly is the body?' he asks, his deep baritone now seriously muffled.

Frank points at a forensic photographer, taking photos from different angles of the blood splatter on the wall.

'Behind that wall.'

'And how do you expect a man of my impressive stature to traverse such an obstacle?'

'Walk on thirty feet and there's a farm gate.'

'Very good. We shall continue our interlocution once I've terminated my primary examination, chief inspector.'

'I'll look forward to it.'

He bends with some difficulty as he ducks under the police tape, then plods his way down the road, lumbering forward like a giant bear on its hind legs.

Frank shakes his head at Zac. 'Do you have to deliberately wind him up?'

'Sorry Frank, but you need some comic relief at times like this.'

'Aye, lad, I suppose we do,' he adds jadedly.

———◦———

The crime scene is nearly dismantled as the last two uniformed officers roll up the barrier tape and all but one of the forensic personnel depart. Apart from the two uniforms, the only people left are the forensics supervisor—Charlene Marsden, Frank, Zac and one of Carmichael's men, a recent addition.

Zac wanders over to him, hands stuffed into his puffer jacket.

'Sorry mate. It's never easy when you lose one of your own. Did you know him?'

He shakes his head. 'No. But it still hurts.'

'Yeah, understood. Let's hope your other guy turns up alive and well.'

'Other guy?' the intelligence officer replies with a baffled expression.

'Yeah, the officer who hasn't checked in for a few days.'

More puzzlement. 'Sorry, but I only arrived by chopper a couple of hours ago from down south. Not had a full briefing yet.'

'Oh, I see. Well...'

'Oi, Zac!' Frank's voice echoes around the countryside. 'Charlene is ready to give us a heads up. Look lively!'

Charlene starts from behind the drystone wall opposite the blood splatter. Her brittle voice and diminutive frame, at odds with the brutality of the crime.

'Gunshot residue on the top of this wall,' she explains, tapping the old stone slabs. 'Directly beneath, the grass is flatter, way flatter.'

'Meaning someone was standing there?' Frank predicts.

'Yes. Early indications would suggest that he or she was a heavy individual.'

'Footprints?'

'Not discernible to the naked eye, but we have photographs we can enlarge and enhance. As usual, Frank, this is an off the record indication of what I think happened. I'm not a detective. I'm just passing on my first thoughts. It's up to you and your team to unscramble the egg.'

'Understood, Charlene.'

'If you draw a line in your mind's eye from the gunshot residue to the blood splatter on the wall opposite, you can envisage the trajectory of the bullet.'

Frank walks out into the middle of the road.

'About here is where the IO would have been shot, then?'

Charlene totters forward. 'Take a couple of steps further back and if you look closely on the ground, you'll see a few dark splats. I believe he collapsed forward, then dropped headfirst to the ground. But yes, you're in the right vicinity.'

Zac joins Frank and stares at the white centreline. 'Someone, or something in the middle of the road creating an obstruction. Car comes around the corner. Stops. Officer gets out, suspicious. Edges forward. Blam!'

'Hmm... something like that,' Frank agrees.

'Tiny fragments of glass were found thirty metres up the road,' Charlene says. 'But it will take weeks, if not months, to find out what type of glass it is. One peculiar thing...'

'What?' Frank asks.

'No cartridge case found.'

'Professional,' he murmurs, staring down the road.

'It fits our suspects, boss,' Zac says.

'Is there anything else, Frank?' Charlene says as she disrobes from her bunny suit. 'Only I have an appointment in York in two hours.'

'No. Thanks, Charlene. As usual, a bloody star! Don't you dare retire before me,' he jokes.

She throws him a wistful look. 'Can't guarantee that. Bye Frank, bye Zac.'

38

They fasten their jackets against the cold, damp weather and pick up a brisk pace, heading south towards an indiscernible structure in the distance.

'So, do you want to talk about it?' Prisha asks.

'About what?'

'Don't play coy. About everything.'

'You may get me on the false passport, but your case against me for the kidnappings is weak to non-existent, Prisha. Why would I tell you anything you could use against me?' Tiffany replies aloofly.

Prisha gently grabs her by the arm and spins her around.

'I'm not asking as a police officer. I'm asking as a human being. I'd like to know what your reasoning was, what your motives were. Anyway, whatever you tell me now cannot be used against you. It would be inadmissible in a court of law. And with the death of Mark Bridges, the kidnapping case won't be going to court. You can't put a deceased defendant on trial. And to be honest, I think I've figured it out already.'

'Then why ask?'

'Curious.'

Tiffany's face softens. 'Okay, what do you want to know?'

'Let's start with the kidnapping of Zoe Clarke and Emma Tolhurst... why?'

Tiffany sighs. 'First of all, let me say, Emma Tolhurst was only taken because she was with Zoe on that day. I... we, had no interest in Emma.'

'Understood.'

'It started off as my silly daydream, a fantasy. Not the kidnapping—that would be sick. I meant the end result—the money. Have you never dreamed of living in luxury? To have money at your disposal to fulfil every wish, to never have to work again?'

'Yes, of course. I'm sure everyone has flirted with that particular fantasy. But I'd never stoop to kidnapping and ransoming a child to fund it.'

'Nor did I, initially. As I said, it started off as a silly daydream, thinking of all the places I'd visit, the life I'd lead, the men I'd meet. Then one day I overheard Zoe Clarke bragging to a friend about how rich her uncle was. It piqued my curiosity, and I did some research.

There's rich, then there's *rich!* From then on, it became like a little game for me, devising the ultimate plot that wouldn't physically hurt anybody but would make me rich. It was like I was writing a script to the perfect crime. I went into everything meticulously, and whenever I found a flaw, a hole in the plot, I'd rework it. Never in a million years did I intend to go through with it. Then I told Mark Bridges about it. He said I was crazy, but after a while I got him to play along. We'd spend evenings acting out possible scenarios, picking holes in it, throwing problems at it, asking—what ifs? It was fun, like a game of real-life Cluedo.

It escalated and became more refined, complex. That's when I put the tracking app on Zoe's phone. We acted it out in real-time. I'd tell Mark where Zoe was and he'd trail her, with absolutely no intention of following through on the plan. However, there was always one major hiccup I couldn't figure out.'

'What?'

'I needed a watertight alibi before, during, and after Zoe's disappearance.'

'This is what I don't understand. When Mark took the girls, why didn't he just drive them all the way to Westerdale Grange?'

'For one, he'd have been missing from school for too long. His absence would have been noticed. And two, a blue Kombi Van with an orange door would have stood out like the dog's nuts. Driving from Robin Hoods Bay to Whitby, to Westerdale Grange, then back again, was way too risky. It also made sense for Mark *not* to know where the hideaway was. That way, if he was interviewed by the police, he couldn't let something slip. And that's where the plan faltered.'

'Why weren't you the one to take the girls to Westerdale?'

'Self-preservation.'

'As I thought. Then what?'

'By that time, I'd started an affair with Charles Murray. He was a good-looking man for his age, but it was his mind that really attracted me. He was extremely intelligent. It was also another silly game I was playing. I wanted to see how long I could manage two affairs without either man finding out.'

'It sounds like you have a low boredom threshold.'

'Quite possibly. It wasn't long before I became suspicious of Charles' behaviour. On the occasions I stayed over at his flat, he'd sometimes wake late at night and disappear. At first, I assumed he was cheating on me.'

Prisha snorts. 'How dare he!'

'Yes, I see the irony. I followed him one night. That's when I saw him.'

'Who?'

'The man who shot Lochy yesterday—the Russian Hulk. Whenever Charles went out, I'd start searching his laptop to see what he was up to. After a few months, I noticed an innocuous looking app, no name, but the icon was of an onion. It was something to do with the dark web. When I opened it up, I knew it was shady, like secret communication software. To get into it, you required numerous passwords and finally a fingerprint.'

'So, you never accessed it?'

'No. I gave up and simply confronted him one night when he returned from one of his secret assignations. I told him when we first started seeing one another that it was a case of friends with benefits, nothing more. But the poor sap fell in love with me, which gave me a distinct advantage in getting the truth from him.'

'What happened when you confronted him?'

'The damn fool told me everything. I don't mean specifics, but that he was working as a spy for the Russians, and they paid him well.'

'Did he say what information he was handing over?'

'No. Just that it was technical stuff, electronics, some surveillance of Menwith Hill. He called it—run-of-the-mill espionage, nothing that was going to alter the course of the world.'

Prisha drops the bombshell question. 'And how much did you know about the murder of Shirley Fox and Charles Murray's involvement?'

Tiffany stops and fixes Prisha with an intent gaze. 'How did you know about that?'

'It was just a theory I had. I was fishing—but now you've confirmed it. Again, probably another crime that will never make it to court. Well? How much did you know?'

Tiffany sighs. 'At the time—nothing, I swear. He told me the Russians planned to abduct someone to obtain classified information from their partner. He swore blind no one would get hurt. Charles asked me if I could get the key to Mark's holiday house on Church Lane, as it was the perfect spot to enact the abduction.'

'Hang on, you said that neither man knew about your relationship with the other?'

'They didn't. Mark had a flyer on the staff room wall at school, asking for people to recommend his flat to family and friends who were visiting Whitby. About a week before Shirley's murder, Charles asked me to get the key off Mark, under the pretence I wanted to check the flat out as I had friends visiting. I took the key one weekend when I was at his place, got a duplicate made, then replaced the original.'

'So Bridges had absolutely no involvement with the murder of Shirley Fox?'

'No. I didn't even know the abduction had been attempted until Charles came home crying and wailing that Friday night. I was staying at his flat. It was terrible to see him in such a state. He said he thought she was dead.'

'Did he say who?'

'Not initially.'

'So how did it go so wrong?'

'He crept up behind the woman with some sort of chemical on a rag, enough to render her unconscious. There was a struggle during which she pulled his ski mask off. He said she recognised him. He hit her with a torch. Stunned her. The Russian, who had been hiding on the 199 Steps in case her husband showed up, came rushing down and strangled her. They locked up the house and made good their escape through the back gardens.'

'Jeez,' Prisha whistles through her teeth.

'It was only the next day when I saw it on the news that I realised the woman was Shirley Fox.'

'Why didn't you go to the police?'

They stop walking again and face off against each other.

'Two reasons; fear for my own life, and...' She pauses and gazes down at the soft earth.

'And?'

'Cold-hearted, mercenary, selfish reasons. I'm not proud of it. In fact, I'm ashamed. I'd found the last piece to my jigsaw puzzle—Charles Murray.'

'You blackmailed him into your own kidnapping plan?'

'Not blackmailed, no. Convinced him. I told him that with the money from the ransom we could start a new life together, get away from Britain forever. Start afresh with new identities. He could forget about his past, his spying, his bungled part in the murder of Shirley Fox, the Russians. He actually breathed a sigh of relief and cried with happiness.'

'And did you mean it, about starting a new life with him?'

'Yes and no. We planned to continue working for six months, then hand our notices in at the school. We'd set up home somewhere overseas, then after a few months I'd disappear. I'd leave a million or so for him to live on. After that, it was up to him.'

'You are something else.'

'I was saving him, but that didn't mean I wanted to be shackled to him for the rest of my life.'

'And what about Mark Bridges? Did you love him?'

'No. Mark was a bit of fun. Nice looking, young firm body, good in the sack. I was fond of him. He was sweet, but love, no. Poor boy. He wasn't the sharpest knife in the drawer.'

'Are you aware he was in love with you?'

'No, he wasn't.'

'Yes, he was. He told me on Tuesday when I interviewed him in prison.'

Tiffany stares wistfully off into the distance. 'I never knew,' she murmurs.

'Would it have made any difference?'

'No.'

Prisha rubs at her sore shoulder. 'Murray obviously knew Bridges was involved in your plan, but Bridges didn't know Murray was in on the kidnapping?'

'Correct.'

'So if and when something went wrong, Bridges couldn't implicate Murray, because he didn't know of his involvement. But he could implicate you, but of course you had a perfect alibi and there'd be no evidence found in your car, because the girls were never in your car.'

'Yes.'

'You devious, conniving cow!'

'Now, now Prisha. Be civil.'

'Bridges was set up to be your fall guy.'

'Not at all! I would have been much happier if the kidnapping had gone without a hitch, and Bridges took off overseas with a new identity.'

'But just in case, you needed an insurance policy, and that was Bridges.'

'I was simply being thorough.'

'The timeframe for Bridges would have been very tight.'

'What do you mean?'

'Once the girls were released from captivity or found, then Bridges would have been on the country's most wanted list.'

'If things had gone smoothly, the girls would have been released on the Friday afternoon by Charles. He was simply going to unlock the cellar and front door and hopefully the girls would wander out and seek help. By that time, Mark would have been overseas with his new identity zigzagging across borders. He planned to rent a place on a Greek island. Once I'd moved the money around, I was going to deposit a million into his account. I told him I'd join him in six months or so once everything had died down. Of course, I had no intention of joining him.'

'Okay, so back to the kidnapping. Bridges initially takes the girls and meets with you and hands them over. He heads back to school. Ten minutes or so later, Murray turns up, and he takes them to Westerdale Grange, where you've already set up everything for the girls' comfort for a few days.'

'Correct.'

'But if your plan was to only take Zoe Clarke then why was the cellar at Westerdale set up for two?'

'A contingency. Zoe and Emma were joined at the hip. It was always a distinct possibility we'd have to take both girls. It was fortuitous in a way. They had each other for company and support. And if you want me to tell you about my perfect alibi and how I could be in two places at once, I'm afraid you're going to be disappointed.'

'I already know.'

'What? No, you can't, you're bluffing!' Tiffany exclaims with a mixture of alarm and incredulity.

'The flotation tanks at Frodsham Spa. You snuck out of the window. Went round the back. The critical security camera was pointing at the horizon. You jumped a wall and walked to your car parked nearby, but out of sight.'

'How the hell did you work that out?'

'I'm a copper. It's my job.'

She nods thoughtfully. 'You may be correct, but it's impossible to prove your theory. Anyway, that's about all I have. The kidnapping was wrong. Not telling the police about Charles' involvement in the murder of Shirley Fox was wrong. But personally, I didn't hurt anyone physically.'

'That's your security blanket, is it?'

Tiffany turns away and continues walking. Prisha chases after her.

'And what did you know about Bridges' involvement in the armed robberies on petrol stations?'

She stops dead in her tracks. 'Nothing! I swear to god, on my life. Is that true?'

'Yes, he confessed all.'

She stares at the ground. 'I wondered where he got his money from. He was always flush with cash. Well, I never.'

'So you've never heard of Jack Turner?'

Tiffany shakes her head. 'No. Who's Jack Turner?'

'Mark's accomplice in the robberies. He was murdered early yesterday morning. Legs tied to a rope, body in the water, strung up from the end of the east pier.'

Tiffany clasps her hand over her mouth. 'The Russians?'

'More than likely. I believe they aim to eliminate anyone who could have had any knowledge of the Shirley Fox murder. You see, Tiffany, every action has ramifications. Like tossing a pebble into a calm pond. The ripples keep extending out. Charles Murray knew too much. That's why he's dead. And Charles was your lover, so that's why they're after you. And Bridges is dead because he was also your lover. And Jack Turner is dead because he was Bridges' partner in crime. Now Lochy's dead because he got in the way. Including Shirley Fox, that's five deaths and counting and you had a cameo role in all of them, either wittingly or unwittingly.'

Tiffany is ashen faced as for the first time she reconsiders the tragic events. Sorrow and remorse are rare and unwelcome visitors.

The sharp cry of a nearby raven gives them both a jolt as they refocus on the present rather than the past. During their conversation, they failed to hear the far off sound of a two-stroke engine.

39

A shaft of watery sunlight breaks through the prison of bruised clouds, illuminating a shallow valley close to the horizon. The women have trudged on in silence for fifteen minutes, chilled, famished, parched. They're still unsure where they are or where they're going.

'If you could have three things right now, what would they be?' Tiffany asks.

Prisha closes her eyes and dreams. 'A bottle of chilled water, a bagel with smoked salmon, cream cheese, and capers, and to eat and drink them in a warm bath, with a fluffy towel warming on a towel rail,' Prisha replies, smiling at the imagery. 'You?'

Tiffany chuckles. 'A large mug of piping hot tea, deep fried spicy chicken and...' she muses over her third option. 'Yep, I think I'll go for a luxuriating bath. So hot it makes me sweat. Then a long sleep in cosy pyjamas on a soft bed.'

'Cheat. That's four things.'

'You had four things too!'

'No, I didn't!'

'What about your warm towel?'

'Oh, yes. My apologies.'

They exchange grins until Tiffany's expression changes to one of concern, as she tilts her head slightly to the breeze as Prisha follows suit.

'Shit!' they both yell.

They gaze towards the valley, and see no movement, but the unmistakable irregular snarl of a wide open throttle assaults their ears in short two-second bursts.

'It's heading this way,' Prisha mutters as nausea and fear punch her in the guts.

'Maybe it's a farmer checking his fences or flock?'

'You're the eternal optimist, aren't you?'

'I try,' Tiffany cringes contritely.

They both assess their options as they spin around. The landscape is desolate. Nothing but grass, sheep, and the occasional crush of rocks. Prisha takes one more look at the bleak terrain. Her eyes fall onto a drystone wall a good half a mile away.

She points. 'There! It's our only chance.'

They break into a sprint, forcing the jelly in their limbs into action. Prisha's senses are overwhelmed. Leaden sky above and ahead. Wind on her cheeks. Wet feet. Scent of earth and pasture. Tang of fear on her dry tongue. Bleating sheep scurrying away.

As they near the wall, they hit a patch of boggy ground that swallows their feet and drains the last vestiges of energy from them. She glances at Tiffany, who valiantly struggles through the quagmire, grimacing. The growl of the engine is distinct, clear, no longer sporadic.

Prisha dares to glance over her shoulder.

'Oh, fuck,' she cries, spotting the motorbike as it momentarily becomes airborne, hitting the crest of a hill. 'Come on, we can do this!'

They plough on as the revolutions of the engine intensify.

Tiffany stumbles, falls, and places her hands out into the mud. She whimpers and sniffs. Prisha hits firm ground and races ahead.

'I can't... I can't go on anymore,' Tiffany croaks, as she drops both knees into the mire and draws in deep gulps of air.

The motorbike advances at lightning speed, the wall still twenty feet away.

Prisha stops and yells. 'Don't give up! We're nearly there!'

'You go... go on. It's me they're after. Save yourself,' she gasps.

For a split second, Prisha considers the offer, before a burning rage banishes her fear. She rushes back to Tiffany and drags her up.

'Move it, you stupid bitch! Another few feet and you're out of the mud. He can't follow us over a wall on a motorbike.'

'No. But he can still shoot us.'

'What happened to your eternal optimism?'

'I've used it all up.'

Prisha drags her towards the wall, the motorbike bearing down on them less than fifty feet away.

She cups her hands together. 'Here! I'll lift you up.'

Tiffany wearily places one foot into the human stirrups and, with an almighty heave, Prisha propels her upwards. She straddles the wall and offers her hand to Prisha as she gazes at the approaching colossus on the bike. He lifts his visor and grins.

'We're fucked,' Tiffany whimpers, as Prisha struggles to climb the wall. They pause, realising their cause is futile.

As the Russian advances, he pulls a pistol from his jacket, one-handed, and aims. Tiffany squeezes Prisha's hand. Boggy ground snatches the front wheel of the bike and sucks it under, bringing the momentum of machine and rider to an abrupt halt. The bike screeches in humiliation as the Goliath is tossed like a rag doll over the handlebars headfirst into the sludge. The pistol spins in the air akin to a broken boomerang and lands with a gloopy splat some distance away.

'The gun!' Tiffany screams, already moving as if to dismount from the wall.

'No!' Prisha yells, realising the risk is too great, as she heaves herself onto the top of the wall, then jumps down into the adjacent field. She grabs Tiffany by the collar and yanks her to the ground. She lands heavily with a thump and a groan. 'Sorry.'

'I bet you are.'

They take one last terrified glance over the wall as the monster struggles in the cloying grime, his bulging muscles neutered by the liquefied soil. With a newfound energy, they race along the edge of the wall, hand in hand, heads down. The ground falls away as the wall rises high above them.

40

Entrails of low mist filter out amongst closely knitted trees, streaking all with a sinister dew. Three crows huddle on a moss covered branch in a tall silver birch. They survey the scene below them... watching, waiting, the custodians of their domain. A long, deep, mournful caw reverberates around the deathly spinney.

A greeting? Encouragement? A warning?

'What do you think?' Tiffany says as she pulls her eyes away from the farmhouse in the distance.

Prisha wiggles her mouth from side to side in contemplation.

'We've watched it for over an hour. No sign of life. No vehicles, no farm animals. But the building still looks in good nick... not abandoned. You're from these parts. What am I looking at?'

'A lot of smaller farms get bought out by bigger farms. They either bulldoze the old farmhouse or use it for itinerant workers or turn it into a holiday rental.'

'And what does this one look like to you?'

'Holiday season is now well and truly over...'

Prisha interrupts. 'You're telling me. A few weeks ago, I was basking on the beach. Now it's like we're in the midst of a nuclear winter. Is it always so changeable in Yorkshire?'

'Yes. It could be hot and sunny tomorrow, but probably more of the same. The end of summer around here is a slow, inexorable decline into death.'

'Cheerful soul, aren't you?'

'Ah! But after death comes rebirth, and it all starts again.'

'I should have transferred south. Okay, let's check the house out. Nice and slow. If we spot anything untoward, we head back to these woods, right?'

'Right.'

Prisha twists the door handle. It turns. She tiptoes inside and gazes around the kitchen as Tiffany follows her.

'Definitely a holiday rental,' Tiffany says. 'It's been renovated recently. It's rustic, but comfortable. You wouldn't do that for casual labour.'

'The place is spotless, no sign of life.'

'They probably had the cleaners in last week.'

'Why would the door be unlocked?' Prisha asks, apprehensive.

'Maybe the cleaners forgot to lock it. Or possibly, because it's so remote, what's the point? It only means paying a joiner or glazier to fix the door or replace a window if someone breaks in. If a person wants to get in, they will.'

Prisha pulls a tumbler from a cupboard and turns on the water tap. She lets it run for a few seconds before filling it, then greedily chugs the liquid down in seconds. She hands the glass to Tiffany, who does the same. It takes three refills to temporarily slake their thirst.

'Okay, let's have a scout around. Main priority is a landline and food,' Prisha says, still cautious of her surroundings.

After a cursory search of the farmhouse, they return to the kitchen.

'No phone and not a single thing to eat, apart from salt, pepper, and sugar sticks,' Prisha moans.

Tiffany grins as she shakes a box of teabags in front of her.

'But we do have tea and electricity. Time for a cuppa. I'm afraid you'll have to take it black,' she says, filling the kettle.

'That's how I normally drink it.'

Tiffany freezes and gazes at her. 'Hmm... me too.'

They huddle around an old, well-worn but fashionable farmhouse table, facing each other, their hands encircling the mugs.

'What shall we do?' Tiffany asks, sipping on the rejuvenating beverage.

'Not sure. We could stay here until the police arrive.'

'And will they?'

'Eventually, as they widen their search. Or we could follow the farm trail which must lead to a road, but then we're in the open again.'

'When you say—eventually—how long?'

'Not sure. Maybe tomorrow, midday. Possibly sooner,' Prisha says, accompanied by a yawn.

Tiffany gazes around the room. 'The bedroom looks inviting, and I could die for a warm shower.'

'Do you feel safe here?'

'Safer than I did outside. We zigzagged across the countryside, changing directions. The Russians wouldn't have a clue where we are.'

'Okay. Let's freshen up, then catch some shut-eye in turns, then maybe our brains will start functioning better. I'm not thinking straight at the moment,' Prisha says as she places her cup down and splays her hands on the table.

Tiffany reaches out and touches the back of her hand.

'Thanks for today. You're the only friend I've got at the moment.'

There's a momentary pause until Prisha snatches her arm away.

'I'm not you friend,' she states, coldly.

'Then why did you come back for me?'

'I was doing my job. My sole objective is to see you in court.'

Tiffany is wounded. She sniffs. 'Sorry... I... it doesn't matter.'

Prisha wavers. 'Look, Tiffany, another time, another place, then maybe we could have been mates. But at the moment, we're on opposite sides of the fence. That's just the way it is. I'm sorry.'

'No need to apologise. Right, why don't you take the first shower, and don't use all the hot water. I'll keep guard.'

Prisha smiles at her. 'Okay. You promise me you will not do a runner?'

Tiffany rises and walks over to the kitchen counter and flicks the kettle on to make a fresh brew.

'And exactly where am I going to run to? As unappealing as a police cell sounds, it's definitely preferable to the alternative. If you don't trust me, feel free to handcuff me to the radiator.'

Prisha pats the pocket of her jacket, feeling the hard outline of the cuffs. She considers the idea for a moment before disregarding it.

———⬩———

Warm water cascades onto Prisha's skin, the needle like stream stinging her cuts and bruises. Weariness flows through her veins like molten lead, the high octane fuel of adrenalin long gone.

As Tiffany quietly opens the bathroom door, she's greeted by a burst of scented steam. The glass surround of the shower, opaque, apart from occasional streaky rivulets which offer a blurred vision of its occupant.

She falters, distracted as she catches a glimpse of Prisha's soft brown skin, the curve of her buttocks, the rise of a breast. A splat of soap suds hits the shower base as hair is rinsed.

She gathers together the jumble of damp clothes and exits the bathroom.

———⬩———

Sitting on the shower floor for a good ten minutes, Prisha tries to ward off the desire to sleep. She trawls over events.

They must have found Lochy's body by now, and the Range Rover. Or maybe the Russians drove the car somewhere else, up the coast or inland, then abandoned it to throw them off the scent. If it's fifty miles away, then they'll be searching in the wrong location, and they won't have found Lochy yet. How did the Russians track the car? We were ambushed, which means they had some knowledge of our route. But no one knew which way we were going, apart from Lochy, and he seemed to make it up as he went along. Frank and Zac, they'll figure it out between them... I'm certain.

Pushing the questions from her mind, she stands and turns the shower off. She steps out and grabs a warm towel from the heated rail and drops her face into it. Breathing deeply, she wipes the steam from the mirror and stares at herself.

Come on, Prisha, think. All I need to do is attract someone's attention and raise the alarm, then this will be over.

'How reliant we all are on technology,' she mutters to herself. 'Without my phone or police radio, I'm completely incapacitated. What did they do in the old days?'

As she finishes drying, she stares at the empty spot where she'd dropped her clothes.

'Oh, no, please god. Surely, not!'

A loud banging emanating from the kitchen sends her pulse racing. Naked, apart from a towel, she realises how completely vulnerable she is, and also how naïve she's been. When is she going to learn to trust no one? She'd let her guard down once too often.

She slides the bathroom window open but realises its way too narrow for her to climb through. Scans the room for any sort of weapon. Nothing but soaps, shampoos, conditioners, and towels.

Not the sort of thing to put the fear of god into two psychopathic murderers.

The thumping ceases.

What the hell was that? Is it the Russians dismembering Tiffany's body with an axe?

Debilitated by fear, her body refuses to move. Her mirrored reflection catches her eye.

What did Lochy and Tiffany say? Control your emotions. Don't let them control you.

The thought galvanises her, as she deftly cracks open the bathroom door and peers out. An unseen kettle is bubbling away, accompanied by the echo of footsteps on wooden floorboards, and the repetitive hum of an appliance. Tightening the towel around her, she steals forward. To her left is a corridor which leads to the laundry. It has an external door. To her right, the passageway leads back to the kitchen, passing bedrooms along the way. She considers her options still battling with fear.

Tiptoeing towards the kitchen, she peeks around the doorway. Her relief is profound, but it's immediately replaced by anger. Marching in, she startles Tiffany.

'Where the hell are my clothes?' she demands.

'Oh, you made me jump. On the settee,' she replies.

Prisha stares at the neatly folded bundle of clothes with the handcuffs sitting atop.

'I gave them a wipe down, then put them in the tumble dryer. You spent so long in the shower they're dry now. You jacket's still in there, it will need another five minutes. I've cleaned your shoes and put them on top of the radiator,' she says, motioning towards them.

A wave of shame and self-hatred floods through Prisha. She cringes and offers an apology.

'Sorry, I thought...'

'You thought I'd stolen your clothes and flown the coop?'

'Yes,' Prisha offers meekly.

'I could have done. But I didn't.'

She picks up her garments and heads to the bedroom. Dressing quickly, she fights with a glut of emotions. She knows she has two priorities: get to safety, and charge Tiffany Butler with numerous offences. The first is a no-brainer, the second is becoming increasingly complicated.

Back in the kitchen, Tiffany hands her yet another cup of tea.

'I hope you don't mind, but I've put some sugar in it. I thought it would at least give us some energy.'

'Thanks,' she replies, sitting down at the table. 'Hey, what was the banging I heard earlier?'

Tiffany places a plate in front of her. 'I used a rolling pin.'

Prisha stares at the offering. 'Where the hell did you find them?'

'In the smaller bedroom in a bedside drawer. Very odd place to keep them. Grab a handful. They're full of protein and nutrients.'

'I'm grateful, I really am, but unfortunately I'm allergic to walnuts.'

41

Gentle fingers of rain waft over the lonely farmhouse in intermittent waves. Tiffany gazes absentmindedly through the window at the winding farm track that carves a swathe through damp fields, before rising next to a peak adjacent to a rocky outcrop high on a hill.

Refreshed from her long shower, dry clothes, and forty minute nap, her mind is lucid as she considers her bleak future: death or incarceration. Neither is appealing.

Prisha stirs in the chair, the heavy woollen blanket like a shroud of protection. Tiffany half smiles at her serene face as she creeps to the kitchen counter. She silently pulls open the top drawer and studies the assortment of knives. After a moment of consideration, she picks her weapon of choice, a small paring knife with a strong blade and vicious tip. She removes her belt from her trousers and carefully slides the knife between the stitched folds of leather until they part slightly. The knife nestles neatly in the improvised scabbard. Refastening her belt, she sits back down to make sure the knife does not encumber her.

'Perfect,' she whispers as she stretches her jumper down at the back to cover the blade. Her hand reaches behind her and rests upon the hilt, offering a modicum of reassurance.

At first, her eyes don't register the enormity of what they see as a tiny vehicle emerges at the top of the hill and begins the downward descent. Then her heart skips a beat with excitement, bittersweet.

'Prisha!' she cries. 'Wake up. We're safe. There's a vehicle heading this way.'

Prisha wakes with a start, momentarily wondering why she's in a farmhouse with Tiffany Butler. She groggily staggers to her feet and joins her at the window, wiping sleep from her eyes. She's desperately praying her brain will move from first gear to second fairly soon as she tries to comprehend the situation. Like a freak wave, her memory returns, and crashes into her consciousness. Excitement and fear push and shove with each other.

'Who is it? Maybe the owner has come to check on something, or possibly a team of officers from JSTAT.'

Tiffany gently squeezes her on the arm in anticipation.

The vehicle rumbles on like a lethargic tortoise.

'Why is it moving so slowly?' Tiffany murmurs.

It disappears from view as it rounds a bend. Both women wait in silence for it to reappear, egging it on, hoping it doesn't stop and turn around. The bonnet finally reappears a few hundred feet away. Prisha's eyes narrow, mouth dry, heart pounding. Affirmation and recollection collide, mutating into realisation.

'Fuck! It's a black transit van!' she screeches as hope is ripped from her heart, replaced by terror.

———◦———

Kira walks into the kitchen in a foul mood, throwing her backpack onto a chair. The muddy, dishevelled, and contrite giant follows behind like a cowed puppy dog.

'Imbecile!' she yells at him again as she paces back and forth. 'We'll never get a better chance. You had them in your sights. We could be on our way home by now. Instead, we have come full circle. Time is running out. We've ridden our luck too often. How long before the blundering police find our location?'

'I'm sorry, Kira. It was the mud. They can't have travelled too far on foot.'

'And what if they've been found, or raised the alarm? Then it's all over. You blundering ape!'

She spots the walnut shells on the kitchen countertop. It's a small thing but infuriates her further.

'What have I told you about leaving everything in a pristine condition? As though no one lives here! Why do you never listen?'

Her anger boils over as she pulls a knife from a sheath attached to her thigh. She prods the tip of the blade under Maxim's chin as he tilts his head back.

'I should gut and skin you like a rabbit right here and now,' she whispers, eyes on fire. 'You are a lead weight around my neck.'

'I... I don't know what you mean...'

'The damn walnuts!' she yells as she puts the blade away.

Maxim stares at the mess on the counter. 'That was not me,' he offers, gently.

'Oh, and who was it then? Maybe we have mice who can wield a hammer.'

'I swear on my mamma's life, Kira. It was not me.'

She eyes him coldly, then studies the rest of the room. A blanket on a chair. Two empty cups on the kitchen table. The heat from the radiators. She yanks her knife out again and rushes around the house, inspecting each room. In the bathroom, she spies two wet towels hung over a handrail. She darts back into the kitchen breathing heavily, her temper frothing. Glaring out of a side window, in the distance, she spots the quarry as they race across a field towards woodland.

She cackles and grins. 'Maxim, fetch your rifle from the van. We're going on a bear hunt.'

42

Frank is in the teapot position, hands on hips. He peers through his office window into the incident room. People scurry from one position to another, talking, exchanging notes, facts, rumours. DS Cartwright munches contentedly on a jam donut as he taps at a keyboard. James Carmichael shepherds his own team of intelligence officers in front of whiteboards plastered with photos, notes, pins, and red twine. Seemingly uncoordinated activity is, in fact, a well-oiled machine. Each person knows their part, experienced, keen to find answers.

'I wonder if she's any idea what havoc she's caused?' Frank murmurs.

'Who?' Zac asks.

'Tiffany Butler. Prisha was right about her all along—a bloody psychopath. All those man hours out there, four dead bodies, a missing police officer, and intelligence officer, traumatised children and parents, and why? Because of her greed.'

'I can't imagine she's had much fun over the last twenty-four hours... if she's still alive.'

'Oh, she's alive all right.'

'So you think we're right?'

'Yes.'

'It's your call then, Frank,' Zac says, sitting in an office chair as he picks fluff from his trousers.

'Hmm...'

'For what it's worth, I'll back you up all the way. It's the only possible explanation.'

'No. I'll tell the super this is my theory, and mine alone. I'll say no one else knows. If I'm wrong, my career is over. There's no point embroiling you in it, otherwise you'll remain a sergeant for the rest of your career and be handed all the shitty jobs. Do I make myself clear?'

'Yes, Frank. Of course, if we are right, you'll be regarded as a superhero and get all the praise,' he replies with a chuckle.

Frank turns to him and grins. 'Don't worry, I'll share the esteem. I'll tell everyone it was my brilliant, up-and-coming DS who first joined the dots together.' He returns his attention to the incident room. 'And here she is now. Just walked in. Detective Superintendent Anne Banks, North Yorkshire's answer to Miss Havisham. Wish me luck, Zac.'

Both men saunter through the hustle and bustle of the incident room. Frank gently takes Anne's elbow and pulls her aside.

'Excuse me, ma'am, but could I have a word?'

Zac melts into the background.

She offers him a rare smile. 'Yes, Frank, what is it?'

'In private, if you don't mind. Your office.'

———◆———

Anne drops her face into her hands and sighs wearily. The clock on the wall clicks along, recording every second of the drama.

'I'm sorry, Anne. It's the only explanation.'

'It's not much to go on, is it, Frank?'

'No. But it makes sense.'

She lifts her head and pushes back in her chair, puffs out her cheeks, stares at him.

'Do you understand the ramifications of your accusation?'

'It's not an accusation, Anne, it's a suspicion.'

'In this instance, it's one and the same. This will go to the very top, Whitehall, the corridors of power. And if it's true, heads will roll, internal investigations. The minister would probably have to fall on his sword.'

'I'm aware of that.'

'And if you're wrong, they'll haul us both over the coals for this. It won't be pretty. They'll put you out to pasture and I can kiss goodbye to a Chief Superintendent's promotion. I was hoping one day to reach the lofty heights of Assistant Chief Constable.'

'I'll go gracefully and resign. Meera's been on at me for some time to put my feet up and call it a day. At least one person will be happy.'

'Are you one hundred per cent sure about this?'

'About my suspicions, or to pursue it further?'

'Both.'

'No, to the former. Yes, to the latter.'

'Great! I'd have preferred it the other way around.'

'I can rephrase it if it would help, ma'am.'

'Very funny. Last chance, Frank. There's no going back once I'm sitting in front of the Chief Constable.'

Frank nods. 'I wouldn't have asked if I thought it wasn't true.'

'No, I know you wouldn't. I'll make the call to his secretary now. Of course, I'll have to drive over to Northallerton. This is not a matter to be discussed over the phone.'

She reaches for the receiver, then pauses. 'Who else knows of your suspicions?' she asks with a furrowed brow.

'No one.'

'Not even Zac?'

'No, ma'am.'

'Are you protecting him?'

'Would I?'

She shakes her head. 'I see. Okay, you can leave.'

Frank stands and opens the door. 'Thanks, Anne. It's always reassuring to know your boss has faith in you.'

'In this case, blind faith.'

43

Hot breath, clammy skin, foggy head. Panic rising like a nuclear submarine about to penetrate the surface.

Prisha's voice falters as she tries to respond to Tiffany's question. An anxiety attack closes in. Blocks out rational thought.

If she's going to die, let it be quick. A bullet to the back of the head. Please don't let it be long, painful, drawn-out.

Not by hanging. Not a knife wound, slowly bleeding out. Not a frenzied attack. Nothing weird, freakish. Just quick, clean.

Tiffany is still talking, but her words are muffled jargon, a foreign language. Her face is expressive as she communicates.

Prisha tries to read the signals.

Inquisitive, thoughtful, a half-smile, consideration.

'Prisha, can you hear me? Are you listening?'

Unsteady on her feet, she feels her body rising. She observes two women below in the dark wood. All she sees is the top of their heads. One woman puts her arms around the other and pulls her in close, tightly, like a mother with a distraught child. The other does not respond, limp, emotionless.

Voices.

An engine.

A black van trundles across a field towards the copse.

Blackness.

White hot light stings her retinas as her senses ignite.

Faint smell of scented soap. Warmth of a body.

Birds chirrup, leaves rustle.

A breeze brushes her cheeks. Damp in the air.

Leaves, sticks, moss on the ground.

And something else, intangible—another human being, a kindred spirit.

Emotion, care, understanding transferred from one beating, bruised heart to another.

A lifeline thrown to her as she resurfaces from a wrathful, raging sea.

'It's a panic attack, that's all. Don't fight it. Let it wash over you, accept it, it will pass. The less you react, the less power it has.'

Prisha sniffs into Tiffany's shoulder and slowly embraces her.

Breathing resumes.

Distant, two doors slamming shut.

Tiffany gently pushes her away, hands on Prisha's shoulders.

'There... feeling better?'

Prisha nods as she hurriedly fills her lungs with air.

'Thanks.'

'Okay, what's the plan?'

'Run!'

'This is déjà vu!' Tiffany yells as though it's a game of hide and seek.

Prisha does not share her enthusiasm as they tramp, scurry and rush through thickets and bushes, bypass trees, and slip and slide on sodden leaves beneath their feet. The incline is steep. The sonic whistle passes inches from her temple before embedding with a thwack into an ancient oak tree. Splinters explode into the frigid air. The booming crack of the gunshot follows a second behind. It reverberates throughout the wood, sending a myriad of roosting birds into mayhem. A cacophony of cries and screeches erupt, almost as loud as the rifle shot itself. She falls to the ground as Tiffany rushes on.

'A bullet to the back of the head? Be careful what you wish for, Prisha,' she murmurs to herself as she stares at the dirt. 'So much for Carmichael saying the Russians would not harm a police officer.' She picks herself up and crabs forward, bent double. 'Don't run in a straight line!' she shouts.

'Not much chance of that,' Tiffany replies, now some distance ahead.

Another whistling sound. This time, she senses the heat of the lead on her cheek as it passes over her shoulder. She darts to the right, then back to the left. She reaches Tiffany, who is catching her breath behind the wide girth of a giant beech tree.

'If... if we get out of this... I have a prop... a proposition for you,' Tiffany gasps.

Prisha bends, resting her hands on her knees, blowing hard.

'Don't tell me—you want us to go into business together and set up a shop selling scented candles?'

Tiffany grins. 'It sounds rather relaxing, but we'd both be bored after the first week.'

'Speak for yourself. Come on, let's get to the top of this hill and see what's beyond.'

Maxim cracks a walnut between his biceps and picks at the kernel. He drops to his knees and lays prostrate, resting the barrel of the rifle on a fallen limb of a tree. Rubbing his wet hands against his fleece, he fixes his eye against the scope and gets comfortable. The two figures continue to dart in and out of bushes, zigzagging, occasionally disappearing behind a tree. They vanish from view for a moment before re-emerging, then stop. The crosshairs slowly fixate on the back of Prisha's head.

Maxim grins as his finger applies pressure to the trigger.

'Proshchay moy vorobey,' he chuckles, as he swallows the remnants of the nut.

His finger curls. A black shadow swoops in front of his sight. He involuntarily jerks. The bullet explodes into a tree twenty yards ahead. The crow takes off with some alarm, a worm wriggling from its beak. Maxim curses and quickly reloads. The two heads disappear from view. A buzz from his mobile. He groans.

'Well?' Kira's voice snaps.

'No. They are now making their way down the hill.'

'You big, dumb, neanderthal mutt! Come back to the van.'

'But Kira...'

'Now!'

———◦———

'What's that in the distance?' Prisha asks.

Tiffany squints, then grips Prisha's arm in excitement.

'I think it's the ruins of the monastery—Rievaulx Abbey!'

'Will there be people there?'

'No, it would have closed hours ago. It's nearly seven. But a mile further on is the village of Helmsley, and if my memory serves correctly, there are several dwellings near the abbey.'

'Good. Let's make our way there and keep our heads down until it's completely dark, then we'll knock on someone's door and this nightmare will be over.'

Tiffany pulls a handful of sugar sticks from her pocket and passes some to Prisha.

'Here, have some instant energy.'

'You're sweet.'

'Very funny.'

———◦———

They pick up a trail through the heather, dappled with pink blossom, their footsteps encouraging the plant to release a comforting musky smell.

'Under normal conditions, I'd be enjoying this, tramping across the moors, breathing in the sweet, clean air,' Prisha states.

'An outdoor girl, are we?'

277

'Yes.'

'Why?'

'Not sure, maybe it's because I was brought up in an impoverished part of Birmingham. When you pull open your curtain each morning and stare out at grimy, litter-strewn streets, and walls stained with crap graffiti, then the countryside and coast provide the perfect antidote. What about you?'

'Meh... I can take it or leave it. I like foreign shores and hot weather. Lazing on a beach reading a good book. Lunch at a rustic café, dinner at a posh restaurant, champagne, and canapes.'

'You've got a taste for the high life.'

'Not the high life, just the good life... and don't make any cheap comments about the good life, okay?'

'Never crossed my mind. Do you have any siblings?' Prisha says, bending down to tie her shoelace.

'No. An only child. You?'

'Two older brothers.'

'Do you get on?'

'We do now, not when I was younger.'

'Why not?'

'They got away with murder compared to what I was allowed to do. I resented them. Muslim families can be pretty strict, especially if you're female. But we're all good now. Although, my father still thinks police work is a man's world.'

'There's something I need to say,' Tiffany remarks as she skips in front of Prisha and faces her.

'Not more confessions? Bodies under the floorboards, gold bullion buried in the back garden?'

Tiffany pouts. 'I'm being serious. I owe you an apology.'

'For getting me involved in this mess? Don't worry, it's my job.'

Tiffany glances at the ground. 'No. It's something I said to you at the station the first time you interviewed me about the kidnapping.'

'That seems a long time ago now, even though it's only a couple of weeks. Go on, what did you say to me?'

'It was after you released me. In the entrance of the police station, I made a repugnant remark to you.'

'Ah, yes, I remember. You said my type were all the same, and that we had a chip on our shoulder.'

'Yes. I didn't mean it. It was a deliberate cutting remark intended to hurt. There's not a racist bone in my body. I apologise unreservedly. Will you forgive me?' Her eyes flick back onto Prisha.

Prisha smiles. 'Yes, I forgive you,' she says, now laughing.

'What's so funny?' Tiffany quizzes, completely bemused.

'You! That's what's funny. They broke the mould when you were born.'

'I don't understand?'

'You kidnapped two girls, helped in a bungled abduction which ended in murder. You were having two affairs, one with a Russian spy and the other with an armed robber, and you effectively stole twenty million pounds. We're now being chased across the countryside by two ruthless psychos who intend to kill us and the thing which has been preying on your mind is a slight racist remark you made!'

Tiffany joins in the hilarity as she drops to Prisha's side. They both roll around in the heather, clutching their ribs, crying uncontrollably.

44

Zac jumps into the passenger seat with two large parcels wrapped in butcher's paper. A grin as wide as Whitby Harbour morphs across Frank's face as he rubs his hands together in anticipation.

'Oh, yes! Now we're talking,' he says as he starts the engine, and the car moves off. 'What did you get?'

'As you asked for; haddock and chips, a tub of mushy peas, curry sauce, breadcake, and a can of shandy.'

'What about scraps?' Frank asks, concerned.

'Yes, and scraps.'

'Good lad. What did you get?'

'Same, apart from a can of coke instead of shandy. I don't like to drink on the job.'

Frank chuckles. 'Daft bugger.'

They drive a short distance and park up in the pavilion car park overlooking the east and west piers. As magnificent as the views are, it's blindly ignored as both men attack their food.

'How are those lads of yours going?' Frank asks as he fills a breadcake with half the fish and a pile of chips.

'Good. Thomas has just been picked for the school football team. He's chuffed to bits.'

'What position?' Frank says through a mouthful of food.

'Right wing.'

'Nay, that's no good. He needs to get himself in midfield. That's where all the action is. He can control the game from there.'

'He's just turned nine, Frank. I hardly think the Leeds United scouts will be turning up to watch him play.'

'You never know. They get them early these days. And how's Samuel?'

Zac laughs. 'Oh, the same. A cheeky little beggar. We were called into the school the other day. He called his teacher a witch. Asked her where she parked her broomstick.'

Frank coughs and quickly takes a slurp of his shandy. 'He never!'

'He did.'

'How old is he now?'

'Seven.'

'You've got your hands full there. And Kelly?'

'She's fine. Starts her new job next week at the hospital, so it will mean nightshifts at some point. But she's really excited.'

'That's good to hear. Everything okay between you two now?'

'It's better, but not perfect.'

'And how are you going with the, you know, the gambling?'

'Coming up for three months without a single bet.'

Frank turns to him and smiles. 'Well done, Zac. I'm proud of you. It's an addiction like any other and it can't be easy, but you're on the right path.'

'You won't believe the money I've saved… I don't mean saved, I mean money I haven't lost, which now goes to pay the bills and get the wife and kids a few treats occasionally.'

Frank's mobile rings as he drops a large piece of golden battered fish into his mouth.

'Oh hell,' he mumbles. 'It's the super. Not a word,' he says to Zac, who nods. He answers, hitting the speaker icon at the same time. 'Yes, Anne, how did you go with the Chief Constable?'

'Are you alone?'

'Yes. I'm in the car overlooking the harbour eating my tea.'

'Let's just say the Chief Constable took some persuading. He made it perfectly clear that if this turns out to be a wild goose chase, then he's going to make sure the shit runs downhill, meaning you and I will be in the firing line.'

'I see.'

'He had a robust discussion with the minister who was none too pleased as he was attending a wedding reception at the time.'

'Poor little sausage.'

'Anyway, the wheels are now in motion. They're using an officer from MI6, someone who has never met Suspect One. He's on his way by chopper. Should land at Menwith Hill in the next twenty minutes. You won't even know he's here. He'll be doing the surveillance and whatever cloak and dagger things they get up to. If he discovers any evidence pertinent to the case, he'll report it to his boss, who will report it to me. Then I'll pass the information on to you.'

'Good. We wouldn't want to overcomplicate things.'

'Frank! It's no time for your wise-cracks! This is a very sensitive matter and needs to be handled with complete secrecy. Do not... I repeat, do not mention this to anyone. Do I make myself clear?'

'Yes, Anne.'

'Right, let me know of any developments.'

'Will do.'

Frank puts his phone away and pinches a chip from Zac's lap.

'He'll report to his boss, who'll report to her, who'll report to me,' he snorts with disdain. 'Some people have forgotten what it's like to be at the coalface. Well, here we go then. Let's see if he shows his hand.'

'Christ, I hope we're right about this, Frank. I'm having second thoughts now,' Zac says, suddenly losing his appetite.

'Are you going to eat that batter?'

Zac shakes his head. 'No.'

'Give it here. Waste not want not.'

45

The gothic arches of the abbey witness the last of the anaemic daylight slink away as murky shadows creep along the sandstone walls. A purplish hue hangs in the sky as an uneasy quiet befalls the darkened countryside.

Prisha can hear her own rapid breath and feel the rhythmic pump of her heart. She's apprehensive as she peers out from the safety of the trees. They've already bypassed several remote farmhouses, reluctant to make the same mistake twice. Crossing a country road only once, they scaled fences and walls to make their way through open fields.

As they hide behind a small row of trees, they gaze at the abbey in the distance. Opposite the monument is another farmhouse, but there's no sign of life.

'It's too bloody quiet,' Prisha murmurs. 'What's happened in the last twenty-four hours? Was a neutron bomb dropped that vaporised the entire population, apart from us two and the Vladivostok Vampires?'

'I think we've outsmarted them this time. They can't be everywhere at once,' Tiffany says as she pours another packet of sugar into her mouth. 'Funny...'

'What is?'

'The abbey doesn't look how I remember it at all. It seems a lot smaller, not as grand.'

'The memory can play tricks on you, and it is getting dark. Come on, I'm sick of this. Let's take it nice and easy through the ruins and see if we can get a good vantage point to check out the farmhouse.'

They cautiously leave their haven and creep towards the road they need to cross. They stop and exchange nervous glances as the distant sound of an engine approaches.

'Quick, down,' Prisha encourages. 'Please god, don't let it be them,' she mutters as once again she stares at the cold earth.

The middle-aged couple are bickering in the Corolla as it sweeps down Longbeck Road, passing the abbey.

'I'm telling you, Kate, there's no way I'm having your mother come to live with us. We've only just got shut of the bloody kids!'

'You can be such a wanker, Gareth! She can't cope by herself and she's only going to get worse.'

'Not my problem. It would be the end of our marriage. I can just see her now, nit-picking over everything I do—the grass could do with cutting Gareth. My bedroom hasn't seen a wet paintbrush in years. In my day, men used to shave every day. It was a slovenly individual who had stubble. Oh my god! And what about the TV she watches? Antiques Roadshow, Songs of Praise, Neighbours.

No, it's not going to happen, Kate, and that's the end of the matter,' he says defiantly as he turns to his wife.

'Gareth, look out!'

A squeal of brakes rips through the silence as two wild looking women run out in front of the car, shouting incoherently. One of them waves an ID badge at the occupants. The car halts inches from hitting her. She slams her palms onto the bonnet as the other woman rushes up behind her.

'What's she saying?' Gareth screams at his wife, in a state of panic.

'She says she's a police officer.'

'Oh, aye. And I'm a monkey's arsehole!'

His wife has no time to confirm, nor deny, her husband's claim as Tiffany yanks at the door handle of the car as Gareth hits the central locking and hurriedly puts the car into reverse.

'Stop! Police! We need a lift! We're in danger!' Prisha screams.

'Bollocks!'

Slamming the car back into first gear, he speeds around them side-glancing Prisha. She tumbles heavily to the road.

'You've hit her, you bloody idiot!'

'Tough shite!'

'What if they are police officers?'

'Did you see the state of them? They're covered in mud, their hair's all over the shop! There's no way I'm giving them a lift. Have you forgotten about those grisly murders that have been happening in Whitby? A couple of nutters on the rampage, I've heard. That could be them. And yesterday there was something going on near Fangdale Beck. The police had it cordoned off for hours. It's only twenty minutes up the road.'

'I'm going to ring the police and tell them about it.'

'Aye, you do that. Just don't give them our names. Keep us out of it, all right?'

Prisha hobbles along, one arm around Tiffany's shoulder as they cross the road, open a metal farm gate, and make their way into an overgrown field shielded from the road by a high hedgerow.

'Christ, it hurts,' she whimpers.

'I'll take a look at it when we get to the abbey.'

As impressive as the ruins of the abbey are, it's not Rievaulx Abbey.

'I'm sorry, but from a distance, one ruined abbey looks much like the next,' Tiffany says with a stern pout as she gently inspects the swelling.

'I wasn't having a go,' Prisha replies, grimacing as Tiffany's fingers gently prod and poke at her knee. 'So where exactly is Byland Abbey?'

'I couldn't say exactly. Maybe four or five miles from our intended destination.'

'Ouch!'

'Sorry.'

'It doesn't matter now. Our only option is the farmhouse across the road. I need water and food.'

'Nothing's broken. You've taken a heavy knock to the knee. You really need ice on it to reduce the swelling.'

'Don't suppose you have any on you?'

'Most amusing. I'll gently massage around the bruise. It may help.'

'So, what's this proposition you mentioned earlier?'

Tiffany delicately runs her fingers under the back of the knee.

'With Mark Bridges now dead you said there'll be no trial for the kidnapping. Even if you decided to pursue me over the kidnapping, a dead man cannot testify or be cross-examined. His confession is worthless. You have no evidence against me, and I have my alibi, which you cannot disprove. Emma and Zoe do not know of my involvement. You have nothing on Charles Murray. And as for the money, good luck trying to figure that one out. I also knew nothing about the robberies or Jack Turner.'

'We caught you at the airport about to board a plane to Mexico with a false passport. Or have you forgotten—Ms Murray?'

'There's no correlation between that and the kidnapping. I was fleeing for my life, as proven by the events of the last twenty-four hours.'

'Ow! That's a little too firm,' Prisha complains. 'How did you get a false passport?'

'Charles organised it. Through his dubious contacts, no doubt. All you can charge me on is the false passport—maximum sentence—ten years. Usual sentence—two years. Throw in mitigating circumstances, and I may get away with eighteen months, suspended.'

'This doesn't sound much like a proposition.'

Tiffany carefully rolls the trouser leg back down and stands up.

'My proposition is... if you let me go, I'll split the money with you—fifty-fifty. Ten million pounds,' she states pragmatically.

Prisha screws her eyes up. 'I really wonder about your sanity sometimes. Bribing a police officer is another offence.'

'It's not a bribe. It's a gift.' She becomes animated as she sits at Prisha's side and takes her hand. 'Imagine this; we go over to the farmhouse, and you ring the police. As we wait for their arrival, I take the occupants' car keys and escape. No one can blame you. You're exhausted and incapacitated. In six months' time, resign from the police stating post-traumatic stress disorder. Leave it another month or so, then book a flight to Buenos Aires where I'll meet you. You set up a bank account and I'll transfer the money across. Think of it, Prisha, you'll never have to work again. You'll be free to do whatever you want. We can party and visit places, meet tall handsome men at street carnivals. Learn how to tango, explore Plaza de Mayo, go horse riding with gauchos, sip cocktails on the banks of the River Plate, take a cruise to witness the Perito Moreno Glacier, a train ride to Tierra del Fuego. We can live together and share a luxury apartment.'

'Whoa! Hold on, girl! You've now proved to me you *are* clinically insane. First of all, how the hell do you think you're going to get out of the country without a passport and with every police force in the land on the lookout for you?'

'I had a contingency plan,' she replies coyly.

'You do surprise me. Go on, what contingency plan?'

'When I left Whitby, I had two suitcases with me. You will have only recovered one from the hold of the plane. In a locker at Manchester Airport is the second case, containing another false passport, clothes, cash, and bank cards. The key is in a cistern in a toilet. It was my insurance policy. With a wig, dark glasses, and some expert makeup, I'm confident I'll escape detection.'

'Good grief! You thought of everything. You certainly like your contingency plans and insurance policies, don't you?'

'One cannot be too careful. Without being over critical, you were a little careless in your police work. You may recall I checked in at the airport under the name Ms Murray.'

'And yet at the car hire place you used a credit card for Miss Dolores Fernandez,' Prisha murmurs. 'However, you're missing a very important point.'

'What?'

'You've just told me everything. When the cavalry *do* arrive, and I tell them what you've told me, then it won't take them long to locate your suitcase in the locker at Manchester Airport.'

Tiffany pouts for a moment, contemplative. 'But you wouldn't do that.'

'Wouldn't I?'

'No.'

'And why not?'

'Because of what we've been through together. We have a bond. Now and forever. We're sisters.'

'No, no, no.... we're not sisters! And we don't have a bond! I'm a police officer!'

'That's a job. Never let your profession define who you are. You're so much more. You're human, first and foremost.'

Prisha sports a fierce gaze for a moment until exhaustion and the truth of Tiffany's words undermine her resolve.

'Whatever,' she laments. 'I don't have the energy to argue.'

Tiffany relaxes, then giggles. 'So, my proposition—what do you say?'

Prisha hobbles to her feet. 'The whole thing's ridiculous. If you want to go, then go now. I'm not in a position to stop you. If the police don't get you, then the Russians will. Go on, run.'

Tiffany's radiant smile evaporates. 'I can't,' she mumbles.

'Why not?'

'Not until I know you're safe from those monsters.'

Tiffany's fantastical imagination has distracted both women's attention. Kira and Maxim saunter through the arched entrance, smirking, relaxed. Tiffany makes to bolt but stops.

Maxim smartly karate chops Prisha to the side of her neck with the edge of his hand. It's not a powerful strike, but swift, firm, and accurate. She recoils in surprise. Eyes close, shoulders hunch, limbs sag. She teeters and falls to the ground like a felled tree, landing on the soft grass as her right leg performs a hypnic twitch.

'You fu...'

Tiffany doesn't get to scream her invective, as the same fate befalls her. Kira stands over the two unconscious women and chuckles.

'At last, the two little sparrows have had their wings clipped. Now we can go home and leave this decaying little island behind.

Cuff their hands behind their backs, blindfold, and gag them, then put them in the sacks, Maxim. We'll dispose of the policewoman at sea. Leave any possessions on her. I want to make sure that when her body eventually washes up on shore, the authorities know who she is. A lesson to them. Now, I have a call to make.'

'Yes, Kira,' he replies, pulling a walnut from his pocket.

46

Two cars containing four officers from the firearms unit are speeding along the winding road. Following closely behind are another two patrol cars, and finally a Skoda with Frank Finnegan and Zac Stoker.

The convoy slows on a tight bend opposite the abbey.

'What was the report again?' Frank asks.

'Approximately four hundred yards before the abbey, coming from the south-west. Just before some sort of dirt track to either side of the main road.'

'What is wrong with people? Why are they so scared of leaving their name and number?' Frank grumbles as he spots the dirt track on the GPS.

'People don't like to get involved, boss.'

'I sometimes wonder what's become of society. It was never like this in the old days.'

Zac rolls his eyes. They leave the abbey behind and travel around a tight chicane. The fleet of cars glide to a halt at the side of the road, adjacent to a track.

'Okay, somewhere around here,' Frank says as he heaves himself out of the car. The firearms unit are already strategically placed as the two detectives walk along the road looking for clues, their powerful torches scanning the verges and hedgerows.

'Hell fire, it's over an hour since the call was made. They could be anywhere by now,' Frank notes.

'Not really, Frank. It would have been twilight an hour ago. Even if they kept walking, how fast can they go? Three to four miles per hour?'

'Unless they've hunkered down for the night. Okay, tell one patrol to check the farmhouses we passed before the abbey, and send the other patrol the opposite way to do the same. It's a waste of time, though. If they'd found refuge in a house, we'd have had a call by now.'

'What are we going to do?'

'We'll check the ruins out. Maybe they've found a sheltered spot somewhere.'

Both men do a complete circuit of the abbey, calling Prisha's name, and meet back at the front entrance.

'Nothing,' Zac sighs.

Frank walks under the tall arch into the entrance of the abbey, his flashlight illuminating the dilapidated stone structure.

Zac joins him. 'Bit creepy, isn't it?'

'You scared of the dark, sergeant?'

'Just saying,' he replies as his light falls to the ground. He edges forward and kneels.

'What is it?' Frank asks.

'Shit! I don't believe it,' Zac whispers slowly, tension in his voice. He holds the object up and shines his light on it.

Frank rubs his hand through his silver hair. 'A bloody walnut shell. I reckon our Russians have captured their prey.'

47

Maxim tips the women from the sacks like emptying a bag of potatoes. They land heavily on cold flagstones; muffled groans echo around the small chamber. He roughly drags the women to their feet and dumps them onto wooden chairs.

'Maxim, we have work to do. Drive the van south for half a mile, then push it over the cliffs. Then get back here. The dinghy is on the beach below. We leave in forty minutes.'

Maxim replies in Russian, slowly, softly. Kira rolls her eyes and laughs.

'Very well, but only after you've completed your tasks. I suppose you need a little treat now and then. What is the English expression—all work and no play makes Jack a dull boy? And Maxim, when you're finished...'

She pulls a finger across her throat.

Maxim grins and leaves the room. Heavy sounding footsteps clank down metal stairs. Kira pulls the covering from Prisha's eyes and kneels in front of her. She runs the blade of her knife gently down Prisha's cheek.

She flinches. Rapid breathing. Shakes.

'It seems you have an admirer, Sparrow. Maxim has never had a woman of colour before. Look on the bright side. I'm sure it won't last long. I've seen him in action before and it will be over before you know it. Then he'll wipe the memory from your mind forever.'

The knife now rests on her throat. Prisha's eyes glare with horror and hatred. Kira leaves the room and slams the door behind her. Creaking of metal as a lock turns.

Prisha's brain is ravaged with fear by the thought of a brutal rape, followed by having her throat slit. She pushes it aside and focuses on something else—a puzzle.

Why am I still alive? Obvious—Maxim's plaything. But the bullets whizzing past my head in the forest doesn't make sense. Why haven't they killed Tiffany? If they were trying to eradicate anyone who knew about Shirley Fox's murder, then why didn't they finish the job at the abbey?

Tiffany's chair squeaks as the legs scratch against the slabs of stone. Prisha is desperate to speak. One last comforting word; a goodbye to a human with a soul, with a heart, but the gag is too tight.

Tiffany's hands are steady as she pulls the knife from her belt. It takes a moment before she's confident she has the blade against the rigid plastic of the electrical tie around her wrists. It's slow work. An inch or two, repeatedly back and forth, until the improvised cuff falls to the floor. She rips the gag from her mouth, then pulls the blindfold from her eyes.

'Fuckers!' she declares. 'Pardon my language. I'm not predisposed to profanity, but on this occasion, I think it's warranted.'

Prisha is quickly unbound as they study their prison.

'It's an old lighthouse,' Prisha states, staring at the giant lantern in the centre of the room.

Tiffany walks to the circular windows and gazes out. She notices the black transit van, headlights dipped, edging down the coastal path. There's no sign of Kira. Focussing west, she instantly recognises where she is.

'We're in the old lighthouse about two miles from Whitby,' she states.

Prisha taps at the semi-circle of glass in front of her. 'Storm-proof. No way out through that.'

A growl of a vehicle. They drop to their knees. The slam of a car door.

Voices.

Prisha dares to glimpse.

Darkness.

The flash of a light.

Features illuminated.

A wave of relief engulfs her.

'We're... we're safe,' she stammers.

'How? Why?'

'The cavalry *have* arrived. Better late than never.'

'The police?'

'No. Carmichael.'

'Who?'

'James Carmichael. He's a senior officer with MI5.'

She drops down and shudders as Tiffany embraces her.

'It's over,' Tiffany murmurs.

Prisha doesn't know whether to laugh or cry as welcome endorphins rush through her veins. She sniffs as Tiffany strokes her head. A loose thought is an ice pick to her heart. She jumps to her feet.

'What is it?' Tiffany asks.

'It's not right. Where are the others? Where are Frank and Zac? Why is he alone? There should be a swarm of uniforms and the firearms unit. What's he doing here... alone?'

Her eyes pick out two shadows below, near the entrance to the old lightkeepers' cottages. The whitewashed stone walls are almost luminescent.

Kira leans in and kisses him, soft, tenderly. They embrace as he reciprocates by kissing the top of her head.

'No, no, no,' Prisha whispers, her mind a frenzy of computations. She slumps to the cold floor.

'Prisha, you're scaring me. What is it?'

Her eyes dart from side to side as she picks over the puzzle. The ultimate piece slides into place.

'It's him, Carmichael. He's the double agent. That's how the Russians knew our route.'

'You're not making sense,' Tiffany says, edging away, spooked.

'They're after the money. The twenty million. And the only person who can give them the money is you. Charles Murray must have told them everything before they murdered him.'

'If I could give them the money to save our lives, I would. But it's not that simple. I invested half of it in stocks, shares, gold, long-term deposits. It's not sitting in a suitcase somewhere. It's all over the world.'

'That's why you're not dead. They plan to take you away. Probably overseas. They'll keep you alive for a few days and torture you until you give them all your accounts, usernames, and passwords—then they'll kill you.'

48

The Skoda leaves the market town of Pickering behind, then accelerates away, flagrantly ignoring the maximum speed limit signs.

'This confirms our suspicions,' Frank says, pulling his seatbelt tighter across his barrel chest.

'And it means they're both still alive,' Zac replies, increasing his pressure on the accelerator.

'Tiffany Butler—yes. Not necessarily, Prisha. They may have killed her back at the abbey.'

'Then why not leave her there? It would have tied up police resources, bought them more time.'

Frank pulls at the loose skin on his neck nervously.

'Not sure. Possibly a mistake, an error of judgement. Or maybe they're keeping her alive until the last minute to use as a bargaining chip should we corner them. I know one thing for sure though; they intend to leave the country tonight, which means they'll use a boat. And if Prisha's not yet dead, then she will be once they hit the water.'

'I think you should call the Coastguard. Get some boats out there, ready for them.'

'And what do I tell them? Can you look for two Russians and possibly two young women—late twenties, abducted in a boat—description and size of vessel unknown, possibly somewhere in the North Sea? They'd tell me to piss off.'

'Fair point.'

'If you were in their shoes, the Russians, what would your plan be?'

Zac ponders for a moment as he overtakes an oversized truck.

'I'd stick to my patch. Places that I know. But obviously somewhere remote. If I were escaping by a big boat, that would involve a mooring at a harbour or a quayside. Too risky. Too conspicuous.'

'That would leave only one option; some sort of dinghy or smaller boat, to take you out to sea, then a transfer to a larger vessel.'

'And a dinghy can be launched from almost anywhere. You know how many coves and inlets there are along this coast.'

'Northwest of Whitby would be too dicey. The A174 runs alongside the shoreline,' Frank says.

'Which would mean somewhere southeast. No roads, remote, and no walkers at this time of night. What about that scrap of paper you retrieved from the Russian's bolt hole, you know, the one that was half burnt?'

'Hell, I forgot all about that,' Frank replies he pulls out his notebook, flips to the page where the scrap of paper is nestled, and turns on the car's interior light. He studies the letters and numbers.

metered 0399060

There's something about the word—metered, which intrigues him as he falls silent for a few moments.

'Dracula!' he yells, way too loudly.

'Jesus H, Frank! You scared me to death!'

'The ship that brought Count Dracula to Whitby was called Demeter,' he says excitedly.

'Thanks for that. I'll sleep easy on a night now.'

'Metered is an anagram of Demeter, which was the Russian sailing ship.'

'Oh, I get it. What about the numbers?'

'Hmm... 0399060.' Frank reads the numbers out slowly, deliberating. 'What's the date?'

'Sunday,' Zac replies.

'The date, not the bloody day!'

'Sixth of September. Why?'

Frank chuckles. 'Reverse the numbers and guess what we get?'

'A headache?'

'06-09. Sixth of September.'

'What about the rest of the numbers?'

'Not certain but I'd wager it means nine-thirty. This is a date and time telling them when to rendezvous offshore with a boat or ship. Now I can call the coastguard. It's not much to go on but at least it's something.'

Frank's phone vibrates. 'Eh up, it's the superintendent,' he says as he accepts the call, automatically putting her on speaker.

'Where are you?' she snaps.

'About twenty minutes from Whitby, ma'am.'

'I've just had a call from our man at MI6. Apparently, Carmichael made an impromptu visit to the old lighthouse on the coastal path about ten minutes ago.'

'Did he indeed.'

'When I quizzed his team, they said he'd nipped out to get a bite to eat. He was there for about five minutes, then left. It looks like he's heading back to HQ.'

'I see. That's narrowed it down. I believe the Russians plan to leave the country tonight, at approximately nine-thirty, by way of a ship or boat.'

'That's cutting it fine. It only leaves thirty minutes to get things in place. We need to act fast.'

'I suggest we proceed with stealth, ma'am. I'll organise the team, now. Dogs, firearms unit, and paramedics on standby, and a few uniforms to cordon off the entry road to the lighthouse.'

'I agree, Frank. It looks like you were right about Carmichael. Good work. Now bring Prisha back alive... and Tiffany Butler.'

The call ends as Zac pushes the accelerator to the floor.

'Time to call the Coastguard and arrange some backup,' Frank says as he holds onto the safety strap for dear life.

49

Their eyes follow Maxim as he strides back towards the lighthouse. As he nears, Kira confronts him. Raised voices in Russian. Maxim nods as Kira picks up two backpacks and sets off down the steep trail leading to the beach. She stops.

'Oh, and Maxim... once you have finished with Sparrow, do not slit her throat. Too much mess, and we don't have time for that. Stick the knife into her spine and twist. Incapacitate her. She will have a welcome bath later.'

He grins and nods.

———◦———

'Can you do this?' Prisha asks as she takes hold of Tiffany's hands and stares into her vacant eyes.

'I... I think so.'

Prisha shakes her head from side to side, vigorously. 'There can be no—I think so—involved. Either you can do it, or you can't. And if you can't, then give me the knife and I'll do it.'

Tiffany takes a deep breath and releases the air with a whoosh.

'I can do it... for you. I'll have the element of surprise. It makes sense.'

'Good. You need to be swift and accurate. You'll only get one chance. He's a mountain of a man and a slight wound will not stop him. In fact, it will only infuriate him further,' she replies as she rests her hand on Tiffany's shoulder. 'Remember what you told me? Don't let your emotions control events. Right, come on, let's get these gags and blindfolds back on.'

With each thud of a heavy boot on a cast-iron step, both women swallow hard. Prisha's breathing is erratic. Her head throbs, mouth dry, heart battering her ribcage.

The lock clinks in its housing.

A blast of frigid air rushes in. Salty. The faint smell of seaweed.

Light breaches Prisha's blindfold. A lamp at her face.

She bites the inside of her cheek. A copper tang, like an old penny. Light recedes.

The door slams. Outside world snuffed out. Movement as he places his lamp on mute flagstones.

Prisha's band is ripped from her eyes as she stares at the ogre, silhouetted by a creamy glow.

He lifts her chin up.

'Krasota,' he murmurs gently, flashing his teeth, as he pulls her gag away. He turns and yanks the blindfold from Tiffany.

'Don't be jealous,' he chuckles. 'You'll get your turn once we're on the boat. For now, you can watch. It may turn you on.'

'You know that she'll kill you,' Prisha blurts out. Maxim turns and refocuses on Prisha, puzzled. Her eyes are on fire. 'Kira. She'll kill you. She's in love with Carmichael. We've had them under surveillance for some time. They're like young lovers,' she lies.

The hulk shrugs. 'So?'

'You don't *really* imagine she'll share the money with you—do you?'

Now he's annoyed. 'You speak lies!'

'No, I don't. Is that what Kira told you? A three-way split? You must be dumber than you look if you believe that.'

He steps forward and swipes her with the back of his hand across her cheek. Her head snaps to the left as a trickle of blood pools at the side of her mouth.

'Show some respect, sobaka!'

She's uncowed. 'Think about it, Maxim. Kira is ruthless. It's her and Carmichael. You've been her pack mule, but tonight you've outlived your usefulness... you're finished.'

He grabs her ponytail and jerks her head back, moves closer, sticks his tongue out and licks the blood from her lip. She squirms in disgust.

'You taste good,' he drawls.

He places his oversized hands on her neck, then rips at her blouse. One hand slips inside, fumbles past the bra, squeezing, mauling. Prisha gazes past his arm to Tiffany, who has quietly removed the gag and is sitting bolt upright, ready. Prisha shakes her head ever so slightly.

Maxim moves to the other breast, as his spare hand pulls the leather from a belt loop. Prisha looks up at him and lets out a gentle moan.

'See, Sparrow, if you relax, you will enjoy it,' he says, as he unfastens the top button of his trousers, then pulls at his zipper.

Prisha arches her neck, yearning for him.

He smiles and bends to kiss her on the lips.

She smiles back... then spits in his face—the signal.

Surprise, followed by rage, flashes through his eyes.

A rush of movement.

Tiffany brings the knife down, hard and fast, into the base of his neck. The excruciating scream of agony is deafening as he thrashes around, knocking the lamp over, as he drops to his knees. A smash of glass and darkness.

Prisha pulls her keyring out and flips on her micro torch.

Maxim's face is grotesque. He claws at the back of his neck reaching for the knife. A cracking sound, a wet squelch, and the blade is removed. He glares at the weapon. Prisha yanks at the iron door as Maxim roars, like a wounded bear, and staggers to his feet.

Tiffany rushes him, her slight frame only strong enough to make him stagger back a step towards the stairwell. It's not quite enough to send him reeling. The heel of his right foot hangs in thin air, his left foot still firmly connected with the floor. He desperately reaches for the frame of the doorway, as Prisha slams the heavy metal door shut on his fingers.

A gut-wrenching scream of pain bounces off the hard walls as Prisha immediately yanks the door open... three severed fingers attached to the door frame.

Maxim's eyes register the horror and pain as he flounders against gravity. His huge body tumbles backwards, down the spiral staircase, clattering, banging.

Silence.

50

Both women stare at one another in disbelief and shock, trembling violently. Prisha pulls a key from her keyring, and pushes it into Tiffany's hand.

'My house is 12C The Terrace, on the west cliff. It's the top flat. Up the steps to the dormer loft is my bedroom. At the back of my knicker drawer is an unused credit card I have in case of emergencies. Take it. Get a quick shower and change into some of my clothes, we're a similar size. Order a taxi and go. I'll tell the police you escaped during the fight with Maxim, and you'd mentioned something about a friend who lives in Brighton. It should buy you some time. Leave the key under the wheelie bin on your way out.'

Tiffany's eyes fill with tears. 'I meant what I said about the proposition.'

'Tiffany, I don't want the money. I never want to see or hear from you again—ever! Understood?'

She nods as tears stain her cheeks. 'Do you mean that?' she sniffs.

'Yes... and no,' she sighs. 'Dry your tears and listen to me. I'll tell the police I was the one who stabbed Maxim. It will just make things a lot simpler if this should ever go to trial. If you don't make it, and get picked up, stick to that version of events, right?'

'Yes.'

They hug each other tightly before Prisha pulls away. She carefully unravels the tie from Tiffany's ponytail and fashions her locks around her shoulders.

'You shouldn't see anyone on the coastal path back to Whitby at this time of night, but once you hit the town, keep your head down and pull your hair forward to hide your face.'

She glances out of the window and notices the distant figure of Kira heading back up the narrow track from the beach.

'Go on, get going!' she urges.

Tiffany steals down the steps with Prisha close behind. They step over the crumpled body, sprawled against a wall as blood begins to pool.

'What are you going to do?' Tiffany asks as they stand on the threshold, the stiff breeze blowing through their hair.

'Follow the road. Flag someone down. Raise the alarm.'

Tiffany leans in and gives her a peck on the cheek. 'Goodbye, Prisha.'

'Goodbye, Tiffany. And good luck. You'll need it, but then again, good luck seems to follow you around.' She watches for a few seconds as Tiffany sprints around the corner and disappears into the dark night. A melancholy sense of loss threatens to overwhelm her. 'Not now, Prisha,' she murmurs sadly.

Scanning the gloomy room she spots a backpack in the corner and quickly rifles through the contents, pulling out a bottle of water and a flare. Guzzling the water down in seconds, she discards the bottle and picks up the knife at the side of Maxim's prone body and wipes it down on his shirt, ensuring Tiffany's fingerprints are removed.

Kira's voice cries out. 'Maxim! Enough, we are ready to leave.'

'Shit!'

Dropping the flare back into the bag, she hauls it on ready to bolt through the door. She takes a deep breath.

'Come on, Prisha, dig deep. Summon the last of your energy.'

Her upper body lurches forward ready to bolt but her left leg is caught fast as a hand of iron reaches out and grips her around the ankle as if snared by a bear trap.

51

The convoy of cars creeps along the narrow gravel track towards the lighthouse. Only the front vehicles sidelights illuminate the way.

'It's too quiet for my liking,' Zac murmurs.

'What were you expecting? A brass band playing Mull of Kintyre and a chorus line of dancing girls waiting for us,' Frank says, peering into the murkiness.

'What I meant was, I think the Russians have gone. I'm dreading what we might find.'

The Skoda slows as they near the last bend in the road. Frank speaks into the police radio.

'Lights off, everyone. Once I give the word, firearms unit to secure the building. Oh, and dog unit, keep those bloody K9s under control. The last time we used them, I ended up in emergency with a vicious bite mark to my arse. I've still got the scar.'

The fleet of cars edge forward to within a few yards of the structure.

'This will do,' Frank says. 'We'll go on foot from here.'

52

Prisha desperately tries to prise the fingers back. Maxim's eyes flash open, ghastly, deathly.

'Sparrow,' he croaks.

He coughs up a thick slurry of blood onto his chin. Footsteps approach. She raises the knife and punches it into the back of his hand, cringing at the sound of crunching bone. He smiles one last time as his chest heaves, then releases a laboured death rattle as his grip loosens.

'Maxim! Your fun is over. Put the sparrows in the sacks and get down here!'

The light swings back and forth in an arc as she steps through the doorway and freezes, taking in the scene. Prisha desperately yanks at the blade in the back of Maxim's hand, but it's lodged fast. Kira pulls her diver's knife from the sheath on her thigh.

'If I had time, I'd skin you alive,' she snarls. 'Instead, I'll just cut your heart out.'

Prisha reaches into the backpack and fumbles for the flare as Kira approaches.

'Take one more fucking step and your face is going up in smoke!' Prisha screams, pointing the flare at her.

Kira flips the knife in the air and catches it by the spine, then raises her elbow.

'Dumb bitch. That's a hand flare, not a rocket flare,' she says with a laugh as she raises her arm to launch the knife.

Prisha pulls the cap off. A burst of orange smoke explodes into the room, blinding them both as she feels a draught pass her head followed by a dull crack. Barking, and gruff, blazing voices compete with the hiss of the flare as she falls to the floor to escape the fumes. She tosses it through the doorway, watching as it rolls across the flagstones, illuminating a figure sprinting away. On her knees she crawls forward, coughing, choking. She collapses outside, trying to suck in fresh air as a slew of commands are screamed at her.

'Lie down! Hands behind your back! Do not move!'

A rumble of boots stomp by her head as a gun is trained on her. She tries to speak but can only cough up sputum.

A minute passes until someone yells, 'Clear!'

53

Kira starts the onboard motor and speeds away, bouncing over the choppy water. She peers back at the clifftop, where an orange mist still hangs in the air. A troop of bodies snake their way down the narrow trail to the beach.

She curses in Russian. 'Suka blyad.'

The dinghy slows as she puts distance between herself and the coast. Removing her hand from the tiller, she tugs up the hood on her wetsuit, pulls on the flippers, and dips the facemask into the water. The distant throb of the large Coastguard vessel dances over the waves. Its giant flashlamp erratically skimming the surface. She throws one last glance back at the twinkling dots on the mainland.

'You'll pay for this, you bitch. I'll return and when I do, you'll beg me to kill you.'

She puts the mask on, clamps down on the mouthpiece of the snorkel, pushes the rudder hard to the right, then flips backwards into the water.

———◦◦◦———

Tiffany finishes drying herself and squirts deodorant under her arms. She picks up a perfume bottle and smiles as she sprays a touch onto her neck and wrists, the scent immediately transporting her back to the previous day in the Range Rover, a lifetime ago. A smile creeps across her face.

'So this is what I could smell—My Way by Giorgio Armani. Classy.'

After quickly wolfing down a cheese toasty and two strong cups of coffee, she collects the credit card, picks up the landline, and orders a taxi. As she waits, she stares at herself in the full-length mirror in Prisha's bedroom.

Baseball boots are on her feet, sitting below a snug fitting pair of jeans. A black Nike hoody is comfortable and warm, and a brown beret finishes off the disguise, with a pair of sunglasses resting on top. A short blast from a car horn indicates her taxi has arrived. As she turns to switch the light off, she spots a family photo of Prisha. She picks it up. It can't be that old, as Prisha looks no different. Smiling out from the centre of the photograph, her arms are draped around two young attractive men who Tiffany assumes must be her brothers.

Placing the frame back down, she kisses two fingers and places them on Prisha's face.

'I'll miss you.'

She drops the latch and pulls the door shut behind her, crouches and slides the key under the wheelie bin. The taxi driver leans across to the passenger-side window and calls out as she approaches.

'You Miss Kumar, love?'

'Yes. That's right.'

'Hop in. Where yer heading?'

'Manchester Airport.'

'You can't be going on holidays, you've no luggage.'

She opens the back door and climbs in. 'That's right. I'm meeting my best friend who's flying in from Buenos Aires.'

The car trundles away and makes its way through the old town. A wailing siren and flashing lights makes the driver pull over to the side of the road. Tiffany freezes for a moment until the police car speeds past and the taxi moves away again. The driver eyeballs her in the rearview mirror.

'Not sure what kicked off tonight, but the place has been crawling with coppers coming and going. Apparently, something happened up at the old lighthouse. Have you heard anything about it?'

'No. Not a thing.'

54

A scene of organised pandemonium ensues at the lighthouse.

'Get those bloody dogs under control before they have some bugger's arm off! And put some lights on! It's supposed to be a bleeding lighthouse and we're stumbling around in pitch black!' Frank thunders. 'Get down yer vicious bastard!'

Prisha is sitting on a low stone wall next to Zac as he nears the end of his preliminary questioning. DS Cartwright waddles up and pours something from a flask into a cup as bright lights erupt, bathing the setting in ghostly daylight.

'Here you go, Prisha. A cup of hot chocolate. I know it's your favourite,' he says, handing her the drink.

She gratefully accepts it as he places a heavy woollen blanket around her shoulders.

'Thanks Jason. You're a star.'

He wanders off as uniformed officers unroll barrier tape around the perimeter of the lighthouse.

'He's got to be good for something,' Zac says. 'Because he won't make a decent copper whilst he's got a hole in his arse.'

Prisha half smiles. 'Don't be cruel,' she says, sipping on the hot chocolate.

'Okay, wrapping up; you're certain Tiffany headed off down the coastal path towards Robin Hood's Bay?'

'Yes. Saw her as clear as day.'

'But it's night.'

'You know what I mean. A couple of times, she mentioned a best friend who lives in Brighton. I'm guessing she may try to hitch a lift there.'

'Hmm... Let's go back to the scene inside the lighthouse. You said Maxim was about to rape you, and you pulled the knife out and stabbed him in the back of the neck?'

'Yes.'

'Where did you get the knife from?'

'The farmhouse I told you about on the moors.'

'If they captured you at Byland Abbey, how come they didn't search you?'

'Not sure. Anyway, the knife was hidden. I'd cut a slit in the back of my belt and hid the knife there. Is he definitely dead?'

'He has a twelve inch knife embedded in his forehead and he didn't greet us as we walked in—so I'd say, yes, he's well and truly dead.'

'That was Kira. She had a divers' knife. She was about to throw it at me when I let the flare off.'

'I see. Back to the fight. After you stabbed him, Tiffany opened the door and ran down the stairs. Maxim was staggering around in obvious discomfort with a paring knife lodged in his neck. He held onto the doorframe, and you slammed the door on him, severing three fingers?'

'Yes. I pulled the door back open, and he fell down the spiral staircase.'

'So how come the paring knife is stuck in the back of his hand?'

'He pulled the knife from his neck in the lantern room, then fell down the steps. As I was about to bolt, he grabbed me by the ankle. I saw the knife, picked it up and stabbed him in the hand. Then she walked in.'

Frank ambles over, buttoning his coat against the cold.

'Okay Zac, finish up for tonight. We'll get a full statement tomorrow.'

'Yes, Frank. Just two more questions. Prisha, is there anyone else we should look for apart from Tiffany and Kira?'

She shakes her head. 'Not as far as I know.'

'She didn't mention anyone else?'

'No.'

'You've had a hell of a time,' Frank says. 'Stuck with that psycho bitch for over twenty-four hours.'

Prisha cannot hold back her emotions. 'Don't call her that! She's not as bad as we all initially thought!' she yells.

Frank pulls his neck back and grimaces. 'She organised the kidnapping of two young girls and was in the process of absconding to Mexico, and you say she's not as bad as we all first thought?'

'You don't understand! I've spent the last day with her being hunted like a wild animal! Have you any idea what that feels like? She saved my life on at least two occasions. And without her companionship, reassurance, and sheer bloody determination, you'd be slipping me into a body bag right now!'

Frank and Zac exchange concerned glances.

Frank lowers his voice. 'Okay, let's call it a night. We'll get you to the hospital and checked over. I suggest an overnight stay as a minimum. You've been through a hell of an ordeal.'

'I'm not going to the bloody hospital. I'll see the on-call doctor and she can check me out at the station. I've told you, I'm fine. A few cuts and bruises, that's all. I'm going to sleep in my bed tonight.'

'I'm not sure that's a good idea, Prisha,' Zac says gently. 'Trauma and stress can play havoc with a person.'

'It's over. How many times have I got to tell you—I'm fine.'

'I can sleep on the couch if it would help?' he offers.

'It's hardly likely Kira's going to break in during the night and finish me off, is it? But thanks for the offer. Anyway, I can take care of myself—I've learnt that much.' She stands up, pulling the blanket around her.

'One last question Prisha, then I'm done for the night,' Zac says.

'Go on?' she replies wearily.

'Having been in North Yorkshire for just over three weeks—everyone wants to know—are you enjoying it?'

She smirks. 'What a comedian.'

'Daft bugger,' Frank chortles. 'Come on, lass, I'll drive you back to the station.'

'Detective Chief Inspector Finnegan!' bellows a voice with a strong West African cadence.

'Oh Christ! Raspberry Whipple—I need him like a hole in the head. Wait here. I'll be back in a moment. Ah! Doctor Whipple. What a pleasant surprise,' he replies with false cheer as he saunters over to the doctor.

'Considering you were anticipating my attendance, it is hardly a surprise, chief inspector. And I could never deem the scene of yet another fatality, pleasant.'

'Fair point.'

'I was looking forward to a gratifying evening of Titicaca with Mrs Whipple.'

'Nice work if you can get it.'

'It is a board game, inspector, a board game!' he yells.

'Is it indeed? No need to shout. Let me show you to the body.'

As Frank wanders off with the bombastic doctor, Zac joins Prisha.

'So where's Carmichael?' she asks.

'Under armed guard at Menwith Hill.'

'Has he been arrested and charged?'

'It's complex, sensitive.'

'You're not telling me he's going to get away with this!'

'Calm down. He's not going to get away with anything, but considering his position and who he works for, it's sort of out of our hands.'

'So when did you first suspect him of being a double agent?'

'Two things got me thinking. How did the Russians know where the Range Rover was? They must have had inside intel, which meant someone from JSTAT. Then, at the site of Lochy's murder, I was chatting to one of the intelligence officers. I offered my condolences and said it was always a sad day when you lost someone from your team, and hopefully, the intelligence officer who was missing would turn up alive and well. He didn't know what I was talking about regarding the missing officer, but said he'd only just been pulled onto the case.'

'I don't understand.'

'I suspected there was no missing officer, and the person who Charles Murray met on the top of Sutton Bank was, in fact, Carmichael. On the sly, I questioned two other guys from the JSTAT and they confirmed they weren't missing an operative, which was contrary to what Carmichael had told us. That's when me and Frank were convinced he was the mole. Frank spoke with the super, who then fronted up to the Chief Constable. They pulled in some hotshot from MI6 to track Carmichael.'

'And Carmichael turned up tonight to bid farewell to his lover—Kira.'

'Yes.'

'Has he confessed?'

'Don't know. It will be a few days, maybe even weeks, until we unravel all the threads.'

'Devious, cold blooded, murdering bastards,' Prisha murmurs as Frank returns, appearing slightly frazzled.

'That man's a challenge,' he grumbles. 'Come on, let's get going, Prisha,' he says, draping a fatherly arm around her shoulder.

'If you want me to stay the night, just yell out,' Zac calls after them.

'Jesus H! What the hell's that!' Frank's voice booms as he pulls his arm from Prisha's shoulder, disrobing her blanket as he inspects the sole of his shoe. 'Bloody dog shit! My god, will this day never end? Those K9s are a bleeding liability!'

As Frank drags his foot back and forth across the grass, Prisha bends to pick up the blanket. Her jacket rides up at the back as Zac watches on with a grin. His eyes drift from Frank and focus on Prisha's waist.

She's not wearing a belt...

55

Two Weeks Later – Monday 21st September

Prisha locks the door and skips down the steps in her jogging gear. She runs along North Terrace, through Whalebone Arch, and down onto the winding Khyber Pass.

The sun breaks through and bathes her in a warm glow, as seagulls swoop and cry above the leaden waves. It takes her ten minutes to reach the station.

As she walks through the entrance, the desk sergeant greets her.

'They're all waiting for you,' he says with a welcoming smile.

'Oh no... I hate things like this. Are there many up there?'

He shakes his head. 'Nah. Just the usual suspects, pardon the pun.'

She jogs up the stairs and into the CID room. The small gathering erupts into song.

'Happy birthday to you, happy birthday...'

Her face flushes crimson as she fidgets uncomfortably with her fingers.

As cake is handed out, Prisha chats with Frank and Zac.

'So how have you been?' Frank asks.

'A little sluggish the first week, but then I came good. I spent last weekend back in Birmingham for my Nanni's birthday. I don't know what you said to my dad when you spoke to him, Frank, but his whole attitude towards my job has changed.'

'Simply told him the truth. I said he had a wonderful daughter who was intelligent, diligent, had balls of steel and one day may even make it to the lofty heights of Chief Constable.'

Prisha chuckles. 'It certainly worked, although I have no aspirations to be Chief Constable. I like to be where the action is. Talking of which, I'm ready to return to work, Frank.'

'Oh no. The superintendent was adamant you were to have three weeks' rest and recuperation.'

'But Frank, I'm bored. I want to get back to work.'

'No can do. Another week. That's my last word on the matter.'

'Bully,' she pouts.

'By the way, have you been seeing the counsellor?'

'Yes. I've had two sessions,' she mopes.

'Has it helped?'

'There's nothing to help with. I wish everyone would stop worrying about me. I'm not depressed, in denial, in shock, traumatised or feeling suicidal. I'm perfectly fine. I just want to get back to normal.'

He glances at her heavily strapped knee. 'Should you be running on that thing?'

'It's okay. Just a little sore in the mornings.'

'Hmm... Right, I'm going to snaffle another slice of sponge cake before Cartwright devours it all,' he says, wandering off.

She focuses on Zac. 'Any news?'

'About?' he replies, sipping on his tea.

'Carmichael, Kira, Tiffany?'

He puffs air out. 'They're dealing with Carmichael internally. There's been a task force set up to investigate how long he's been playing for the other side, what secrets he's divulged and who else, if anyone, was involved. It's going to be a long drawn-out process.'

'And Kira?'

'Nope. They found the dinghy she escaped in, but no sign of her. She either swam to a rendezvous point with a vessel or drowned.'

'Tiffany?' she asks, trying to appear nonchalant.

'Nothing on that front, either.'

'Any theories?'

'I reckon someone's covering for her,' he says peering into her eyes.

She laughs nervously. 'Covering for her?'

'Yeah. She'll be holed up at someone's house. Lying low. She can't leave the country, well, not by conventional means, without a passport. And she can't start splashing money around otherwise it would raise suspicions. She's trapped in a gilded cage of her own making. We'll get her, eventually. She'll make a mistake, or whoever's covering for her will get a stab of the guilts and snitch on her. Don't you think?'

'Yes, I suppose,' she replies thoughtfully. 'And the official cause of Maxim's death? Was it the knife to the back of the neck?'

'No. It was the fall down the steps. He took some heavy blows to the head, which caused internal bleeding on the brain. I can get Doctor Whipple on the phone if you'd like a more in-depth synopsis, and an instant headache?'

She chuckles. 'No. That won't be necessary. Right, I'm going to say my farewells to everyone, then continue my run.'

'Where are you heading?'

'Thought I'd jog the Cleveland Way, heading towards Robin Hood's Bay. Probably turn around at the halfway mark.'

'That will take you past the old lighthouse.'

'So?'

'Do you think that's a good idea? It must be still quite raw.'

'As Frank said, I have balls of steel.'

———— ◦ ————

As Prisha nears her flat, she slows to a steady walk to let her heart rate return to normal. She spots a young man on the top step, holding a brown paper bag and ringing the bell.

'Can I help you?' she asks, pushing the gate open.

'I have a delivery for Prisha Kumar.'

'That's me. What is it?'

'Takeaway food delivery.'

'I haven't ordered anything.'

The man drops the bag into her hands. 'Well, someone did. Ordered online and paid for. Have a nice day.' He turns and scoots down the steps.

She immediately thinks of Zac and Frank. As she opens the door, she collects the mail off the floor and makes her way upstairs.

Sitting on the couch, she places the mail onto the table and peers into the paper bag. She pulls out a bottle of water, cracks the top and takes a hearty gulp, then removes a cardboard sandwich box and lifts the lid. Her pulse rate increases as she inspects the bagel.

'Smoked salmon with cream cheese and capers,' she whispers. Her eyes drift to the mail on the table. She picks out a postcard and studies the four pictures on the front.

An elegant man and woman performing the tango; a man in a white shirt, neckerchief, and bolero hat leading a horse; an aerial view of the Perito Moreno Glacier, and lastly, a picture of an old-fashioned, colourful steam train.

She flips the card over and reads as a lump comes to her throat.

"On my way by train to Tierra del Fuego. Wish you were here! Maybe one day? The proposition still stands. Not the same without you.

Love, Dolores Fernandez

p.s. Miss you like crazy!"

She sniffs and wipes away the tears from her cheeks.

56

Sunday 27th September

The church bells reverberate over the abbey. Seagulls screech high in the pale blue sky. A damp, cool breeze blows in from the sea as Frank wraps a generous bunch of rhubarb in newspaper and places it in the wooden crate on top of tomatoes, cabbages, beetroot, and turnips.

'It's been a damn good harvest this year, and still plenty to pick at,' he mumbles to himself, glancing at his watch. 'Church service has finished. No doubt Meera will spend twenty minutes chewing the cud with the vicar and a few parishioners before she wanders over. Just enough time to update my journal.'

Sitting snugly in his shed in front of his bureau, he unlocks his briefcase and removes the journal. He lights a cigarette, takes a gulp of whisky, and picks up his pen.

Diary Entry

"September –Russians, Traitors, and the Shirley Fox Case."

The nib of his pen glides effortlessly over the paper, creating a comforting scratching sound. Facts, suspicions, supposition, and his own lucid interpretations are all committed to history.

"James Carmichael finally made a full confession, and without blowing my own trumpet, my small team was not far off the money with our theories and educated guesswork. It was Carmichael who got wind of the project which Dudley Fox was working on at Menwith Hill. Being in the pay of the Russians, he thought this information would be useful to them. It was he who hatched the plot to abduct Shirley Fox and use her as leverage to get the good oil out of Dudley. Unfortunately, Shirley saw her attacker—Charles Murray, and Maxim decided she had to be eliminated. Everything went quiet for about six months until guilt finally got the better of Charles Murray and he arranged a meeting with the secret service to broker a deal. Unluckily for him, the operative who turned up to meet him late at night on the top of Sutton Bank was none other than James Carmichael—the traitor. Murray was unaware Carmichael was also working for the Russians.

After the rendezvous, Carmichael realised Murray was becoming a liability and ordered Kira and Maxim to dispose of him, after first torturing him to find out if anyone else knew of his covert activities and his involvement in the Shirley Fox murder. Prisha was right—they employed waterboarding to extract the information from him.

Murray told them of his affair with Tiffany Butler, the kidnapping and subsequent ransoming for twenty million pounds for the safe return of Emma Tolhurst and Zoe Clark, and lastly, of his suspicions that Tiffany was having an affair with Mark Bridges.

He sowed the seeds of many people's demise during his confession, including his own. But who could blame the poor man? Carmichael decided to eliminate anyone who may have known about the Shirley Fox plot, mainly for his own self-preservation. But he also hatched his own plan, along with Kira—his lover.

The lure of twenty million pounds was too much for them. Once they'd covered their tracks by eliminating the others, they planned to abduct Tiffany Butler. They would whisk her away to some foreign shore, then with a little friendly persuasion she would transfer all the ransom money over to them, and Carmichael and Kira would start a new life together, after disposing of Tiffany, of course. Carmichael had already handed in his notice and was serving out his last six weeks, so confident was he of their scheme.

When Carmichael first came to us and asked us to drop our investigation into the murder of Murray, he was becoming edgy. His threat to go to the very top to thwart our investigation was mere bluff. Hats off to Superintendent Banks for standing up to him.

When Carmichael realised his threat was toothless, he figured the best way to hinder our investigation, and keep a tab on events, was to work alongside the police.

We know Maxim murdered Shirley Fox, and we know Kira and Maxim killed Charles Murray, Jack Turner, and SE17—or Lochy as Prisha referred to him. We still don't know who murdered Mark Bridges but assume either Carmichael or the Russians organised his death. Prisha, and eventually Tiffany, would have also been eliminated if we hadn't arrived at the lighthouse in time.

We have no clues as to the whereabouts of Kira or Tiffany Butler. Kira could have drowned at sea, but I have a gut-feeling she didn't. As for Tiffany, well... for all her duplicitous actions in the ghastly events, she helped Prisha stay alive, for which I am thankful. It is some recompense for her actions, but it does not absolve her from her sins or prosecution. She still has her conscience to live with, but that is small comfort to me.

I had the unenviable task of relating a lot of this information to Dudley Fox. He listened in silence until I finished. I hoped it would bring some resolution for him, knowing the how and why his beloved wife was murdered. If it did, he did well to mask it. He appeared lonelier and sadder than usual. I'll make the effort to call on him occasionally to see how he's going. Alas, I fear he's a broken man and I'm not sure he'll ever be fixed.

I must make a special mention of several officers. Prisha for her initial theories, which at least gave us something to go on. She's a rare species—the intuitive copper who stitches together the threads of crimes like a bespoke tailor creating a wedding suit. How she survived being hunted for twenty-four hours by two ruthless assassins is a testament to her guile and inner strength.

Zac for bringing to my attention his inkling that someone was working on the inside, and for also giving me a few chuckles along the way. If you don't laugh, you cry.

Superintendent Anne Banks for giving me her full support, despite being a hard task-master.

And lastly, DS Jason Cartwright, who actually showed some nous for once. Maybe there's hope yet?

In my last diary entry for August, I ended by writing I was looking forward to a quiet September—I got that one wrong.

There was a propaganda campaign during the Second World War—Careless Talk Costs Lives. I think it's a fitting epitaph for this series of tragic events.

DCI Frank Finnegan, signing off."

He enjoys one more nip of whisky, clears away then drops his journal back into his briefcase.

'Frank! Are you ready?' Meera's voice calls out, followed by footsteps on gravel.

He pulls the shed door shut, turns the lock, and closes the padlock.

'Ah, Meera, my love! How was church?'

'Wonderful, as usual. I'm now ready to face whatever next week has to throw at me. It's a tonic.'

He kisses his wife on the lips, hands her the briefcase and picks up the crate of vegetables.

'A tonic, you say? I tell you what, next week I'll accompany you to church. After the two months I've had, I could do with a tonic and something to believe in.'

Meera guffaws. 'My, oh my! The Lord moves in mysterious ways. At last, Frank Finnegan has seen the light!'

'Steady, love, steady. Did you put the roast on?'

Let Us Keep In Touch

Thank you for reading. I hope you enjoyed the book. If you would like to read the next instalment in the DCI Finnegan series, book 3, **Vertigo Alley - Text K For Killer** is available now.

Ely North Newsletter

Why not sign up to my entertaining newsletter where I write about all things crime—fact and fiction. It's packed with news, reviews, and my top ten Unsolved Mysteries, as well as new releases, and any discounts or promotions I'm running. I'll also send you a free ebook of the prequel novella to Black Nab, **Aquaphobia – Your Worst Fear Can Kill You.**

Type the following link into your browser and it will take you to BookFunnel.

https://BookHip.com/QHXNXCK

———◆———

And lastly, if you enjoyed Jawbone Walk, then a review (or rating) on **Amazon**, **Goodreads**, or a share on **Facebook** would be appreciated. Or even better, why not tell someone you know about the book? Word of mouth is still the best recommendation. I thank you for giving me your time, a very precious and finite commodity.

All the best,

Ely North

Also By Ely North

DCI Finnegan Yorkshire Crime Thrillers

Book 1: **Black Nab** – Text M For Murder

Book 2: **Jawbone Walk** – Text V For Vengeance

Book 3: **Vertigo Alley** – Text K For Killer

Book 4: **Whitby Toll** – The Bell Rings... But For Whom?

Book 5: **House Arrest** – Escape Can Be A Deadly Road

Book 6: **Gothic Fog** – The Strawman Cometh

Book 7: **Happy Camp** – Discipline, Godliness, Fun!

DCI Finnegan Series Boxset: **Books 1 – 3**

DCI Finnegan Series Boxset: **Books 4 – 6**

Prequel – **Aquaphobia** – The Body in the River (Free ebook for newsletter subscribers)

*Note: All books are available from Amazon in ebook, paperback, and in **Kindle Unlimited** (excluding Aquaphobia). Paperbacks are distributed widely via online retailers (Apple, B&N, Kobo, Amazon etc). **Boxset print editions are one book compiled from three books. They do not come in a box. *** Pre-orders only apply to ebooks.

Contact

ely@elynorthcrimefiction.com

Follow me on Facebook for the latest
https://facebook.com/elynorthcrimefictionUK

Sign up to my newsletter for all the latest news, releases, and discounts.